'A compelling adventure story told with lyrical panache'
Daily Mail

'Impressive . . . far more than mere historical reconstruction, it is quite a feat of storytelling . . . Compelling . . . few first novels could draw a reader to it as effectively . . . An exciting, almost cautionary, well-told tale about a dangerous hunger for escape and self-fulfilment.'
Irish Times

'A grand sweep of a book, combining both derring-do plot with tingly love story . . . the perfect read for armchair adventurers everywhere.'
Elle

'A tense, moving début novel . . . in Michaels's mix of grit and grace, a personal tragedy is realised.'
Independent on Sunday

'A courageous love story'
List

'A novel about love, life and loss that succeeds on every level'
Financial Times

Lisa Michaels

Grand Ambition

A Novel

S

SCEPTRE

Hodder & Stoughton

Copyright © 2001 by Lisa Michaels

First published in 2001 by W. W. Norton & Company, New York
First published in Great Britain in 2001 by Hodder and Stoughton
A division of Hodder Headline

The right of Lisa Michaels to be identified as the Author of
the Work has been asserted by her in accordance with the
Copyright, Designs and Patents Act 1988.

A Sceptre paperback

2 4 6 8 10 9 7 5 3 1

A CIP catalogue record for this title is available from the British Library

ISBN: 0 340 81922 7

FRONTISPIECE: Glen and Bessie Hyde, Grand Canyon, 1928
Photographs by Adolph G. Sutro

Typeset in Sabon by
Rowland Phototypesetting Ltd, Bury St Edmunds, Suffolk
Printed and bound in Great Britain by
Clays Ltd, St Ives plc

Hodder and Stoughton
A division of Hodder Headline
338 Euston Road
London NW1 3BH

For Mauricio

Reith Hyde

I wasn't always a cautious man. I did things when I was young that astonish me now – walking through a blizzard to get to a dance, chopping wedges into trees as thick as wine barrels, sure that I'd step the right way when they fell. But life has a way of blind-siding you, and once I had a family, I could never be so careless again. Still, in this case, I was grateful for my vigilance, because I didn't let myself wait until they were over-due. If I had dawdled, assuming all was well, I could never have forgiven myself.

My son, Glen, and his wife started their voyage in central Utah, on October 20, 1928. They built a boat and planned to follow the Green River south until it became the Colorado, then run that west through the Grand Canyon of Arizona and out to the flats of southern California. This was their honeymoon, a rather strenuous one, by any standard, but she was game. The whole trip was to take seven weeks; they were hoping to set a record for speed. But even if they missed that, Bessie would be the first woman to run the rapids of the Colorado River.

I passed those weeks on tenterhooks. So much time to think. Then, in the middle of November, I got a letter from Glen, posted from a ranch halfway through the Grand Canyon. He said that all was going as planned, and that they expected to pass through the Grand Wash Cliffs by December 2. From there it was a full week of easy drifting to Needles, where they would send a telegram. So when the 9th arrived and there was no news, I packed a knapsack with things I thought might be of use and went directly to the station in Twin Falls. My daughters tried to dissuade me from going. Even Jeanne, the more practical of the two, had to say her piece. But I made it clear I wasn't going to curl up in my rocker and wait for word.

After a full day's travel, the train let me off at a point near the river – a whistle-stop, right about where California, Nevada, and Arizona come together. Nothing but a board deck jutting off into nowhere. I found a track that led toward the water and started walking upstream. It took me two days to find anyone. I came upon several settlements, but when I got closer, I saw they were ghost towns – doors swinging open, roofs full of holes. This had to be the most desolate country I'd ever seen. A big bleached-out valley, nothing but clay and salt flats. The river muddy and wide. No wonder everybody gave up and moved on.

At sundown, on my second day on foot, I found a man in a shack by the bank. He said he hadn't left the river for several weeks, and that no one had come by during that time. My son was never a big talker, but after nearly a month in the canyon, I figured he would have pulled over to speak to just about anybody – you get hungry for companionship after a while. So I knew they hadn't passed that place and must be farther upstream.

That got me nervous – they'd been delayed for a week. I knew they might have lost a few days here and there to bad weather, but this seemed too long. It gave me the sinking feeling that the boat had got loose and left them stranded. I had never seen the Grand Canyon, but I knew from books that it was wild, inhospitable country, what with the dead-end gorges and lack of springs. Still, I couldn't think of anyone who had better odds of managing himself out there than Glen. Like most Idaho boys, he was ranch-bred. Not prone to panic. He could walk thirty, forty miles in a day if he had to. He knew how to gather dew with candle wax and a bit of flour sacking, and he was a crack shot. When he was in high school, I once watched him fell a deer from three hundred yards. That might not sound like much. But at that distance a deer looks like a mouse. And the bullet drops so far you've got to aim for the head to hit the heart.

I had faith he'd weather this out.

Now his wife was another matter. Bessie was new to the outdoors. She was dreamy, accustomed to cities, thin and always bent over a book. When he first brought her home to the ranch, I wasn't sure how it would go. But she surprised me, that summer before they set off. She put her head down and worked. It was like watching a filly that had looked good for nothing but munching dandelions buck up and start taking fence lengths. She had more strength than you'd expect, given her size.

By the time I'd mulled all this over, pacing along the riverbank, it was dark, and the homesteader was kind enough to let me sleep on his floor. He was a humble fellow, eking out a living on the shore, surviving on fish and stunted vegetables watered by bucket in a salty plot. I had once started out with as little, but he was nearly my age – perhaps seventy – and I didn't see things improving for him soon. After he gave me his extra blanket, he asked if I knew what day it was. When I told him it was December 11, he nodded and carved a few marks on the doorjamb. Said he was off by a couple of days, and it didn't matter most of the time, but he liked to celebrate Christmas with the rest of the country.

The next morning, we shared a cup of coffee and said our goodbyes. I was just setting off when he came out of the cabin with a folded handkerchief in his hand. 'What's this?' he asked. It was my pocketknife, which I'd left rolled up in the spare blanket. I had hoped he wouldn't find it till I was gone. 'You don't owe me nothing,' he said, looking offended.

I told him it was a gift, not a payment, and he wasn't

supposed to use it until the 25th. Man ought to have something to open on Christmas morning. Still, he tried to hand it back. Finally I told him he'd be doing me a favor if he kept it. I had the feeling I was going to need the help of quite a few strangers before I was through, and I figured what I passed on to one might come back from another. He nodded then, and shook my hand, and when I got to a bend in the river and looked back, he was still there, outside that dismal little shack in the middle of nowhere, watching me leave.

I headed back toward the railway line, turning over scenarios in my mind, keeping the river on my right. Just at sundown, I spotted the cairn I'd left for myself and came out at the tracks. I was prepared to sleep on the platform, but as luck had it, I arrived in time to whistle down the evening train. As soon as the engine chugged east, following the river upstream, I started to feel better. I was headed in their direction. I just had to keep my mind on the task at hand – bettering their odds. Making sure that, if they were holding out somewhere, help went to find them.

Glen and Bessie Hyde

On the 20th of October, 1928, they waved goodbye to the spectators on the bank: watermelon farmers and railroad men with seamed faces and dusty coveralls, who'd heard there was an expedition setting off and dropped their work. Magarel stood apart, a head shorter than the rest, waving his battered Stetson as if fanning away bees. A half-skilled handyman, clinging like a limpet to the Santa Fe line, he'd come by to offer his help building the boat, and when Glen said he couldn't pay, he had offered to work for free. He was the only one who knew them beyond a passing hello. The rest of the crowd stood watching curiously as the scow caught the thread of the current and began to move. Then the owner of the dry goods started to clap, and the rest joined in, until an old drunk started whistling wildly, bent back at the waist, fingers in his teeth, and the applause dissolved into laughter. A less than rousing send-off, but soon the figures were as smooth as clothespins on the duff-colored bank, and Bessie couldn't tell one from the other.

She sat on the bare box springs in the center of the boat, while Glen stood on a cross plank, working the long sweeps. They were plowing through a caramel river – thick, with a greasy sheen. It ran flat and smooth to the banks, which were bare and just high enough to block the views on either side. A deep ditch, really. A canal. Within it, the boat looked rather substantial: a flat-bottomed barge the size of a peddler's wagon, piled with supplies. A box stove, a .30–30 rifle, two cartons of bullets, crates of canned peaches and tomatoes and

5

beans, rope and blankets. Bessie kept her things wrapped in oilskin: a box camera, twenty-seven dollars in a beaded purse – a sentimental object, frivolous for any occasion ahead – pencils, charcoal, a sketchbook, and blank diary.

The thought of that notebook made her pulse quicken. All those empty pages, which would soon be filled with accounts of days she could hardly imagine. That was the thrill of beginning: a burst of pent-up tension, mixed with curiosity. As if someone, somewhere, knew how it would end and wouldn't tell her. For a moment, she imagined that the story was already written, and she was just waiting for the words to appear.

When she looked up, Glen was tying the sweep oars out of the water with a bit of rope. 'What are you doing?' she asked.

'Letting us drift for a minute.'

She watched him, puzzled. Then he pulled the camera from its crate. 'I wanted to take your photograph.'

She laughed. 'While we plow into a sandbar? That's one way to make the papers. "Expedition runs aground half a mile from launch. Captain taking girlie pictures."'

'I never said anything about getting undressed.' He pressed his lips against a smile and opened the case.

'Not yet,' she said. And with one eyebrow arched, she buttoned her leather jacket to the throat.

Glen stared at her through the viewfinder. She was browned from their summer on the ranch, her bobbed hair side-parted and combed close to one cheek. He took in her dark eyes, her slim neck framed by a shearling collar. He never quite managed to tell her how lucky he felt.

Of course, she didn't think she was beautiful. She always shook her head when someone suggested it. He used to think that strange – how could someone be so blind to herself? – until he saw her portrait in an old high school annual. She was eighteen, wearing a white-collared dress with a bow, her hair in a wavy bob with a fringe in front, and though no one would have called her homely, neither would anyone have stopped to look at her twice. He remembered glancing up from the photograph. He didn't know her at that age, and the intervening five years had planed the curves from her face, bringing out the fine bones and throwing her eyes into relief. Suddenly he had understood. She still thought of herself as she looked then. Next to her name in the yearbook was a lighthearted horoscope. 'You will travel in foreign countries accompanied by a blue-eyed, brown-haired young man who pays the bills. Disposition: jolly, but bashful.'

Now, framing her face in the camera lens, he tried to set her at ease. 'You look like you're about to get your teeth drilled.'

Bessie broke into a smile, relieved to hear the shutter click. She'd never liked having her photograph taken. She wasn't sure why. Perhaps because the camera reserved judgment. Even a nickel sketch artist at an arcade showed his hand more quickly – you could peer over his shoulder and see what he'd made of you. But the camera would capture her, at good angle or bad, and it would be more than a month till she'd see the result. But that wasn't the only source of her shyness. A year after she and Glen had met, six months into their marriage, she still felt the need to hold herself in a flattering light. She supposed it was natural. In the first rush, they had shared what seemed to be everything – childhood hurts, their tiny quotidian likes and dislikes – but there were things that she still hadn't revealed to him, out of fear of what he might think. They had come together so quickly, as if they recognized one another in some physical way. Often when he was absorbed in a task she would find herself staring at the cords in his neck, the firm set of his lips, and a current of pleasure jangled her to the root. Perhaps, she thought now, the two went together: the passion and the uncertainty.

Glen wrapped the camera in oilskin and looked out at the

riverbank, the soft crumbling ledges. 'God, am I glad to leave that gloomy town. Did you see the way those brakemen looked at you when we were loading the boat? One of them called you "scrappy."'

'No, he didn't.'

'Yes, he did. He said, "That's the kind of gal you could use in a camp."'

'Some distinction. But really, I haven't been good for much except passing you the tools.'

It was true; she had felt restless in the weeks it had taken Glen to build the boat. Her drawing materials were packed away, and at first she'd spent her days sitting on a pile of grain sacks in the barn he'd borrowed for the work, keeping him company. But watching her husband hammer and plane wore thin after a while. He worked quickly and with confidence, marking the planks with a pencil and sawing through with rhythmic strokes. As she listened to the slowly rising notes of a hammer spiking a nail home, she felt a strange light-headedness steal over her. She had given up so much to make this trip, turned her life inside out like an old shirt. They had been dreaming and planning for a year, and now that the moment had nearly arrived she was anxious to set out. It was one thing to talk of adventure, another to push back from the bank and begin.

While Glen finished the boat, she decided to make it her job to examine the town. If she was going to write an account of their trip, she ought to begin with a thorough description of the launching point.

That lasted about half an hour.

Green River, Utah, was a pitiful place, huddled around a railroad stop on the Rio Grande line. Wide dirt streets without a tree to offer contour or shade, the intersections held down by squat brick buildings: the Midland Hotel & Café, Bebe and Sons Dry Goods, a bank, a barbershop. It was like a model for a place where people might one day live. No point jotting these impressions in her journal – a place of such unrelieved loneliness tends to echo in the mind. Instead she retreated to the hotel, where they had taken a room. It was early October, cold even when the sun shone. They would leave in a week. She made tea on a small burner the proprietor had loaned them and set about straightening their gear.

Glen was glad to see her spending less time in the barn, though he tried not to show his relief. When she sat nearby he felt the need to keep her occupied, to explain each step as he did it, and the talking wore him out. Language was his wife's terrain and he was glad to cede it. What he really wanted was to finish the boat swiftly and in quiet and get on the river before the weather turned colder. On the days when he talked through his work, he felt redoubled gratitude toward Captain Guleke, who had taught him everything he knew about boat making, back when he was nothing but a fence post with an Adam's apple. The old man had spiced these lessons with all his superstitions about how to survive on a river, and so far they had served Glen well. He had the sudden urge to send Guleke a telegram, just a quick word to say they were setting out. He could just picture the pissy expression such a show of feeling would summon in the old man. Good thing he was beyond the reach of telegraph lines most of the time, or Glen would have to dip into their meager cash supply just for the pleasure of getting his goat.

Guleke had made his name running machinery and supplies to miners in the deepest canyons of the Salmon River, and the men who relied on his services claimed it was like having someone deliver you tea in the bowels of hell. He shot through those canyons in his heavy barge, running rapids that made other men bite their tongues with fear, and pulled in at some rocky bank to hand out flour as dry as talc. They said that on the one occasion when Guleke flipped and lost his gear, he lived for two weeks on plug tobacco and river water.

Maybe a telegram wasn't such a bad idea. Under his crust, the old man might be pleased to know they were building a scow like the ones he had mastered. It was a boat designed to take a beating, sixteen feet long and six wide, with long sweep oars extending off each end, and doubled floorboards as a caution against rocks. One of its virtues: it didn't require any special soaking and bending of wood. It was a rectangular box, with the bow and stern tipped outward, so from the side it made a perfect trapezoid, like a child's paper boat.

Still, even Guleke, hard to impress, would have been drop-jawed to hear what they were planning to do with it – run the scow down the length of the Grand Canyon. Since 1869, when John Wesley Powell first explored the river by boat, only nine expeditions had attempted such a trip. He and Bessie would be the tenth, and the only ones to do it for pleasure. Most of the men who'd made it through had been surveyors – exploring sites for a dam or a railroad – or grizzled outdoorsmen, after gold and furs. Only lately had a few parties gone through for publicity, taking photographs and motion pictures. But never had a woman attempted the journey.

As soon as he got the scow roughed together, Glen brought his wife to have a look. They would stow their duffel in two piles – front and back, for counterbalance. In the center was a clear place to stand and a high bench, nailed across the width of the boat, where they would man the sweeps. Bessie watched as he jumped up to take the handles. A shaft of sun came down through the hayloft window and fell over the scow. She had to admit it looked bizarre, sitting flat on the barn floor, without water softening its lines. The sweeps jutted off the back and front like giant hockey sticks, resting heavily on the floor.

'You stand sideways to the stream,' Glen said, turning to

face her. 'And try to keep the handles about waist height, like this.' He slipped a weight sack over each handle, and the long articulated blades lifted as gently as false limbs. There was a little delay, a little creakiness, but they did all right.

'Come and try it,' he said, giving her a hand up.

She found it awkward at first, judging the right amount of pressure, but she soon got the knack and worked the oars in soft circles, trying all the points of the blades.

'Of course, they feel different when you're in fast water,' Glen said. 'Sometimes you'll be going along just fine and an eddy will yank one right out of your hand. And if the blade hits a rock, you fly like a spit wad.'

'God, do you have to put it like that?' She laughed and jumped down from the bench. The sides of the scow nearly reached her shoulders. 'If you need me during rough water, I'll be right down here,' she said, pointing to the floor. 'We could rig up some cushions, a little bell.'

'All right, Cleopatra.' He stepped down to the floorboards and pulled her close. Her hair smelled like lavender. 'Do you know what today is?'

'Friday?'

'Friday, October twelfth,' he said.

She scanned his face, trying to guess the significance.

'It's our six-month anniversary,' he said finally, smiling a little. 'I thought women kept track of these things.'

She stood on tiptoe and gave him a kiss. 'You're sweet to remember.' She wrapped her hands around his waist. 'So what do you give a girl you've been married to for six months? Napkins, hemp?'

He brushed his thumb along her jaw. 'I'm giving this one a boat.'

Later that week, he was putting the finishing touches on the scow when he heard footsteps heading for the barn. It was

Magarel, who'd helped him rough the thing together, and a few men he'd never met. Glen was used to gawkers, but these fellows seemed different. One of them took a turn around the boat, giving it careful scrutiny. Finally he spoke. 'You going down the Colorado in this?' He was stout as a barrel, with thin legs and a Stetson perched too high on his head.

Glen felt the bile rise in his throat. As long as he'd been running rivers, there'd been people who felt the need to bet on his doom. Caution was cheap prophecy. If you were wrong, you could shrug and say the fools had been spared by luck; if you were right, everyone gave you credit for foresight.

'I've run the Salmon,' Glen said. 'Figure I can run anything.' This came out surly, but there it was. He didn't need advice from strangers.

Magarel jumped in and tried to smooth things. 'Now, listen, Glen. Howland here knows a little about rivers. He's been down the Colorado. You ought to hear him out.' He was a skittish little man, with greasy hair and a beak nose. When he talked, he hopped from foot to foot as if his heels were hot. This had been amusing when they worked together, and Glen had secretly dubbed him Magpie, for the way he scurried around at the end of the day, gathering scrap wood for his stove. But he didn't appreciate Magarel's summoning a chorus of naysayers now that the work was almost done. He took a dollop of tar on his spatula and went on sealing the planks.

'Are you planning to cover it?' Howland asked, tipping his head toward the open boat. It looked like a boxcar without a roof.

'Doesn't need decks,' Glen said. 'The gunwales are plenty high.'

Howland nodded. 'What about life preservers?'

Glen smiled at him. 'I swim better without a bunch of cork hiked up around my neck.' He watched Howland's face turn sour and took a strange pleasure in it. How many people had told him and his sister that they would never make it across Idaho on the Salmon and the Snake? He could almost taste the satisfaction when they pulled in at the bank in Lewiston, that fall of 1926, the scow battered but watertight, Jeanne grinning and cured brown by the sun. My God, how those people had stared.

'Looks to me like you're building yourself a coffin,' Howland said, but before he could say more, Magarel hustled him out of the barn.

The evening before they set out, Glen stood outside the barn giving the scow a last checking over. A horse would pull it down to the river on skids, and he was plotting the best route when he saw Bessie coming up the road. It was twilight, the only time the town looked forgiving: when the low-hanging dust snuffed the glare out of the sun. She was framed by a black tracery, a big rectangle of coils – fingers hooked above her head, the plum-colored sky showing through the wires. Glen watched her approach, feeling a flush of elation: here was the boat nearly done, and this generous light, and his wife coming up the road with a set of bedsprings. It was a crazy idea – bringing a bed – he didn't know how they'd fit it on the scow. But looking at her, the way she balanced the thing on her back, her quick determined step, he was won over.

'Where'd you get that?' he asked, grinning.

The springs hit the ground with a faint twang. 'I saw it yesterday, leaning outside the dry goods.' She was out of breath. 'Mr. Bebe sold it to me for a dollar. I figured a good bed for two months was worth that much.'

'We'll find out what it really costs when we try to portage.'

'I thought you said we couldn't portage.'

She was right, of course. Portaging around a rapid meant emptying the boat of its contents and pushing it over dry land – usually by rolling it on logs. But the banks along the rapids would be jumbled with boulders, and this wasn't the kind of boat you could drag easily, even on flat sand. Empty and dry as a bone, it had to weigh over six hundred pounds. Glen went over to the bed, turned around until his heels were at the edge, and fell back onto the rack of springs.

'There's no ticking, so it can't get wet,' Bessie said, rubbing the dents out of her fingers.

He closed his eyes and pictured the waves that would lash over them, how they'd sluice right through the coils. He scrambled up and grabbed hold of the bed. 'Get the other end,' he said. 'Let's see if it fits.'

'Oh, it'll fit,' Bessie said, as they slid the thing over the side. It dropped into the bottom, neatly spanning the width of the scow. She smiled. 'I came out last night and measured for it.'

The next morning, the horse dragged the scow to the same bank where, one year before, another party had set off – three boats and twelve men, led by a New Yorker and war veteran named Clyde Eddy. Most of the citizens had come to watch the boats embark: women in felt cloches, their high heels digging into the sandy bank; men in overalls; kids waving tiny American flags. Bessie had seen the pictures. Of course the Eddy party had much to attract publicity: a crew of handsome young men, recruited from Harvard and Coe, and a mascot, in the form of one bewildered bear cub. For a week they took over the town. They were shooting footage for a documentary on running the Colorado. MGM had expressed interest. But as it turned out the International Newsreel cameraman they hired never made it as far as the Grand Canyon. After the run through Cataract, a chilling preview of what lay downstream, he decamped. In the stills, reprinted in the newspapers, the crew looked only slightly less miserable than the bear, who was drenched and shivering, his claws dug frantically into the deck.

It had occurred to Bessie that she might be considered the bear's equivalent – a passenger brought along for novelty – but Glen never treated her that way. He behaved as if she would pull her weight. She would man a sweep in fast water, take notes, and make sketches. And it fell to her to keep track of their whereabouts, using a set of U.S. Geological Survey maps of the canyon. The government had been surveying the river for a hydroelectric project, but five years later 'the biggest dam in the world' was a federal pipe dream, lavishly investigated and never built. Bessie would use the meticulous maps to anticipate the rapids and measure their progress. In Glen's company, it was easy to forget what was expected of her sex. But of course there were other people to remind her. When the 20th of October arrived and her husband pushed the scow into the river and clambered aboard, she heard startled murmurs among the few men gathered at the bank. 'What's he got there, a little woman?'

But now the muttering couldn't be made out, the bleached roofs of the town had sunk out of sight, and the banks drifted by on each side. The water didn't lap at the shores or break into riffles – it slid along like a flat, oiled belt. There was no sound but the chirr of a bird nearby. Just when she had grown accustomed to the silence, it was broken by a wild shout. A Model T churned up a train of dust along the bank. Someone was waving out the driver's window.

'What on earth?' Bessie exclaimed, laughing a little at this extravagant farewell.

The truck ground to a halt at a small lookout formed by a bend in the river, and a man stepped out of the car. It looked like Mr. Sykes from the telegraph office – Bessie had been in several times in the last week, sending farewell wishes to her mother and father in West Virginia. She recognized his portly form and sleeve protectors. Indeed, he waved a slip of paper, cupped his hands to his mouth, and shouted, but the wind was blowing upstream and the words were torn from his lips.

'It must be from your father,' Bessie said. 'I think he said Reith.'

Glen let go of the sweeps and waved his hat in the air. 'Can't – hear – you!'

On the bank, the telegraph clerk tried his message one more time, but the words bounced off the far bank and collided with ones that followed, muddling the phrases.

'Christ,' Glen muttered, his face flushing. 'He just wired yesterday.'

All summer and early fall, while they had worked on the family ranch, Glen's father had held himself in check. He had listened to their plans, but never rendered an opinion. After years working side by side in the orchards, Reith and his son had developed a current of understanding, but this trip forced the taciturn father to put his thoughts into words: he wanted to go along. Glen thought it a ridiculous plan – they both knew Reith couldn't swim – and after that the talk had turned salty and finally dried up. Now they were on the river and moving, it was too late to turn back, and his father still had something to say. Glen took one last look at the telegraph man waving on the bank. Then he turned back to the sweeps, banishing the spectacle.

Bessie envied his composure, but she couldn't resist staring until the boat took the bend and the truck slipped out of view. She felt a small pang to have missed this last message. She drew comfort from her father-in-law. He was nearly seventy, yet still lithe and strong, with an aura of quiet competence that had been passed down, in large measure, to his son. Nothing like her own father – dear as he was, she never sought the solace of his protection. Once, he had shown great courage in helping her out of a difficulty, but that had been a matter of moral, not physical, courage. Out on a river like this, under the open sky, with a rough journey ahead of them, he'd be more liability than asset. She wondered what was he doing at that very moment. Two thousand miles east, in West Virginia, it would be evening already – no doubt he was seeing to the dogs. She hoped that she hadn't given him too much cause to worry.

Bessie's father was a wallpaper hanger and sometime decorator, a melancholy and observant man with hands as smooth as chalk. His precious greyhounds were lodged in a kennel in a corner of the yard, beside a white lilac bush, and though the shack was weathered and listed to one side, the inside was clean and spacious, and every detail of the dogs' comfort had been attended to: faded rag-coil rugs for each pen, fresh water set out in heavy earthenware bowls. Mr. Haley wore a special smock when he fed them, in order to keep the hair off his clothes. It was adapted from a barber's apron, made of canvas with long sleeves, and it wasn't idle protection: the dogs were ecstatic the moment they heard his footfall in the yard. High-strung, deerlike animals, they leapt up when he crossed the threshold, touching their forelegs gently against his chest.

Even when he was at the bottle, William Haley saw to the dogs, lavishing on them an affection that caused envy in his daughter. When she considered the word *longing*, she thought of a muggy night with fireflies, the air like a sweetened washcloth held to the face. She would slip out over the warm grass and stand under the lilacs, tugging on the fat clusters of flowers in a way that would have made her mother scold, and listen to her father mutter soothingly to his pets. Most young girls love their fathers, but Bessie admired Mr. Haley in ways she thought objective. Everyone knew he would have been a celebrated painter if he didn't have a family to raise. He had wet, sad eyes and put down a fifth of bootleg whiskey each evening, but he possessed an acute irony that made his daughter laugh. This was in welcome contrast to her mother, who was sweet, and blameless, and – it seemed to Bessie – unbearably dim.

'You're going to see Tom Mix, dear? Does he live in town?' her mother had asked once, pausing in her sewing and smiling vaguely in Bessie's direction, like a woman fumbling for a water glass in the dark.

'He's a movie actor, Mother,' Bessie said, embarrassed for them both.

It wasn't lost on Mr. Haley that he was relegated to using his eye for color and perspective to enliven the living rooms of women more flinty and more fortunate than his wife. Mrs. Haley, as he called her, had never raised any particular passion in his blood – she had been a brief accident of his early twenties made into holy law – but she loved him in her trusting way, never mentioned his indulgence in drink, and when his wall-papering income fell short, she did alterations at Broida's on Market Street. In this way they paid the cost of the children's music lessons, the Sunday roasts – the small pleasures that made life feel supportable.

Bessie remembered one evening when her father had come home looking particularly pale. He dropped his heavy sample books on the dining-room table. 'Mrs. Cotrill has decided,' he said, 'now that the whole room has been hung, that the flocking was a terrible mistake.' He often brought home mordant snippets of his customers' lives, the only consolation for work he called 'commissioned flattery.' Now he lifted his hand to an imaginary bosom, several inches out from his boyishly flat one, and assumed his client's voice. 'It's so – so – assertive. I feel the very leaves are pressing on me.'

'What did you do?' Bessie asked, unable to hide her anxiety. She was already acutely conscious of accounts, of cash flow and the cost of yardage.

Mr. Haley paused for a moment and sighed. What he didn't say: one large unpaid account like that and the bank would put a lien on the house. Then he glanced over at his daughter and saw that she was riveted – standing in the doorway with her arms out like a marionette.

'I told Mrs. Cotrill that I was sorry. I had been gravely mistaken. I thought if one woman in Parkersburg could pull off such a look – but, no. I picked up my briefcase, promised her I'd tear up the bill as soon as I got home, and started for the door.'

Mr. Haley had moved to the kitchen by now, Bessie trailing in his wake, and he was pulling down his highball glass, lifting a bottle of Scotch from the pantry and popping the cork. He let out a dry laugh. 'And I *was* wrong about Mrs. Cotrill. She let me get halfway out the door before she relented. Then she called me a shameless silver-tongue.' He lifted the glass toward his daughter's beaming face and took a sip. 'Wrote out a check on the spot.'

It had been four years since Bessie left home, but still she fretted about the family finances. Winter was a lean time for a decorator: people sank their money into holiday parties and expensive gifts and put off wallpapering until the spring. Still, if Glen's plan worked as well as they hoped, they wouldn't have to worry. None of them. Even as the trip was beginning, she was already thinking of the prize at the end, the savor of sharing it among the people she loved. They would have their picture in the papers: Girl Navigator Braves the Rapids of the Grand Canyon. She would write an article or two: 'My Honeymoon Voyage.' The offers from vaudeville would roll in. She would buy her father a new automobile, her mother a Chanel suit –

She pulled herself up short. What lay between their present point and the soft-banked river at Needles, California, was a series of fantastically deep canyons, with walls in many places too steep to climb, and chains of fast-water rapids whose very description made her chest clench. She mustn't lose her concentration. Mustn't think about taking her bow before she finished the performance. That was when you stumbled. When you looked too far ahead.

Reith Hyde

I arrived at Pearce Ferry, a few miles downstream from the
Grand Wash Cliffs, early on the morning of December 13.
When I told folks there my son and daughter-in-law were late
coming out of the canyon, the ferryman shook his head. 'You'd
best pray for them,' he said. I didn't reply, because he seemed
a kindly man, but I don't put much stock in prayer. I was
raised Episcopal and went to church while my wife was alive,
but when she passed away young, I quit trying to talk to God.
I think the last time I entertained any hope of Him intervening
in this world was on Wilson's Peace Sunday. If ever the human
spirit might have had influence with the divine, that should
have been it. A whole nation putting in a plea to the heavens
to stop the bloodletting in Europe. Most of a nation, anyway.
Even the atheists wanted their sons back and no doubt muttered a few words. But as far as anyone knows, the death
count went undiminished that day, and the Germans had to
be routed the old-fashioned way – with bullets and bayonets.
So when my son was late, I figured there was no point praying.
I had to make a plan and put it into action. My poor Maggie
might have disagreed, but I only hoped she was working in
her realm just as I was in mine.

People at Pearce Ferry said I ought to head further east, to
a town up on the Kaibab Plateau, where I might marshal help
for a search of the canyon. I caught the train and was in Peach
Springs by late afternoon. There I sat in my hotel room with
a sheet of paper and a pen and made a list of everyone I
might go to for help: the governors of Idaho and Arizona, the

superintendent of the National Park Service. I drafted a telegram to Bessie's father in West Virginia, saying that she and Glen were four days late, and while it was too soon to assume the worst, I wanted to do all I could to be sure they were safe. Perhaps he might lobby with the governor there for an official search. In the morning, I took my list to the telegraph office and had them send wires all over the country, feeling the deepest gratitude to be living in the modern age. Letters, in this case, would have been useless.

Bessie's father wired back within an hour. Said he'd go directly to Charleston to see the governor of West Virginia, hoping he'd take an interest. That was a good start, but what I really needed was someone local, someone with expert knowledge of the river. Then I remembered Emery Kolb. He and his brother, Ellsworth, had run the Grand Canyon in 1911, and I knew he was still living at the South Rim. Glen and Bessie had stopped in for a visit halfway through their trip, and in his letter my son had mentioned Kolb's hospitality. I sent him a wire, letting him know that the two of them were late and asking for his assistance. Two days later, on December 15, Kolb sent a telegram back and we arranged to speak by phone. I took a liking to him right away. He was calm and matter-of-fact.

'Well, they left here on the seventeenth of November, and they're running on low water, so it will be slow going,' he said.

That reassured me a bit. 'Let's say they made minimal progress each day,' I ventured. 'How long would it take them to get to Needles?'

'Well, they should have been there by now, but other things could've hung them up. We've had some squally winds lately – that can slow you up considerably. And they might have smashed a sweep or cracked a hole in the scow. Then they'd have to lay over to make repairs.'

What relief to have someone think it through with me, someone with better knowledge of the possibilities. Still, it didn't add up. 'I checked the postmarks on their letters from Lee's Ferry and Phantom Ranch,' I told Kolb, 'and it looks like they made that stretch in seven days. According to the maps, that's eighty-seven miles. Hard to believe it would take them a month to make the final hundred and ninety miles to Pearce Ferry.'

'Glen did mention they were going for speed,' Kolb said.

I told him I had a feeling they got separated from the boat. It was a scene I had already imagined in great detail. 'They're lining a rapid and the boat gets away from them, and now they're stuck on some beach, running out of food. You met my daughter-in-law, Mr. Kolb. If Glen lost his grip even for a minute, there's no way that Bessie could hold that scow alone.'

Kolb took this in, and then he seemed to make a decision. 'We'll need to get the Havasupai tracking on the rim. You'd best post a reward.'

I couldn't miss that 'we.' It made my heart leap. 'But what if they're walled in?' I asked him. 'They may be stuck on the river. I need somebody who can take a boat down.'

Kolb laughed – a short, high-pitched rasp. 'Take a boat down from where, Mr. Hyde, Lee's Ferry?' He thought I didn't know what I was asking for.

'Doesn't anyone have a boat at Phantom Ranch?' I asked. 'We know they made it that far.'

Kolb seemed to think this over. 'What you really need is someone to fly a plane over. See if they can catch sight of the scow.'

I told him I'd already asked for the army's help, and that I was waiting for word. 'Don't know if they'll hunt for civilians, though.'

'Can't see why not. They sent a plane out after the Pathé-Bray party,' he said. 'Damn movie people, trying to make a melodrama: *Bride of the Colorado*. Running the rapids in yellow wigs.'

It was the first time I'd smiled in a week.

I told him how grateful I was for his advice, and we agreed to meet at the South Rim in two days. I figured I'd have to pay dearly for Kolb's help. He ran a business at the settlement there, taking photographs of tourists, and a search would take him away from that. I had a small amount of cash set aside to hire hands for the next harvest. I resolved right then to use it if I must.

Glen and Bessie Hyde

They were drifting down the lazy river. Glen, anxious to make time, turned the boat broadside to the current and used the sweeps as oars. He followed the quickest thread in the water, which spooled from one side of the channel to the other, under-cutting first the left bank and then the right, leaving a small bluff near the fast water and a soft wide beach on the opposite shore. The landscape flipped from side to side, setting up a strange visual monotony, as if they were stuck in a scratched dream. But the banks were rising, an uplift so gradual that at first they hardly noticed the shrinking sky. Then the change became clearer: the bluffs gave way to low sandstone cliffs, layered like saltwater taffy. Between them, the water moved so smoothly that at times Bessie had the illusion that the boat was holding still, a punt secured in the stream, while the cliffs scrolled backward on each side. A heron startled up from the shallows and flapped over them. Then it was quiet.

She settled back on the pile of supplies and took out the Eddy party clippings. She had pored over the articles countless times, but nervous fascination made her look again: it was the best information she had about what lay ahead. The first was from the *New York Times,* September 11, 1927. She didn't bother with the text, which she knew by heart, but focused instead on the photographs. There was a large shot of a rapid that looked like a field of detonated chocolate milk. A boat pitched through this torrent, half swallowed by a ragged hole, the men inside hunched over like infantrymen dodging shells. Bessie shuddered. Better not to look too long at that one.

Instead she turned to the portrait of the crew: the college boys in rolled-up shorts and loose tanks. They posed on a beach, around Eddy, the trip's captain, bandannas over their foreheads, legs casually crossed. One of them cradled the bear cub like a baby. Another chewed on a corncob pipe. A few of them were beautiful – lean, intelligent faces and a varsity ease. The trip had been underwritten in part by the makers of Mercurochrome, who expected photographs of their product in action. She could just imagine the fun they'd had with that: staged daubing of fake wounds. That is, until they hit the real rough water. Studying their faces, Bessie felt a poignant tug, the nostalgia one feels at photos of the elegant dead. But in fact they had all lived to tell the tale. Even the bear had survived unscathed.

She turned the clipping over. On the back was an ad for Rengo Belt Corsets, which pictured an elfin woman, kneeling demurely under a banner:

MATERNITY ABDOMINAL BINDERS

For the woman not accustomed to wearing corsets

She stared at it for a moment, then out at the deserted cliffs, and started to laugh. It seemed absurd, in a place like this. To cinch yourself in for anyone else's sake.

At sundown on October 20, their first day on the river, they picked a dry beach and made camp. Glen pulled the mattress onto the sand and began making the bed, layering wool blankets over the metal springs and wadding up their coats for pillows. Bessie went in search of driftwood for the fire, heading toward a few scrubby trees clinging to the bank. Above them, a ragged slope of boulders bordered the cliff. She was picking her way among the rocks when a set of strange markings caught her eye. She called to Glen.

'Indian petroglyphs,' he said when he came near. There were

white daubed figures with udderlike fringes for feet. What looked to be elk or deer. Ladders with curled tops, as if they were hooked over the rim of the heavens.

'So beautiful,' Bessie said. She knew a few art students in San Francisco who would be quick to steal the motifs.

'Lots of animal figures,' Glen pointed out. 'Must have been good hunting around here.' He turned and squinted at the cliffs. 'Maybe I should get the rifle.'

'Kind of old news, isn't it?'

He smiled. 'Probably right. Or maybe there never were any elk nearby, and these were just gloomy doodles.'

'Hard to imagine someone doodling here.' She looked around at the stark banks, the muddy river. 'Out in the middle of nowhere.'

'Well, it wasn't nowhere to them.'

'I suppose you're right.' She moved to sit on a flat rock higher up, and from her new perch caught sight of the back of the boulder. 'Oh my God, look at this.' She pointed to the stone. In yellow paint, a more recent graffito: *Olive Meecham Feb* 1923.

'How did she get here?' Bessie asked. They hadn't passed a ranch or a railroad in miles.

'Probably kidnapped by Indians,' Glen said, deadpan.

She gave him a soft push. 'Honestly. You've read too much James Fenimore Cooper.'

'Maybe she was a trapper's wife,' Glen ventured. 'Went along on hunts.'

This made more sense. Still, what was she doing painting her name on stray boulders? It gave Bessie an eerie feeling. But it was more than that. She was surprised to find that it bothered her – the thought of another woman in this isolated spot. She had started to enjoy thinking of herself as a pioneer.

When they returned to the beach, arms full of driftwood, Bessie rummaged around in the food crates, trying to decide what to make for dinner. They had to be careful with supplies, making them last until they could restock at Lee's Ferry, twenty days ahead. It made sense to use the most perishable items first. The weather wasn't cold enough to prevent spoilage. She settled on the idea of a stew, with smoked meat, carrots, and onions, and started pulling the ingredients out onto a small oilskin.

Suddenly she sat up from her crouch, bowie knife in hand. 'Damn.'

'What is it?' Glen was down at the scow, getting kerosene to light the stove.

'We forgot a cutting board.'

He walked over with the gas can. 'Maybe we can rig something up.' He glanced around the beach.

'Don't tell me you're going to use driftwood.' Glen loved to whittle, and she could just see him spending an evening by the fire, planing a cutting board out of a decomposing log.

'Why not? I've heard grubs are nutritious.' He stifled a smile.

'It's a little early to be stooping to grubs.'

'Well, I'm glad you haven't ruled them out.' He went down to the scow, untied the oilskin over the pile of duffel, and moved things around. A few moments later, he stepped onto the sand with a long oak board over one shoulder.

'I thought we needed that for repairs,' Bessie said when he reached her.

'We do. I can't cut it. But a few knife marks won't make a difference.'

The board was as long as a teeter-totter. 'You expect me to balance that thing on my lap?' She grinned in disbelief. 'I'll be chasing the onion from one end to the other.'

Glen pulled out his pocketknife, then sat down beside her. He settled the board over their knees. 'Pass me a carrot.'

She gave him half the ingredients, then planted a kiss on his cheek. Together they worked quietly, no sound but the nicking of wood, the vegetables gathering in piles at the side of their knives. After a while, as if in reward for their silence, a swarm of bats spilled out of the cliff opposite and began hunting for insects over the river. They stopped to stare at the black bodies, darting like shuttlecocks through the dusky air.

By the 22nd of October, it was clear they had entered Labyrinth Canyon. The channel had narrowed and the cliffs rose straight up for three hundred feet. The river made sinuous curves, as tortured and backtwisting as a length of intestine. Here was the same alternating pattern of cliff and beach, except the scenes became more varied and the palette more vivid: banded rust faces and scallops of lush, green bottomland. For the first time, Bessie pulled out her sketchbook and started drawing the river. It was a place of eerie beauty – and they had it all to themselves.

Late on the afternoon of their third day in Labyrinth, they made a long jog to the left – Glen guessed it was eight miles – and then curved back to a point several football field lengths from where they had started. Bessie picked it out on the map: the river making two wide loops, like a child trying to tie a shoe. Bow Knot Bend, it was called.

The sun was low in the sky. 'Want to hike to the top?' Glen asked, pointing to the thin wall of stone around which the river had doubled.

They moored the scow, changed from their canvas sneakers to their boots, and started hiking up the cliff. Half an hour later, winded and damp with sweat, they reached the top.

The scarp was lower than the surrounding plateau, but they could see the deep trench in which they traveled and the miles of weathered stone undulating away on all sides. Bessie had never seen a landscape like this: purely sculptural – warped stone and a range of color so narrow that it seemed at first to be lifeless. Then she saw that it was full of foliage: strange, withered, sand-colored plants, matched to the rocks. It was nothing like the rumpled West Virginia hills, so green in springtime they almost hurt the eyes. The land had seemed old back east – worn down to soft nubs. But this place, jagged and scoured, was older still. It reminded her of O'Keeffe's abstract landscapes, which she had pored over in *Vanity Fair*: hollowed ribs of reddish stone, massive arches, lone towers topped by what looked like human heads. The river ahead of them carved straight through the rock, a shining blade of water. It was all worth it, she thought – all the difficult times of the last few years – for having led to this place.

Glen turned in a slow circle, pulling off his hat. He ran a hand through his hair. The scenery dwarfed them, two tiny figures perched on the top of a monolith. They were utterly exposed, but their size gave them a kind of privacy. He took a swig of water from the canteen, offered some to Bessie, then pulled a blanket from his rucksack and spread it out in a hollow. The wind was dampened there. He lay down, arms behind his head, squinting against the sun, and smiled at her.

She stretched out beside him, staring up at the blue lid of sky. The stone beneath them was cupped and warmed by sun – as if they were curled in the shelter of an enormous palm. Glen kissed her temple, which tasted of salt, and ran a finger under her collar. Turning toward him, she reached through the open diamond of his arms and worked at his buttons. They laughed a little, then peeled the shirts from their shoulders and pressed skin to skin. They were stripped to the waist, out in the wide world for anyone to see, except there wasn't anyone, only a hawk riding the updrafts overhead. How delicious, she thought, to be naked, beyond walls, in the frank sun.

Glen wasn't her first lover. First, there had been Earl Helmick, her classmate at Parkersburg High – Gardening Club, Lit Club,

Quill Staff, Chorus. They both enrolled at Marshall College, and in the fall of 1925, when they were sophomores and had been sweethearts for two years, they lay down in the Helmick family fishing cottage, under three quilts and two wool blankets, and stared at the ceiling.

'Shall I get more covers?' Earl asked her, tucking the quilts down around her shoulders.

'No,' she told him. She was shivering out of fear.

'I'll be right back.' He disappeared into the bathroom for what seemed like an eternity. When he returned, stripped down to his underwear, he had to burrow through quilts, blankets, sheets, and clothing to reach her. So much fumbling and haste. They moved together briefly, both of them hesitant, their breath filling the room. Then Earl made a sudden gasp and lay still.

Bessie felt tears wet her shoulder and then slide, warmed by her skin, down into the crook of her neck. She felt a strange sense of – not quite pity, but a kind of tender responsibility. She smoothed the hair on the back of his head, stroked his shoulder blades until his breathing slowed.

'That was lovely,' he said finally, kissing her cheek. 'You're lovely, Bess.'

She lay there for hours after he fell asleep, watching moonlight sift into the room. It was a great disappointment to her, this first knowledge of sex. She expected something more, but then chided herself. This is what sets us apart from men: the ability to tolerate the gap between dreams and the possible. In this way she coaxed herself into quietude. It would be months before she let herself admit how in that first night of mild lovemaking, that stilted pressing of limbs, the only thing roused had been her fury.

She was half relieved that they would have few occasions for such privacy. The dormitories were strictly patrolled, and neither of them had an auto, which the church fathers had dubbed 'mobile petting rooms.' So it was with particular irony that she realized, in the spring of the following year, that their few encounters had been enough.

It was late May 1926. She was home from college for the summer. The mercury was rising into the eighties, and all week she had woken feeling faint. The night before, she and Earl had got into a tiff, and moments after she opened her eyes it all came back with exhausting clarity. She phoned down the street to the Helmicks', but Earl had already gone to his father's accounting office, where he was learning to clerk. 'Oh, he left *hours* ago,' Mrs. Helmick said, a note of reproachful pleasure in her voice.

Bessie hung up and stared out the kitchen window. Her mother was at Broida's already, hemming summer dresses. She tried to force down a few bites of boiled oats but at one point she had to pull the full spoon out of her mouth – even the idea of eating seemed tedious. She did manage to drink some milky Earl Grey, so at least she was alert and queasy. Then she went to the bathroom, splashed her cheeks with cold water, and stared at herself in the mirror. How she hated that round, gloomy face. She had to tell him, that was all. They would come to an understanding.

The subject was finally broached on the porch at her parents' house – a long, creaky wraparound with deep eaves, set here and there with faded wicker furniture. It was high noon and sweltering. Only the ferns dangling between the columns seemed suited to the climate. Mrs. Haley brought out iced tea on a tray, the tin buckling as she set it down. She approved of Earl, approved of the whole Helmick family, who lived down the street in a house more substantial than their own. After some small talk about Earl's mother's confederate violets, she begged off with a feeble flirtation: 'I'm a little like a violet myself, Earl. I wilt in the heat.'

Then she let out a sigh that made Bessie think of a form of

torture – medieval, if she remembered correctly – where people were flattened to death by heavy stones.

As soon as her mother had withdrawn, she delivered the news: 'I'm in the family way.' What a coy phrase. Still, she couldn't bring herself to say it more plainly.

Earl blanched, looking nearly offended. 'Surely you're joking,' he said, glancing in the direction of the screen door. Sweat broke out on his upper lip. He sat rigid in his chair. Bessie poured him a slosh of iced tea and sugared it liberally.

'You act as if you can't fathom how this happened,' she said, holding out the glass. When he still didn't break from his daze, she grew short with him. 'Do you have nothing to say?' She put down the tea. His shock galled her. He seemed to be saying, One of those pitiful nights?

'Oh, Bessie, you're absolutely right. My God. I'm sorry.' He picked up her hand and closed it in his palms. They were damp as steamed rolls. He leaned forward in his chair – the wicker creaking – and looked into her face. 'There's only one thing to do.'

She felt a wash of relief: how could she have doubted him? He must know someone in the capital.

'We'll have to elope,' Earl said. 'If we announce the engagement my mother will expect a wedding, and that takes time.' He sounded strangely calm. 'You know, it's funny, Donald Mayhew was just telling me about a town in Kentucky where the preacher doesn't ask questions. I'll have to look into it.'

Bessie saw it pass before her in a rush: the two of them at the altar, dressed in their good dark clothes, flowers pinned at their lapels. His parents' faces when they heard the news, their shock and disappointment and eventual giving in. And then the baby, her whole life given over to this small accident of fate.

'How will I finish my studies?' she asked woodenly, staring over his shoulder. It wasn't a real question, but rather a line delivered to confirm his reply.

'You don't need any more art lessons. You should be teaching them,' Earl said. 'You could do portraits here in town. Teach our son to sketch.'

He was wrong, of course. She wasn't beyond any useful teaching; she had hardly begun. But she might do worse than Earl, a man who could admire a son's ability with charcoal and brush – provided it was balanced by a good dose of business sense. All the girls thought him a lucky catch. He talked firmly of their plans, slowly brushing the back of her hand. 'Like a little bird,' he said absently, and for a moment her hand did look like a wren, huddled on his palm.

Bessie pulled her fingers free. 'And what if I'm not ready to have a child?'

Earl took on an expression her mother often wore – the pleated brow, the suffocating *concern* for her welfare. She pushed on, a cornered animal making a lunge. 'I'm not sure either of us is ready,' she said. 'You're not exactly in a position to provide for a family.'

This was a desperate rebuke. Earl looked stunned, as if she were rearing about breaking china. She choked out a laugh. This boy she had first loved in a kind of drunken swoon appeared suddenly foolish to her – the very portrait of a delicate swain. His flushed cheeks, his bow tie and round collar, the volume of Byron peeking out of his satchel. He didn't have the faintest idea what she was capable of.

But then again, she didn't have the full measure of Earl. He grabbed her hand and hurried her down the steps, around the house, and into the backyard. 'This is my child as much as yours,' he hissed, pinching the bones in her hand. 'I can't believe you'd suggest something so –'

Behind him, the dogs began barking in their kennels.

'So *what?*' She pulled back at arm's length, her chin drawn down and shaking, but she met his eyes.

'So dishonorable!' he blurted, looking satisfied with the word.

'This is hardly a matter of honor,' she said hotly, but she felt as if she were shouting over an engine's roar – the words would never get through.

'It is precisely about honor!' Earl was nearly breathless, his tie askew. 'I've treated you with nothing but courtesy and respect these past two years. I had the impression you returned my feelings.'

'Of course I returned your feelings, Earl. Don't be ridiculous!'

'Then why won't you be my wife?' His voice bounced off the clapboard, and suddenly he let go of her hand and stood there awkwardly. After a pause, he said, 'There are plenty of girls who would be glad for the offer.' He meant it as a jab, but it came out brokenly. The color welled up in his face.

Without his fury, something to resist, she went slack as a windless sail.

And so on the 6th of June, 1926, they borrowed his father's Cadillac phaeton, claiming they were going on a picnic, and motored over the state line to Catlettsburg, Kentucky.

After seven days on the river, Glen and Bessie passed out of Labyrinth and into Stillwater Canyon. The river sliced deeper into the stone, and for miles the water filled the canyon entirely, the surface smooth as a sheltered pond. No rapids, very few places to land. The quiet was deafening. Glen whistled through his fingers, listening to the notes ripple back to them.

'It's like we're in the bottom of a well,' he said, craning his head to look at the rim.

Just then an elk startled on a high ledge and sprinted off, letting loose a crackle of stones. They watched as the rocks bounced down the cliff and then arced outward, heading straight for the scow.

'Jesus!' Glen said, flinching as they pierced the water. 'Hate to get brained by a pebble here at the start.'

Their laughter bounced back at them like dice off a wall. When it had died out, they were quiet for a while, watching the stone cliffs drift by. Behind them, the scow left a scar on the water, catching the light.

'I wonder what Reith wanted,' Bessie said.

'Probably wanted to come along.' Glen adjusted the sweep, nosing them toward deeper water. After a while, he spoke again: 'He used to farm ten acres on the other side of the Snake, when we first moved to Twin Falls. Got the land cheap. Put in clover.'

He sat down on the cross plank, one hand lightly on the sweep handle. 'He drove the team down to the ferry and took them across. Six days a week. I'd stay at home with Jeanne and Edna. Then one day, just as the horses were coming down to the ramp, one of them spooked. They were good horses. Must have been a snake. Reith yanked on the reins, but there was no stopping them, they just barreled down the dirt ramp, men leaping off to either side, hit the ferry at a full gallop, and went right off the other end, wagon fishtailing behind. The ferry's gone now – they have a bridge – but it used to be set at a bend in the river. On the south side the bank drops off.' He made a steep cliff with his hand. 'And then it slowly shallows out to a gravel bar on other side. The team dropped into the deep water and sank like a stone.'

Bessie was quiet, picturing the scene.

After looking downriver for a moment to check their course, Glen went on. 'Everybody ran to the edge of the barge, watching for Reith to come up. The horses were yoked to the wagon and it had the plow in it and all sorts of heavy stuff, so they figured they'd be dragged along the bottom and drown. Thirty seconds, a minute, went by. Nothing happened. The ferryman pulled off his boots and was about to jump in when a horse's head popped up halfway across the river. Then another one popped up, swimming like mad, and finally they hit the gravel bar and dragged the wagon out of the river. And there was my papa, sitting on the bench, still holding the reins.'

'Why didn't he let go?' Bessie asked.

Glen smiled, rubbing his jaw. 'That's what everyone asked. And when he caught his breath, he said, "Cuz I can't swim a lick."'

They floated deeper into Stillwater Canyon, passing abandoned Indian dwellings cut high into the walls, camping at night on narrow beaches hard against the cliffs. Later, Bessie would come to think of this time as their honeymoon: the privacy and quiet, the effortless gliding. No chores, no one in the bedroom down the hall. They would sleep late, make love, boil up coffee on the box stove. While Glen packed the boat, she would draw in her sketchbook. Then they drifted through scenery more striking at every turn.

On the afternoon of October 28, they made camp on a thick crescent beach on the right bank. The cliffs formed a curving wall around the sand, giving it the feeling of a giant buttery room. Bessie went down to the river and filled the water bucket, so the silt would have time to settle before supper. Glen pulled the mattress up against the wall and made the bed. The weather had been clear since they set out, but there was a slight nip in the air. 'Let's go sit in the sun,' Bessie said, pointing to a wedge of golden light at the far end of the beach. Glen picked up the Kolbs' book and followed her. Halfway there, he stopped and stared at the cliff face.

'What is it?' she asked.

'Come look,' Glen said. Just at his shoulder level, scratched into the sandstone, were the names of previous river voyagers: Ellsworth and Emery Kolb, 1911; the Eddy party, twelve names in all, dated June 1927. Bessie looked down at the volume in Glen's hand, *Through the Grand Canyon from Wyoming to Mexico*, by Ellsworth Kolb, then back at the same name, carved in the stone in front of her. That leap – from crude scratching to finished book – gave her a thrill. Perhaps her own plans were possible.

'Should we add our names?' she asked. There was an odd hitch in her voice.

'Why not?' Glen asked.

'I don't know,' she said. 'I guess it seems presumptuous.' She ran a finger over the list. 'They've written books, made the papers. We haven't exactly braved much so far.' In fact, their first week on the river had been so peaceful she could hardly call it an adventure.

Glen smiled at her. 'Neither had they when they got to this point. That didn't stop them.'

'I suppose you're right,' Bessie said with a laugh. She watched as Glen got out his penknife. A few minutes later, he had still only made the downstroke of a B. The stone was harder than it looked. 'Blade won't be good for much after this,' he said. 'I can't believe I forgot my whetstone.'

'Why don't you use a nail?' Bessie offered. They had brought along a whole sack, in case the scow needed repairs.

'Good idea,' Glen said. He went down to the scow and dug among the crates, coming back with hammer and nail. He stuck the point into the rock and tapped, carving a thin path in the stone. 'Works like a dream.'

Bessie went to sit in the sun. With her back against the cliff and her heels dug in the sand, she closed her eyes and listened to the tap of the hammer. Suddenly it stopped. She heard Glen laugh softly to himself.

'What?' she asked.

'I feel like I'm fourteen,' he said. 'Carving a girl's name in a tree trunk.'

Bessie came over to look at his handiwork. 'It's a bit more permanent than bark,' she said, admiring the neat lettering. BESSIE + GLEN HYDE 10/28/28.

'How do you like those eights?' Glen asked, slipping the hammer in his back pocket, the nail in his teeth. 'Those were tricky.'

'Neat as a figure skater's,' she said, smiling up at him.

He cocked his head. 'Now I know why they charge so much for headstones.'

Together they stared at the fresh cuts in the wall. It was the same primitive impulse that prompted memorials. To leave something for those who followed. A way to say: We were here. We lived.

That night, as they fed driftwood to the fire, Bessie looked over and saw his handiwork, flickering in relief on the cliff behind him. 'Strange, isn't it? To leave your name in a place like this. It might be years before anyone sees it.'

Glen didn't answer, just broke a stick over his knee and tossed it on the fire. Flames stole up around the fresh wood, lighting the crease between his brows.

'What are you thinking about?' she asked softly.

He lifted his head and stared for a moment. 'My mother.'

Bessie held very still, as if a dragonfly had alighted. He never spoke of her.

'We had to leave her in Prince Rupert. Her grave, I mean. It always bothered me.' He looked at her with a bare expression.

The canyon was silent. No sound but the snap of wood breaking down in the fire. 'What was she like?' Bessie asked.

Glen picked up another stick and worried the coals. 'She was a polished person. Very elegant.' He smiled faintly. 'She used to wear her hair piled up on her head, never a strand out of place. When I was little I thought that it grew that way. One day I passed by their bedroom and saw her with her hair down – it came all the way to her waist – and I started crying. I must have been four or five. She came out and picked me up. Asked me what was wrong. I said, "Your hair's all wrecked." She just threw her head back and laughed.'

He fell silent for a while. Bessie watched him but didn't speak. She sat cross-legged on the sand – her chest radiating from the fire, her back cold – as if she were poised between the present and the past.

At length he looked up. 'I know it sounds stupid, but I never expected her to die. Edna told me later that she used to imagine it all the time – sort of trying it on for size – what it would be like to lose her. Of course, she's always been the nervous type. But I had this absolute faith that she and Papa would always be there. So it hit me like a ton of bricks. I couldn't even cry at the funeral. I felt terrible about it. Even Reith had tears streaming down his face. I was sure people would think I didn't care. I just sat there with this pain in my throat. Felt like someone was breaking my windpipe.'

Bessie imagined the skinny boy he had been, twelve years old, frozen with grief on a country church pew. She got up and put her arms around him from behind, tucking her chin over his shoulder. 'What did she die of?' she asked softly.

'My father never said exactly,' Glen said, rubbing a hand over his face. 'I think life on the ranch did her in. We were homesteading, and she hadn't been raised to that kind of labor. Pumping water, working a garden. She used to name the chickens and cry when they were killed. For the first three years of their marriage my father did all the cooking – she hardly knew how to boil water. He used to spend all day clearing the land, cutting timber, and then wash up and start in the kitchen. She was stubborn. Tried to do the work anyway. I guess it just wore her out. Then she got sick, and went back to her parents in Vancouver to recover. We never saw her again.'

There was something about the stillness of the canyon, the fire burning a brief hole in the darkness, that made him want to talk. And in the silence after, the things he said drifted up through her mind like smoke. Strange that a loss like his – a beloved mother – hadn't made him cling to life. Instead, it seemed to have done the opposite. He had told her once, shortly after they met: he figured it was all chance. He would die in some unexpected way, impossible to guess and most likely mundane, and so he forged ahead. Death didn't miss you because you stood still.

By midday on Halloween, eleven days after setting out, they came to their first junction, the meeting of the Green and Colorado rivers. At first the transition looked benign – a muddy Y, with logs collecting in the slack water. But within a few yards, they could feel the change in the river. The water had doubled in volume, the scow picked up speed, and for the first time Glen used the sweeps as they were designed, as front and back rudders. They were being drawn swiftly into Cataract Canyon. Five miles downstream they would face the first white water of their trip.

The walls widened here, a shock after Stillwater's tight, protected canyon, and the wind picked up, scudding the surface of the river. Several hours later, they heard a rapid ahead. The sound was ferocious – a wall of noise advancing toward them. Glen steered over to the bank and tied off the scow. They would camp here for the night, resting before they ran the first rapid. Bessie scraped a level patch in the sand and laid out the mattress and stove, hunching her shoulders against the thunderous sound.

Glen spoke to her from a few yards away. She could hardly hear him.

'What?'

'I'm going to batten down the gear,' he shouted, holding up a length of rope.

How could water make a noise like this? It wasn't constant; it moved through phases. First a deep vibrating bass note, then a sound like garbled human speech. A grinding of gears. A thunderclap that unfurled and unfurled, as if the sky were a colossal tapestry ripped from end to end. All that from a river pouring over stones. She'd read a little about Cataract in books. The canyon was like a massive fish ladder, the water making its descent toward the sea in quick, white steps. And where it dropped, a violent roar filled the canyon, vaulting up between the cliffs like the puff of dust between clapped erasers.

Cataract was only twenty miles long (a mere prelude to the 270 miles of the Grand Canyon), but there were fifty-two rapids along that stretch. According to the Eddy party's accounts, they had often made only a mile a day. The walls rose up almost two thousand feet, keeping them in shadow for all but a few hours near noon. They had cracked holes in their boat, elected to line most of the rapids instead of running them, and often thought they wouldn't make it out alive.

That night, Bessie could hardly choke down her dinner. Across the fire from her, Glen balanced a tin plate on his knees. He looked nearly content.

'We're making good time,' he said, taking a forkful of beans. 'Already a day ahead of schedule.'

'I'm starting to wish we'd gone slower,' she said, glancing downstream.

Glen smiled at her. 'Come on. This is where it gets interesting.'

'I know,' she said. 'I'm just nervous.'

He put down his plate and leaned toward her. 'Look, so am I,' he said. 'I always feel this way before the first few rapids. Wondering how the boat will handle. Then after a while you start looking forward to white water.'

She couldn't imagine that. But it was a relief to hear him admit to his jitters.

Glen laughed suddenly. 'The morning that Jeanne and I were supposed to run the first big rapid on the Salmon, she was just cool as a cucumber. I asked if she was nervous and she said no. I have to say I was impressed. Then I took a sip of the coffee she'd made and spit it three feet. Turned out she'd salted it.'

He went down to the water to make sure the boat was secure, then lay back on the mattress and dropped off to sleep.

Bessie scoured the supper pans with sand and water. In the faint moonlight the river had a strange glassy quality, but when she tossed a stick into the current she was alarmed at how quickly it swept out of view. She went back up the beach and threw a few logs on the dying fire. Curled next to Glen, the covers drawn up to her chin, she studied his face as the flames leapt up: the whorl that began each eyebrow, the skin drawn taut over the bridge of his nose. He didn't sunburn, but turned a ruddy brown, a face planed out of teak. Who was this man, her husband? Asleep, he looked older and younger at once – the hollows deepening under his eyes; a dark lock curved over his forehead, as if someone had combed his hair for a picture.

Hours later, after the coals were nearly out and she'd grown tired of lying awake, she crawled out from under the covers and found the beach bathed in a silvery light. The moon had swung high overhead, turning the sand into a mound of frozen sugar. She crouched a few paces from the bed and relieved herself, watching a rivulet form in the crust. It was as black as the trickle of blood in a silent picture, its faint hiss drowned out by the river. She didn't think she'd ever been so afraid. Well, that wasn't true. But it had been fear of a different kind.

Bessie's first marriage was performed by a Reverend A. P. Keyser, an adenoidal man in a creased suit and a string tie who blessed the unions of desperate couples from three states around. Please be brief, Bessie thought, when she and Earl gathered at the makeshift altar. But if the reverend noticed her pleading expression, he didn't show any sign. He read several long passages of scripture, and extended the service with a few impassioned flourishes.

Driving home down a Kentucky side road, the woods and undergrowth converging on each side, Bessie couldn't draw a decent breath. Earl was quiet, lost in thought. The beams of the headlights splayed weakly in front of the car, lighting only a small section of the road. That foreshortened view seemed to stand for her circumstances. She was twenty years old, and the months that stretched ahead of her seemed empty of purpose. How many times had she stared across the dinner table at her mother and father, that hopelessly mismatched pair, and sworn to avoid their fate? Instead she had followed them, like a girl in a hypnotist's trance. She hadn't even had the substance to make an original mistake.

When Earl pulled into Parkersburg it was dark, and the church bells were ringing ten. He parked in front of her parents' house, set the hand brake, and came around to help her out the door.

'Thanks for the lovely picnic,' he said with a wink.

She managed a weak smile.

'I'd better get the car back or Father'll think I ran it into a ditch.' He gave her a peck on the cheek and roared off.

Bessie stood on the front lawn, holding her purse. All the house lights were out. Her mother would be in bed by now, having polished the kitchen and said her evening prayers. Her brother had no doubt slipped out to play stickball with his friends, though he was long past the age for such games. They were all trudging in the daily furrow. Nothing had changed. She was a married woman, she was going to be a mother, and still she would sleep tonight in her narrow child's bed.

She opened the front door and paused in the hall. Water ticked in the sink. The joists settled. Then she heard a cough in the living room.

'Who's there?' she called.

'Bessie?'

Her father's voice. She could guess at the level in the flask from a single word. 'Dad, you startled me.' She moved to turn on a lamp, but her father protested.

'It's nice in the dark. Come sit with me.'

She wanted nothing more than to go upstairs and pull the covers up to her neck, but she went to the sofa and sat down.

'How was your outing?' he asked.

'Fine.'

'How's our Mr. Helmick?' he asked in dry tones. Her father had never been fond of Earl.

'He's fine,' she said with a sigh.

Her eyes were slowly adjusting to the dark. Her father was right: it was peaceful. She could just make out the outlines of the piano's lathed legs, her mother's sewing chest and the soft contours of a half-finished garment, folded neatly on top. Above her father's head, a mirror caught the moonlight from the street, an oval of hoarfrost on the wall.

Mr. Haley broke the quiet. 'The hounds were quite upset the other day.'

She could hardly abide talk of his dogs, but there was something strange in his voice.

'Quite unlike them to bark that way in the afternoon. I got home early from the Flemings' and I could hear them all the way out front.' She heard the clink of metal against glass, the slosh of liquid, then saw him wedge the flask down beside him in the chair.

'How is Mrs. Fleming?' Bessie asked dully. The Flemings' son, Max, had been a senior with her at Parkersburg High. They'd performed in the class play together.

'As loose-jawed as ever,' Mr. Haley said. 'She's to be a grandmother again and can't stop nattering about the joys, the joys. I had the mind to wrap her neck in a curtain rope.'

'Do you ever wish for that?' Bessie asked, stirring a little.

'To murder a client?' Her father chuckled in the dark. 'Not exactly good for business.'

'No, to be a grandfather.' She looked at him directly, trying to meet his eyes in the shadows.

Mr. Haley sat forward in his chair – grateful for the opening. 'What I want, my dear, is for you to be happy.' His voice was hoarse. 'I want you to further your talents.'

Bessie felt as if someone had clutched her by the throat. 'I'm not sure I have any particular talents.'

'Poppycock. I've seen your marks. Drawing, design – all A's.'

'Marshall College isn't exactly known for its standards,' she said.

'Then it's time you went to art school. Did you ever send off to San Francisco for the forms?'

The mention of that plan, so impossible now, made tears spill down her cheeks.

'Don't cry,' Mr. Haley said. He rose unsteadily and sat beside her on the sofa. 'I know what you're thinking.'

'No, you don't,' she said fiercely.

'Yes, I do,' Mr. Haley said. He was nearly breathless. 'I was at the window. I heard the dogs and I went to the window and I heard you two in the yard.'

She could see him clearly now. His eyes were brimming. 'What did you hear?' she whispered, suddenly afraid.

'That he's in some kind of fool rush to marry. If he wants to elope he ought not shout it to the rooftops. What's wrong with that boy? What's the hurry?' He didn't wait for her answer. 'It's his parents, isn't it? They think we're not good enough.'

Even in her misery, she felt a small flare of relief. He didn't know about the baby.

Mr. Haley caught his daughter's hand. 'I won't let him force you into anything. You've got just one chance to be young, my dear. Don't louse it up the way I did.'

This advice, only hours too late, made her break into sobs. She pulled her hand free and covered her face. 'I don't know what's right anymore,' she said.

'Forget about what's right. Your mother and I did what was right and look at us.'

Hearing him admit to their unhappiness, as much as she had named it in secret, made her weep even harder. It was her arrival, after all, that had forced them to swallow their hopes.

Her father tried to brush away her tears, but in his excited state he only succeeded in poking her in the eye. He settled for squeezing her shoulder. 'Your mother and I get by. But there's got to be something more, hasn't there? I always thought you'd have more.'

She took a deep shuddering breath. Mr. Haley offered his handkerchief. 'You know the one thing I regret?' she asked. 'That I never studied with a good teacher.' She felt almost calm now, surveying this lost avenue. She blew her nose and leaned back against the couch cushions.

'My God, girl, you sound like you're ninety years old. Now listen to me.' He took her by the chin. 'You're going to enroll in the California School of Fine Arts, and I'm going to pay for it.'

'But, how?'

He puffed up a little. 'We'll find a way.'

At the mention of 'we,' Bessie's heart sank. 'We' meant her mother would take in more sewing, wearing out her eyesight so her daughter could draw still lifes of fruit.

'I'm grateful for the offer, Dad. Really. But I can't put that strain on you.'

But her father went on pressing his case, and by the time they said good night in the hall, she had begun to grasp at the rope he had thrown her. In her darkened bedroom, she stripped off her suit – her wedding suit! – already spinning desperate plans. She and Earl might weather this, but he had to see her side of things. She couldn't have the baby. She must continue her studies – No, it was hopeless. She might as well face the truth: she and Earl were already worlds apart. She would have to make a clean break.

She climbed into bed and lay awake for hours, replaying the things that her father had said. It was the only time in her life she could remember that someone had seen into the absolute heart of her troubles and offered a way out. But even as she knew that she would take it, that she would leave Earl and go west and enroll in art school, try to find a doctor who would end the pregnancy, she felt guilty at her presumption. Sleeping in the next room, divided from her by a thin wall, was her mother, for whom such a choice had been impossible. Still, by the time the sun began seeping under the window shade, Bessie had convinced herself this was yet another reason to make her escape.

On the morning of November 1, 1928, Glen walked downstream to scout the first rapid in Cataract, his stomach knotted with expectation. He had waited so long for this moment and now it was here. He would see what the river was made of. Bessie had stayed in camp, saying she would face the 'boiling cauldron' soon enough, so he picked his way alone through the boulders, keeping his eye on the water. The roar grew progressively louder, and soon he saw plumes of spray lofting up from the river. He reached the drop and caught his first glimpse of the white water. The current poured over an invisible ledge and broke into furious waves. Boulders studded the waterway. What was startling was the thickness – the density the water took on when it was riled up. It went frothing over truck-sized rocks and poured into shadowy holes.

Not too bad. He made his way to the end of the rapid and crouched down as Cap Guleke had taught him. At water level, staring upstream, he could make out the half-submerged rocks.

When he had taken quick stock from above, the right-hand run had looked best, but from this angle he caught sight of a huge rock just glazed by the current. After studying the rapid a while longer, he thought he saw a better route along the left. There was a big boulder in the way at the top, but if he cut hard around that, the rest looked like an easy shot. He scrambled up some scree near the cliff and picked out a bush on each shore to mark the crucial turn.

A bit of movement caught his eye. It was Bessie, picking her way along the cobble below. He climbed down to meet her.

'I was worried you'd fallen in,' she yelled, taking a nervous glance at the rapid. Her face was pale.

'This is an easy one,' he shouted. 'I've found a good route.'

They packed up quickly and pulled into the current. The scow lingered for a moment, holding back. People speak of being swept into rapids, but there is often a section of eerily calm water before the falls, the river backed up by the ledge, and a good oarsman can row in place in front of the maelstrom without being pulled over. Still, it's not a good place to linger, or you'll lose your nerve. Glen remembered the feeling well from his trip down the Salmon. When he was poised at the head of a rapid, trying to find the markers he'd picked out from the shore, his stomach climbed into his throat. Then he dropped over the lip and into the roaring channel and his mind went clear and calm. He watched each shift of the scow's position, making pulls on the sweeps, moving through a stretch of expanded time, so that the minute or so it took to make the run became some indefinably longer period. It was as if he were working counter to the current, slowing down its quick sections so they could be parsed minutely. He didn't feel anything he would call fear in those moments, only a heightened sense of clarity. Even in the furious bucking waves, when the boat stood nearly on end, he observed it all from a remove. It was only when he was safely riding out the chop that his heart began to thud and things speeded up again. Then he was filled with a rush of elation – for the boat, reliable beneath him, for the brisk wind in his face. All this let him know he was alive. People sometimes asked him why he ran rivers, why take the risk? But to give up this heightened feeling for the sake of caution, to go about guarding your life like a miser – as far as he was concerned, you might as well be dead.

Now he aimed the scow toward the tongue and felt it slide over the ledge. He skirted the boulder at the head of the run, but they were a few feet off their line and the boat grazed the rock – a glancing blow, but enough to jar them off course. Glen pulled hard on the stern sweep, trying to correct, but it felt like trying to pilot a steamboat with a twig. He had forgotten how hard the river pulled back. The scow climbed up the face of a standing wave and slid down into the hole behind, water pouring over the gunwales. Bessie was clinging to the front sweep, too frightened to steer. They were still keeping roughly to their line, a little off to the right, but if he pulled hard here –

He didn't see the rock – it must have been just deep enough to miss scouting – but he felt it. They struck it at an angle and out of the corner of his eye he saw Bessie jackknife over the side.

Reith Hyde

Peach Springs, Arizona, isn't worth calling a town. It's set up on the mesa near the west end of the Grand Canyon, at the head of a big drainage that carves north and down to the river. I passed two restless days there, waiting for replies to my telegrams. Luckily I had a set of maps – a copy of the USGS survey of the river, which Glen had left pinned to their bedroom wall at the ranch – and I spent my time studying the route. After eating breakfast in the hotel, I went to the store to see if word had come from the army – I must have gone in there twenty times a day. On December 16, there was a wire from the Park Service, asking for more information, and I penciled an immediate reply. The rest of the day, nothing came. To pass the hours, I'd walk out into the desert and back ten times, trying to keep my stiff knee ready for hiking. Of course this brought me past the store ten more times, and it was only through the strictest discipline that I didn't stop in. It had occurred to me that we might have missed each other, that Glen and Bessie arrived at Pearce Ferry after I left, and that even then they were heading toward Needles, just as I was working my way east. But I figured the ferryman would tell them I had stopped in, and that Glen would send a message home as soon as he could. Jeanne had instructions to forward any wires that came to Twin Falls, and one sentence, even a word, from my son would put an end to my torment, but I was starting to feel pity for the clerk, so I made myself wait an hour between visits. I ate supper at the hotel and sent a final telegram to Jeanne, giving her an update. I didn't bother wiring Edna. She was always in a high state of nerves, and this situation hadn't helped things. Her sister would pass on what she could handle.

It was hard not to stew over that last telegram to Green River – if it reached them, Glen didn't mention it in his letters. On the morning of their departure, I sat bolt upright in bed, realizing that they might have forgone the life vests as a cost-saving measure. My son was very stubborn where money was concerned – he would never ask for help. I threw on my boots and rushed into town to send a wire: PLEASE BUY LIFE VESTS STOP I WILL PAY. Not that Glen was likely to heed my advice. He valued my opinions around the ranch, but he never listened to me about rivers. When he proposed running the Salmon, and taking Jeanne along, I made a few comments about the risk, trying to appeal to his reason, and then got hot under the collar in spite of myself and forbade him to go. He just looked at me and shrugged. 'We'll talk about this when I get back,' he said.

At first I was furious. But when I saw the set of his jaw, I pulled up short. I thought, You want him to live like you, a slave to worry? It's the nature of youth to spit in the face of hazard. They don't know how life's capable of handling them, and there's power in that.

It's no surprise that I could never bring myself to gamble. Even after Maggie died, and a fellow in town invited me in on a weekly hand of poker – and what could it have hurt? a whiskey, a smoke, and some regular company – I preferred to stay out at the ranch with the children. For a number of years after my wife passed away I was like a captain at the wheel of a sunken ship. I was presiding over the wreck of my married life, and I probably thought it was noble to suffer like that, a way of honoring my wife's memory. Then I saw that I had children left, and that I had a responsibility to raise them as Maggie would have wanted, so I made myself come up for air.

But I wasn't the same. I was nervous. Not the kind of nerves that show on the outside – I didn't jiggle my leg under the table, I never chewed my nails – but the kind that whittle you down from within. I went around taking care of the ranch, making sure the three of them were clean and well fed, but I kept seeing bad omens everywhere – the corral that looked latched and wasn't, the ladder that hadn't been properly braced. I can't tell you how many times in a given day I'd imagine the ordinary thing gone wrong. It was like a side rail that I couldn't help switching on, a kind of parallel track to my life, in which – truth told – nothing much bad happened.

Then my son went off to California, came back, and said he'd met a girl. Said he was going to marry her, and they were going to run the Colorado together.

You can imagine my fear. What you can't imagine was my relief.

I'd been worrying for so long about things unlikely to happen – so unlikely that I couldn't even bring myself to speak of them. I'd gone around locking up the lye and the kerosene, and all the while holding my tongue. And even though fifteen years had gone by since Maggie died and the children were old enough to see to themselves, worrying had become a kind of habit, like a stain rubbed into wood. But now my son was set on a plan so dangerous, so rash, that I had a right to speak up. Plenty of men had died running that river. Only a few score of them had made it to the end. Glen and his new wife planned to live with me on the ranch for the summer. They'd leave after harvest. I figured I had time to change their minds.

But one by one the months passed, and I couldn't bring myself to say a thing. You should have heard them talk around the dinner table. They had faith in themselves. I could see that my son wouldn't be swayed, and I was afraid that if I spoke out, I would drain the confidence he needed to pull off their plan. Only once in my life had I held him back, and though he minded me then, I had come to regret it. So I tried to remember the way I was taught: you never wake a sleepwalker. And you don't startle a child who's climbed too high on an orchard ladder. You just keep quiet and watch and hope he knows where to put his feet.

Glen and Bessie Hyde

She was still in the air when Glen reached out with one hand and caught her by the heel – a move of pure reflex, the way you'd ward off a blow. For a moment he was frozen there, holding his wife by the foot, her head and shoulders lost in the froth. Then he came to his senses and pulled her in.

The scow bounced its way through the tail waves while he crouched in the bottom of the boat, wiping the hair out of her face. Her clothes were drenched and she was shaking.

'Are you all right?' he asked.

'I think so,' she said, her teeth clenched. She broke into a hacking cough.

Glen put his hands on her shoulders. 'Take shallow breaths.' He cast an anxious glance at the river. They were heading into the second rapid.

'Hang on to the ropes,' he said, leaping up to grab both sweeps. There was no time to pick a course. He'd have to go straight down the tongue. This time luck was on his side. They dropped over the ledge and into the waves, grinding against several rocks but somehow battering through. At the bottom of the rapid, Glen caught an eddy and pulled them over to the bank.

For an hour he paced on the beach, trying to convince Bessie that her dunking was a fluke.

'You'll get a feel for the water after a while,' he told her. 'How to brace yourself.'

She was wrapped in a blanket, a human teepee with a shivering head. 'What if you hadn't caught me?' It was all she could think of – how narrowly she had escaped.

'I'd have fished you out at the end,' he said. 'If you go in, flip onto your back and keep your feet pointed downstream. That way you can push off the rocks.'

At last he persuaded her to get back in the scow, and they ran two more rapids without a mishap. That night it rained, and they curled together under the blankets, an oilskin pulled up like a bedspread to ward off the wet. Even under all those layers, Bessie couldn't stop shivering. Glen shifted on the mattress, pulling her close with one arm, rubbing her foot with the back of his own. She loved that about him – even half asleep, his instinct was to comfort her.

'Are you cold?' he asked.

'Just a little.'

'That was a bad first day. But you were getting a nice feel for the sweep there at the end.'

Indeed, she had started to notice how the waves rose and fell, and could sense when to shift the sweep and when to brace herself in readiness. Perhaps going overboard early was a good thing. There was a comfort in having faced the worst. Still, she couldn't stop replaying the scene: the bone-jarring impact, and then the helpless flight into the waves. She hadn't felt Glen catch her foot. Just found herself in the bottom of the boat, taking gulps of air.

'Are you asleep?' she whispered to Glen.

'Not yet,' he said softly. But in a moment, she could hear the regular soughing of his breath.

In the morning, the sky broke clear and they woke refreshed. But they made an unfortunate entry into rapid number five and barely made it through. Glen decided to teach her how to line.

Lining was a way to get past a rapid that looked unrunnable, using ropes to coax the boat along the bank. If the rapids had been edged by smooth beach, it would have been safe and easy work, but the banks near white water were always thick with boulders, and edging out and around the bigger ones meant coming perilously close to the fast current. Bessie would stand on the shore, holding the bow line so the scow wouldn't get loose. Glen would wade into the water and push the boat around the rocks. The biggest danger was letting the bow or stern swing wide into the current. If the river got hold of the scow, they would be helpless to reclaim it.

'What would you do?' Bessie asked, when he explained this possibility.

'I'd run like hell and hop onboard,' he said soberly. 'And you'd better do the same.'

They tried their new technique on rapid number six. First they carried the mattress and the heaviest crates to the end of the rapid, so the boat would ride higher and wouldn't hang up in the shallows. Then Bessie took her spot on the bank, put on gloves, and gripped the rope until her arms seemed to tear at the roots. The river kept tugging at the boat, trying to pull it toward the tongue. At times she felt she was restraining a living thing – a headstrong bull. But Glen had the harder job: wading in waist-deep icy water to push the scow free of obstructions, losing purchase on the slick boulders underfoot. His hands were chapped and bitten by the rope, his feet half frozen. He only lined for Bessie's sake. If he had his druthers, he'd run them all. Or so he told himself. Lining was so costly – to their bodies and their will – it made him grow sick of caution. A stretch of water that would have taken two minutes to run took them half a day to line. And, in hindsight, lining looked nearly more dangerous than running. He could have jammed his foot between two submerged rocks and snapped his ankle, or worse, he might have been pinned between a boulder and the scow. That last thought gave him a shiver. Even half unloaded, the boat probably weighed eight hundred pounds. And there wasn't a doctor for fifty miles.

That night, their third in Cataract, they barely had the

strength to heat up a can of beans. Bessie looked around at their situation. The cliffs had risen higher, though a week earlier she wouldn't have believed it was possible. Any deeper and it seemed the river would cut down to molten earth. For hours she had been consumed with the progress of the scow – around this boulder, past that jutting driftwood log – a hundred small hazards passed. Now she had a sudden shift in perspective. They were two specks at the bottom of a mammoth gorge. Ants pushing a bit of bark. The rim, outlined against a milk-blue sky, begged to be reached. But then where would she be? On a mesa, miles from nowhere. With countless gullies and slot canyons to cross before she reached a town. A town – how good it sounded. Better yet, a city, with oily lights and cafés, the streets wafting with the smell of cigarettes and bread.

Bessie arrived in Oakland by train at the end of June 1926. It was a difficult trip. She couldn't afford a Pullman, and had traveled across the entire country in an upright chair. Over the long hot days and restless nights, she replayed her separation from Earl. It hadn't gone well. She had made one last attempt to convince him of the importance of finishing her studies (she had left the matter of her pregnancy aside), but when she pressed the matter, he flew into a rage. They were at his parents' house. The Helmicks had gone off to a Rotary Club dinner. She watched in numb shock as he shouted and paced and thought, This is the beginning. He will always decide what I can and cannot do.

When he seemed to wear himself out, she stood up and put on her coat. 'I'm going, Earl,' she said, and walked out the door, waiting, with each step, for his hand on her shoulder. At home, she packed in a rush – taking only a single trunk – and went to catch the eight-o'clock train. Her father drove, and as they rattled down the familiar streets, she kept glancing back, half surprised not to see the Helmick phaeton pulling up behind. Even after her father had kissed her goodbye and the engine had pulled out of the station, her shoulders were stiff as a wooden hanger. The train stopped at every burg along the tracks, and if Earl drove in his typical breakneck fashion, he would have no trouble catching up. Usually he sulked for a while after an argument, but if he went to the house looking for her, she had told her parents not to lie, it was too much to ask of them.

The train came to a screeching halt. A long platform lit by a single electric bulb. No one was waiting. Bugs swarmed in the funnel of light. Then she saw a familiar figure in the shadows. He stepped forward, making her gasp, and waved at someone two windows down. Wrong face. Still, her heart hammered in her chest. If Earl showed up and tried to drag her off the train, no one would stop him. He was her husband, after all.

Only when the sun rose and she saw that they were well into Kansas did she let herself stretch and look around. She had escaped! Hard to fathom why he'd let her go so easily. She turned it over in her mind in the coming days, as the train chugged toward the biggest mountains she'd ever seen – a dark rumpling of foothills staggering up toward jagged peaks. Then it came to her: he was afraid. A big man in a little town. Despite all his confidence and bluster, he had never ventured more than a hundred miles from home. For days now she had been dreading what he might do with his fury. Go to her parents and confront them with the elopement, the baby? Now she knew this was unfounded. Earl wouldn't tell a soul. There was too much shame in it.

Her husband's small-mindedness filled her with scorn, but when she stepped onto the platform in Oakland and watched the other travelers rush into the arms of family and friends, she began to understand his fear. She had traveled by herself the whole width of the country, and no one so much as gave her a glance. She moved quickly, hoping to shake this feeling, and inquired at the ticket window about the way to San Francisco. A taxi took her to the ferry dock, and once she boarded the boat, her spirits lifted. It was late afternoon and the bay was glittering. There were islands in the middle of the vast waterway – she hadn't expected that – and ahead of her the low blocky outlines of the city, and then the hills, rising into a bank of pillowing fog. Her first glimpse of the city thrilled her. There was a strange, moist sheen to the light. Men gathered on street corners, their shirts open at the throat. She stepped briskly, conscious of her wallet tucked deep in her purse, her white blouse with the little buttons bo-peeping down the front. She had never seen such a place – the varied faces, the clang of the trolley cars mounting the hills.

She took a modest hotel room near Union Square and bought a copy of the *Chronicle*. There seemed to be plenty of apartments, but most of them, on inspection, were either dismal or out of her price range. After a week of fruitless searching, she found an ad that looked promising: 'A quiet, refined apartment house of unusual excellence. Positively fireproof.'

She met the manager at the front door and followed him up the creaking stairs. The walls were the color of putty and marked by kidney-shaped stains, as if the plaster had been oozing some undefined liquid. Fireproof indeed. She took the stairs slowly, squaring her shoulders. When she got to the landing she saw a block of sun falling through an open door to the left, and she paused behind the landlord's narrow silhouette in a state of almost painful hope, willing him to turn in that direction.

He veered to the right and opened a chipped door at the opposite end of the hall. 'This is it,' he said, his voice echoing off the walls. He was a sallow man, hardly bigger than she was. While she examined the place, he tracked her like a cat.

There was a kitchen the size of a closet, a tiny bathroom with a sour mildewed smell, and small bedroom in the back.

'The floor plan seems a bit strange,' Bessie said.

'It was divided out of a larger flat,' the landlord told her. 'They used to call this the fainting room, but now that corsets are out of fashion, girls can do a bit more without getting winded.' Then he shocked her by reaching out and placing a hand on her waist. 'I see you don't wear one.'

Bessie stepped back neatly and pretended to study the room. The single window looked out on a ventilation shaft. She paced off the distance from wall to wall and calculated that a mattress would take up the entire width of it.

The landlord watched all this with cold amusement. 'There aren't many vacancies these days,' he said.

'Oh, that's not true,' she said lightly, slipping past him and out the front door. She crossed quickly to the sunlit flat down the hall. It wasn't much bigger, but there were two windows facing south, and after her eyes had adjusted to the glare, she peered through the smeared glass at the street below. They were in the Italian section. Across the street was a tailor's shop. She glanced over her shoulder to be sure that the landlord had followed. He was stalled in the door frame, looking nervous.

'There's always room for good tenants,' Bessie said, feeling her pulse pound in her throat. She ran a gloved finger along the sill and gathered up a thick hat of dust. 'I'll give you twenty dollars a month for this place,' she said, brushing the fuzz to the floor.

The landlord shook his head. 'This one's rented.'

'Did they put down a deposit?'

'It's rented,' the landlord said again.

'Yes, it is,' Bessie said, stepping forward and grasping his bony hand. The lecher sucked in his breath. 'It is rented to me, for two months advance payment,' Bessie said. And before he could answer she reached into her embroidered bag and peeled off the bills.

When she walked back to her hotel, she had the apartment key in her purse and fifteen dollars to her name. She only hoped that her father would live up to his promise.

Fifteen days after Glen and Bessie set out, they ran the last rapid in Cataract. That twenty-mile canyon had driven them to the edge of their strength. They had lined nine rapids and run forty-one. There were no more upsets, and Bessie had become deft at working the front sweep, but it had rained nearly every day – lashing rain that streamed down their faces and soaked their gear. When they finally drifted into Glen Canyon, Bessie felt they had entered paradise. The river was broad and flat, with castle buttes in the distance, and smooth cliffs eroded into arches above the beaches. The walls had slid down again – perhaps a few hundred feet high and stained a warm ocher color. And in the scoops of green bottomland there were signs of human life. They drifted past the remains of a prospector's camp, then past a log cabin, which proved deserted. A few miles farther on they noticed a boat tied to the bank and pulled in beside it. In a grove of cottonwoods set back from the river, they spotted another cabin. Glen shouted hello, and an old man appeared in the doorway, wearing a men's dress shirt and a pair of gap-tongued boots, his bare legs visible in between.

'Hello!' he said, skittering toward them without a trace of shame.

He introduced himself as Washington Lincoln Pate. 'But I tend to go by Pate,' he said. And then, seeing their expressions: 'My mother had a fine feeling for the presidents.'

'Nice spot you've got here,' Glen said, turning to the swath of lush grass and the red cliffs beyond.

'More than twenty miles from the nearest telephone,' Pate

said with pride. 'I'm pretty sure I'm the farthest removed from civilization of any man in the U.S.'

'Well, I hope we're not disturbing you,' Bessie said.

'Not at all. I always like a visitor. I just don't have plans to go visiting myself.'

She nodded and tried not to stare at his legs.

'How's the mining around here?' Glen asked.

Pate scowled and looked suspicious. 'Terrible, terrible. Nothing but gravel.'

Glen nodded and threw Bessie a quiet smile.

Then Pate caught sight of the scow. 'Is that what you came in on?'

They said yes.

'Where are you headed?'

'Needles,' Glen said.

'Needles?' The old man looked blank. 'Where's that?' When Glen told him, he cocked his head back in surprise. 'California? Lot of rough water between here and there.'

'Did you come down through Cataract?' Bessie asked.

'I did. Carried that little boat around all the rapids, though. Must have been a hundred of them.' He glanced back upstream with a furrowed brow. 'That canyon scared the hell out of me. After that, I figured I'd rest a bit.' He grinned at the dirt. 'Guess I been resting ever since.'

They stood quietly for a moment, staring at the cottonwoods. The sun had come out and the last autumn leaves flashed like coins in the branches. Then Bessie caught sight of the miner's pants, drying on a low limb, and had to stifle a smile.

'Damn, I'm neglecting my manners,' Pate said suddenly. He trotted over to the shack and beckoned them through the darkened doorway. 'I've got a few morsels I've been saving for a special occasion.'

The shack had no windows and smelled of damp earth and

dirty socks. Glen rolled his eyes in Bessie's direction and convinced Pate that they ought to cook out on the beach. Together they made a fire and put together a supper. Pate contributed a pot of black-eyed peas, flavored with a piece of smoked venison, which had been lovingly stored in a scrap of brown paper. It was a chunk of meat about the size of a thumb, but a thumbful of the smokehouse was enough to suffuse the beans with a dark tang. Glen made biscuits with nearly the last of their lumpy flour. Bessie went down to the boat and came back with her shirt hem pulled up on a few offerings: an onion (still firm), six potatoes (full of eyes). They were on thin rations, until they could reach Lee's Ferry and replenish their supplies, but it seemed fitting to splurge for the sake of company.

When the meal was finished, Bessie caught herself staring at the miner. 'Don't you get lonely down here?' she asked.

'Naw,' he said. He pushed his hat back and looked up at the dark cliffs. 'Most men have got pickled hearts. What's to miss about that?'

As if to prove him wrong, Glen went down to the scow and came back with a can of pears in syrup. The old prospector speared a dripping half and looked as if his eyes would pop out. 'Now I *do* miss pears,' he said, lifting his fork in gratitude.

Later, when they'd finished eating, Pate started to sing. He had a high, crackling voice. Since neither Glen nor Bessie knew the words they couldn't join in. Instead they listened as he quavered through ballads about gamblers and benevolent outlaws. Runnels of syrup glistened in the corners of his mouth and his Adam's apple worked up and down.

When the blaze had slumped down to embers, and he seemed to have run out of songs, Bessie pulled out her notebook and selected a piece of charcoal from the edge of the fire. Working in near darkness, she made a quick sketch of their host. He was hunched on a fallen log, shirttail hanging between his bare knees, his creased face turned toward the last of the fire.

When it was finished, she tore out the page and handed it to him.

'What's this?' he said, stirring from his reverie.

'Something to remember us by.'

He threw another branch on the coals, and when it burst into flame he studied the drawing. 'Why, I look like an old hermit,' he said, sounding surprised. A few minutes later he made some excuse to step away from the fire. When he returned he was wearing his pants.

Bessie blushed – perhaps she shouldn't have presumed – but when they shoved off in the morning, he held the drawing in one hand and waved with the other until they turned the bend.

They spent three more days in Glen Canyon, passing through sections more beautiful than any they'd seen. They drifted past undulating golden walls. Along the riverway, streams had cut side canyons into the cliffs, giving glimpses of spring-fed greenery. When they woke on the morning of November 6, the sky was fired a pale blue, the air soft and nearly motionless. They packed up camp and drifted for a few hours, Glen gently nosing the boat down the center of the river, Bessie half asleep on the pile of duffel, her eyes closed against the sun. She was nearly dreaming when she felt the boat scuff bottom and jerk to a halt. She sat up, rubbing her eyes. They were docked at a sandy beach.

'Is that it for the day?' she asked, confused. Glen was always eager to make good time. With their provisions running low, hunger gave them an added incentive to speed.

Glen nodded his head toward a narrow slot canyon, opening at the head of the beach. 'I saw a nice spring in there. I don't know about you, but I could use a bath.'

Bessie smiled. 'A bath sounds like heaven. I've been making liberal use of my lavender water, hoping you wouldn't notice.' She dug their toiletry bag out of a crate and wrapped a bar of soap in a washcloth.

'Why don't you bring the whole kit,' Glen said. 'I'll give myself a barber's special. We can even do laundry. It's warm enough to go naked for a while.'

Bessie packed a knapsack with her notebook and pencils, their copy of Ellsworth Kolb's book, and a towel. Then they crossed the beach and entered the mouth of the canyon, a tight ocher passageway, with a clear stream threading through the bottom, bordered by moss and ferns. After winding upward a hundred yards or so, they came to a small pool, ringed by smooth sandstone, the walls curving around on all sides in shades of caramel and forming a steep face at the upstream end, down which a rivulet of water ran. It reminded Bessie of a room in a Turkish bath – she'd seen pictures in *National Geographic* – and the sun, directly overhead, bounced heat off the stone and warmed the rock underfoot.

They washed their clothes first, stripping down and soaping their garments against the smooth rock, then rinsing them in the outflow of the pool. When the clean fabric was laid out to dry in the sun, Bessie pulled out the washcloth and stepped into the water. She sucked in her breath, ankles aching from the cold.

Glen waded in, smiling at her, then sank under the surface. When he stood up, the water streamed down his chest, over his furrowed stomach. 'Do it quick,' he said, still knee deep, slicking a hand through his hair. 'It feels good.'

She watched him for a moment, not quite trusting, then splashed forward, dunked down in an awkward curtsy, forcing her head under the numbing cold, and leapt up again. 'My God!' She splashed out of the water and hopped from one foot to the other. 'I think I'm clean enough.'

Glen laughed. 'Throw me the soap,' he said. He caught the white bar as it sailed through the air, then wet it and worked up a lather in the sparse hair on his chest. He seemed unfazed by the cold, calmly soaping his armpits and crotch, then breaststroking through the pool to rinse himself. Back in the shallows, he started working the bar through his hair.

Bessie had settled on the hot stone, her skin slowly drying, and watched him. He was so beautiful, his body pared down to sinew and string. Like an anatomical drawing. She got out her notebook and started a sketch – the way his back flared out from his waist, the knobs of his vertebrae showing when he bent over to rinse. The small triangular dent at the base of his spine. He turned and saw her busy with the pencil.

'I hope you've given me a fig leaf,' he said, squinting into the sun.

She didn't take her eyes from the paper. 'I didn't know you were so old-fashioned.' Then she looked up and sighed. 'Oh, you've moved.' She set the notebook aside, giving the drawing a last glance. There was something there, even half-finished – the ease of his body, caught unawares, the oblong enveloping curve of the pool. The sketches she'd made on this trip were different from the ones she'd done in school. Often made on the fly, they were bolder, more free. Wind ruffled the pages while she worked, and the cold cramped her fingers, so she had to be quick. Speed brought a certain clarity of style. She closed the notebook and lay back on the slope at the edge of the water, feeling the heat loosen her limbs. There wasn't a wisp of wind, and no sound but the soft trickle feeding the pool. Her mind was drifting, empty of thought, when she felt a cool soapy hand on her knee. 'Hold still,' Glen said softly. His slid his lathered palm down to her ankle, lifted one foot, and began washing between her toes.

She opened her eyes and smiled at him. 'For a moment I thought I was in a Turkish bath.'

'Good thing you're not. Did you ever read Twain's description of those places?' Glen asked. He moved to her other foot, then squatted near the water and worked up more lather. 'They made him wear these big wooden clogs. He slipped and nearly brained himself on the marble. Then they scrubbed him with some kind of mitt. He said the more they scrubbed, the worse he smelled.'

Bessie laughed softly and closed her eyes, feeling the percolation of suds on her shins, the polished surface of the sandstone beneath her, and then Glen's hands again, soaping her legs, her belly and breasts, one arm and then the other, all the way down to the fingers. She opened her eyes. 'I love you. Do you know that?'

He didn't answer, just slipped his fingers beneath her shoulders, scratching lightly with his fingernails. Shyness broke over his face. She was always amazed by that. He had no physical modesty, only an instinctive, lazy talent for pleasure, but an honest word could unman him. She sat up and pulled him toward her, soap slick between their chests. 'Glen Hyde, I love you to pieces.' She pulled back and stared into his eyes, hazel flecked with gold. 'You're a good man.'

'I don't know about that,' he said. 'A lucky man. That's for sure.' Once again, he looked away. He was more grateful than he could say, for her love, her faith in him, but in some strange way he was afraid to speak of it. Before he met Bessie, he'd only been on a few dates, farm girls he'd known from high school, and though he found them unsatisfying, he hadn't been one to daydream about the perfect girl. He just went on about his work, his plans. Though he felt a small ripple when his childhood friends married – a sense of time passing – he never envied them. He knew what he didn't want: a girl who'd never been over the state line, who would grow plump and want him close to home, who would fret when he set off to run rivers. Then he met Bessie, and saw his way clear to another life. She was well traveled, with her own ambitions; someone to go adventuring with. He still marveled at his good fortune, but he had trouble putting it all into words. For him, love was a matter of gestures, choices made. He was always thinking of her, looking after her comfort. He had to hope that was enough.

Now he looked down at the drying lather on her shoulders. 'We'd better rinse,' he said, 'or you'll start cracking like plaster.'

She stood up and waded into the pool again, confused by his evasion. She knew that he loved her, but so often it seemed that she didn't have the faintest idea what he was thinking. With a little bolt of anger, she dove into the frigid water. She expected it to hurt – wanted it to – but when she surfaced in the center of the pool, she was surprised to find that the sun and his body had warmed her to the core. Dog-paddling slowly, she watched as Glen propped a small mirror in a crack in the wall. He began to shave, rinsing his straight razor in the shallows. Suddenly she remembered one of their first evenings at the ranch. They were sitting on the porch, as they often did, both of them quiet. 'What are you thinking?' Bessie had asked. He turned to her: 'Nothing, really.' She couldn't fathom this. Her mind was always skimming, out toward the future, back through the past, like the bats that darted over the river at night. 'You have to be thinking of something,' she said. Glen shrugged: 'I guess I don't always have words in my head.'

Now she swam to the lip of the pool and stepped out. Glen was packing up his shaving kit. 'Ready to head back?'

'Yes, I'm famished,' Bessie said. The cold swim had made her stomach knot down.

Their pants were still too damp to wear, but Glen pulled on his boots and buttoned his shirt. 'I look like old pickle-hearted Pate,' he said, pointing down at his bare legs.

Bessie smiled. 'We're lucky we didn't catch him on a real wash day.'

They walked quietly back to the river – thinking, or not thinking. Bessie found a smooth rock in the sun and began reading Kolb's book. Glen laid out their laundry to dry in the scow. He had just finished arranging the clothes when a spray of pebbles skittered down the cliff face above. He looked up. A buck. Four-point. They were downwind. The animal hadn't spotted them; it was still picking its way along a high ledge. He slipped his hand behind him and gripped the rifle barrel. Should he slide it up quickly and shoot? Or try to ease it up quietly, hoping the buck wouldn't notice? He'd get a better shot that way. Just then the buck froze and looked down. Glen's body decided for him. In one motion he shouldered the rifle, levered, and shot. The sound ricocheted from wall to wall.

Bessie startled and threw down the book, casting a terrified look in Glen's direction, then, seeing him still standing, followed his gaze to the buck, teetering on the ledge. The impact of the bullet, dead in the chest, had driven its shoulders toward the wall, and if it crumpled there, they'd never get it down. Such a waste of meat. But as its head listed toward the cliff, its hindquarters swung out over the ledge, pulling the body free into space. The shot was still echoing as the buck wheeled down, horns and hooves slicing the air. It landed with a thud at the base of the cliff.

That night they had a feast: a pan of biscuits, stuffed with hunks of venison, seared to a crisp and running with juices. One by one, the simple pleasures were returning to them: food, good weather, company.

On November 8, twenty days after they'd shoved off from Green River, they turned a bend and saw a flat barge attached to a cable – Lee's Ferry. They had reached the beginning of the Grand Canyon. It was an obvious spot for a crossing. The crenellated red walls dipped low here, giving access from both sides. On the right, the Paria River drained into the Colorado, cutting a wide canyon. Set back on the sandy beach near the junction was an old stone fort and a few cabins.

After the long float through Glen Canyon, it was strange to

have air and sky opening all around – a kind of clarifying vastness. Bessie's eyes had never felt so sharp, so able to take in everything, up close and at a distance. There was a lone man down at the water's edge. When he gave a shout, a crowd gathered. What sweet relief to see so many people, moving toward the water and waving their arms. They pulled the scow in nose first and Glen leapt out to tie off.

'You the honeymooners? We heard you might be coming through,' one man said.

Another one stepped up to examine the scow. 'Funny-looking craft. Got a name for her?' He was wearing a hat that looked like it doubled as a pillow.

Bessie spoke up: 'We call her *Rain in the Face.*'

The men laughed and crowded closer, reaching out to shake Glen's hand.

Their first few hours onshore were spent arranging to buy supplies from the ferryman: flour and coffee and beans. The fellow would make a tidy profit on the goods, but he'd have to wait for the next mule train from Flagstaff before he could replenish his stores. Glen was loading the sacks into the scow when a strange grinding filled the canyon. An auto appeared on the far cliff, switchbacking down the dirt road to the river. 'Looks like I've got a customer,' the ferryman said, unlocking the chain that held the barge to the bank and starting across. When he got to the other side, a man stepped out of the auto and boarded the barge on foot. He introduced himself as Keene, a reporter from Flagstaff. Word had made its way along the railroad line that a pair of newlyweds had set out from Green River, hoping to run the Colorado in a homemade boat. He was hoping to intercept them, get a story out of it.

'You're in luck,' the ferryman told him, pointing to the scow.

Once he reached the north shore, the reporter asked Glen detailed questions about the boat and about the means of navigating the rapids. He scribbled the answers on a small pad. When he was satisfied, he approached Bessie, who was writing letters to her family at a table in the sun. 'Do you mind answering a few questions, Mrs. Hyde?' He was a short, ruddy-faced fellow, about Glen's age, late twenties perhaps, and already bald.

'Of course not,' she said, putting her pencil down.

'I understand you're the first woman to run through Cataract Canyon. Did you know you were setting a record?'

'Our main object was to give me a thrill,' she said, flashing for a moment on that weightless terror as she flew off the scow. There was a catch in her throat, and she waited for it to pass. 'But if we set a record in the bargain, that's all right by me.'

'But you are the first woman to attempt to navigate the Grand Canyon, is that right?' the reporter asked.

'As far as I know, yes.'

'And what do you think of the rapids so far?'

She drew a small doodle in the margin of her letter. 'I've been drenched a few times, but I'm enjoying myself.'

He smiled down at his notebook, still scribbling. 'Any trouble keeping house on the boat?' When she didn't answer for a moment, he looked up.

Bessie forced herself to look serene. 'Glen is very good at ironing,' she said lightly. 'And when I'm not chopping wood, I sometimes give him a hand.'

The reporter stared at her blankly. Then he broke into a grin and pointed with his pencil. 'You had me there for a minute, Mrs. Hyde.'

She gave him a shallow smile. Her first taste of public life.

'This is excellent,' the reporter said, closing his notebook. 'The local rivermen are quite impressed with the way your husband handles that scow. Sounds like you're in capable hands.'

Bessie nodded and thanked him for his time. But when she

turned back to her letter, the man's questions burned in her head. It shouldn't have surprised her that he considered this Glen's feat. She could just imagine the way the papers would describe them: 'A strapping rancher and his tiny new bride . . .' Of course, down on the river there was none of that. They both pulled for their lives. All the more reason she would have to write her own account. It was the only place she could tell the full story.

That night, Glen and Bessie were guests of the ferryman, who fed them venison and pumpkin pie and laid out a bed for them in the front room. The cabin was imperfectly sealed. Bessie lay awake, listening to the wind whistling through the chinks. She was half amazed that they were already attracting attention. It was unfolding just as Glen had said it would. But under scrutiny, the purpose of their trip seemed to turn murky. If they made it through, people would call them heroes, but for what? To her mind, heroes did something for others' sake – Madame Curie, Clarence Darrow – facing risk or injustice, at great cost to themselves. She and Glen were certainly courting danger, but whether they succeeded or failed wouldn't matter to mankind. They were on a private venture, trying to make a name for themselves, a new life. And if she faced an adversary, it was within – the fear that lay in her stomach like a cold cinder.

But there, wasn't that true of everyone? When you went to the center of yourself, a trapdoor opened to the world. When Lindbergh flew across the Atlantic alone, he widened our idea of what was possible, of what a man could do. Didn't we all take something from that? That was why he was lifted up and passed across the crowd at Le Bourget: he stood for the best of us. The one who could go without sleep, who could thread between the boiling thunderheads, over the vast empty sea, and not lose hope. As Bessie spun down toward sleep, she held that thought like a filament: perhaps there was a girl out there, awake at her bedroom window, looking over a smug little town, who might take something from her story.

In the beginning of August 1926, Bessie enrolled at the California School of Fine Arts. Her father's check had arrived on time, and she went in person to pay for the first term. God, what a stunning place. The building, finished just the year before, had been modeled after a Mediterranean villa, with arched galleries on both stories, the railings looking down on a brick courtyard and mosaic pool. A few young men were drawing at easels on the patio, a teacher in a black beret – a beret! – leaning over them. She passed a row of large studios, flooded with sun, and soaked up the details: bizarre little drawing benches, each like a child's hobbyhorse – you sat astride them and faced an attached sketch pad – skeletons dangling in the corners, anatomical drawings on the walls. One class must have been studying perspective: lamps casting cones of light, converging railroad tracks. Though the building was new, the studios showed the comforting signs of work – dusty floors, nicked tables, sacks of plaster against the walls. It must have been the lunch hour. The classrooms were empty. At the end of the hall she came to a set of stairs. Of course – the tower she'd seen from the street. Six stories to the top. She was breathing hard as she leaned out over the lapped tile roof. Below her, the city fell away to the wharves. It was mostly industrial land. Warehouses and water towers. In the distance, ships pulled into the bay, their smokestacks trailing black scarves.

She nosed around a little more, then paid her tuition and wrote down her schedule. On the way out, she took a wrong turn and ended up in the sculpture yard, a patio littered with marble chips; half-finished heads and torsos were arranged on stands. A woman in a smock and saddle shoes stopped chiseling a bust and smiled at her. 'Are you lost?'

It was one of those plain questions that echoed wider. 'No,' she said, and then smiled. 'Well, actually yes – but happily so.'

She had signed up for a full course load, drawing classes four mornings a week, and made it her habit to arrive at the studio early. Often the nausea came in a rush – the steep climb from her apartment to Jones Street brought it on – and this way she could slip into the bathroom and crouch over the toilet until the worst had passed. As she knelt there, wiping her chin with toilet paper, a bubble of panic swelled in her chest. She had to find a doctor soon. She had thought it would be easy in the city. There were so many of them, enough that a man who sidestepped the law might still have a measure of anonymity. But that was exactly the problem. Out on a walk one day, she had stumbled on a street lined with doctors' offices. She paced the sidewalk for nearly an hour, thinking, Behind one of those doors . . . But which door? And how to inquire?

Back in the studio, she sipped a glass of water, untied the string from her oversize pad, propped it on the easel, and slipped a length of charcoal from its box. She had a feeling the model would be a man – she couldn't say why – an older man with bandy legs and a slack stomach and the requisite loincloth tied with string. When she had studied art at Marshall College, all she had drawn was bodies like these, or women with voluminous folds of flesh that used up charcoal the way a frozen road takes up salt. No diapers for them – only the male genitalia were out of bounds. She took satisfaction in rendering the missing area quite under scale.

But today, when the rest of the class had arranged themselves around the model's platform, the door opened on a young woman in a silk kimono. She was yellow-blond and unusually tall, and when she stepped into the beam of sun from the eastern windows and dropped the robe, her body looked as if it were molded from butter. Mr. Macky, unfazed, didn't bother introducing her. He made chalk marks on the platform to position her feet and began lecturing on technique.

'The Butter Girl,' as Bessie called her, came each morning that week. She never spoke a word and never flinched when Mr. Macky suggested a difficult pose. There was something magnetic about her – her beauty and unruffled confidence. On the walk to school in the mornings, Bessie thought of ways to introduce herself, but she never got up the nerve. Finally, on Thursday, she left class and found the Butter Girl in the courtyard. She was sitting on the edge of the octagonal pool, in a long linen coat and soft boots, smoking a cigarette. She looked cold, one arm tucked against her ribs. To the west, above the red tile roof, the fog was pouring over the hills in a way that looked nearly predatory. Over the top, Bessie thought – that awful phrase she'd read in the papers during the war. For some reason it gave her courage.

'It's hard work, isn't it? Standing still for so long.' She tried to look casual.

The Butter Girl squinted at her and exhaled. 'I consider it practice.' She held up her cigarette. 'And this is my reward.'

'Fair enough.' Bessie laughed softly. She had taken up smoking since she arrived in the city, though she limited herself to one cigarette in the evenings, the only time the nausea let up. She considered it a kind of ritual, after a difficult day. To sit on the back stoop of the apartment house and watch the smoke drift up through the lines of laundry.

Now she would have liked to linger, but she couldn't think of anything else to say. She started to head toward home, figuring she would work on a still life she had started in oils, but the thought of the static little tableau she had assembled made her mood sink. 'Would you like to get a cup of coffee?' she asked, turning back. How naked she felt, as if loneliness lifted from her in waves.

'Love one,' the Butter Girl said, stubbing out her cigarette.

She extended a pale hand. 'I'm Greta Grandstedt, by the way.'

Bessie reached out and shook it, surprised to find the skin warm and dry. 'Pleased to meet you. I'm Bessie –' She started to say 'Helmick' and then changed her mind. 'Bessie Haley.'

Greta loosened her long coat to wrap it tighter, and Bessie caught a glimpse of the kimono, and beneath that her creamy skin. Apart from her cotton stockings, rolled to the knee, she was half undressed here on the street, and yet as they walked to a nearby café, she carried herself with perfect aplomb, as if she had on a foundation garment and drop waist under her coat. So strange to think that a version of that body – the nipples, the long toes – was caught under the flap of her sketch pad. When she began studying art, her mother had been shocked to learn that they drew from nudes. Bessie tried to explain: drawing was impersonal. You were sunk in concentration and that concentration left no room for petty appraisal. The only thing you judged, when you pulled back from the paper, was your failure to render what you saw.

'But to pose naked in front of strangers,' her mother had said. 'Who stoops to this job?'

Now Bessie told Greta about her mother's opinion.

'Where is she from?' Greta asked, as if geography were the quickest route to character.

'France.. Originally.'

'Really? I thought the Frenchies were sophisticated.'

'She's country French,' Bessie said. 'She and her sisters used cut beets for lipstick.'

'What about rouge?'

Bessie cocked her head. 'They slapped each other.'

Greta's laugh was lovely, the sound of ice tumbling in a glass. By the time they found a café in the Italian district, she had slipped her arm through Bessie's elbow.

'So what did you mean by "good practice"?' Bessie asked, when they were seated by the window. 'Practice for what?'

'I'm an aspiring actress,' Greta said. 'You do a lot of standing around.'

'Would I recognize the productions?'

Greta smiled over her coffee cup. 'So far, I stand around at auditions – until they tell me to go home.'

The waiter returned, a striking man with slicked hair and teeth as white as his apron. Greta ordered a sandwich. Bessie asked for a dry roll.

'Is that all you're eating?' Greta asked, when the waiter had left.

'I haven't been feeling well,' Bessie said, dipping her head.

'Are you ill?' Greta asked, leaning forward, a faint crease between her brows.

It caught Bessie by surprise – that kindness – and gave her the nerve to confide her predicament. That and desperation. It had been three months since her last period. She was at her wit's end. Besides, this was her new way – to be barefaced and see what happened.

Greta didn't bat an eye.

'I have a friend – a society lady. She considers herself a patron of the arts. We can see if that covers indisposed drawing students.'

'You think someone of her –'

Greta waved this aside with a pale hand. 'You think these Nob Hill women don't get abortions? They get them all the time. They just don't die of it.' She turned sober. 'It will cost you, though.'

'I'll find the money,' Bessie said. She resolved to write Earl in the morning and plead for his help.

'Good,' Greta said, shaking out a fresh cigarette, as if she considered the matter solved.

The following Monday, Greta came up with an address – she hadn't heard from her high society friend, but another actress had given her a tip. Bessie took a street car to the

Mission District and then followed the directions toward a narrow alley. Two men burst out of a pub at the corner – laughing and leaning together. The gutters were clogged with trash, and the smell of raw meat wafted from somewhere nearby. It took her a while to find the right door – the numbers had been pried off, leaving only a faint stencil. When she knocked, a red-faced man answered. He had creases on one cheek, as if he had been sleeping.

'What do you want?' he said, his breath smelling of liquor and something she couldn't place, something sweet, maybe anise.

'I understand you do tailoring.' This was what she'd been told to say.

He glanced up and down the street, waved her inside, and shut the door. It took her eyes a moment to adjust to the gloom. She was in a narrow high-ceilinged room with no windows, only a dim bulb whose wire rose up into a circle of pineapple molding. It must have been the back room of a large house, whose front entrance faced Valencia Street. There was a sagging couch against one wall, with a blanket tossed aside, and facing this, a counter cluttered with jars of liquid, old newspapers, a hunk of molding bread.

'This is where you –' Bessie broke off, the word 'work' suddenly sounding inappropriate. Then she noticed a dining table pushed in one corner, with crude stirrups fixed to one end. She took a shuddering breath.

'How far along are you?' the doctor asked. He had already moved to the counter and was pulling things out of drawers. She heard the clink of steel.

'I'm not sure,' she said, afraid to tell the truth.

'Well, we'll soon find out.' He uncapped a bottle of what she hoped was disinfectant, poured it into a small canning jar, and downed it neat. 'Take off your skirt – you can leave the rest.'

Her palms went slick with sweat. She had expected some kind of preparation – not forms to fill out, but at least an anteroom, a few questions before he began. My God, this man's life. Eating and sleeping in full view of that table. What kind of doctor was he? Then it occurred to her – maybe he wasn't a doctor at all. 'Excuse me,' she said, her voice cracking.

He turned around and gave her a bleary stare. 'What?'

'I was thinking you might explain –'

All his glassiness vanished. He looked livid. 'My methods?' He moved quickly to the counter, and turned around with a cracked china plate twined with roses, a pattern, she noted dully, quite like her mother's wedding china. In the center, his instruments lay in a gleaming pile. She found it difficult to breathe. All that exhaled sorrow in the room – the sighs of the women who had lain on that table, the sour breath of this man in front of her.

'This is a dilator,' he said, lifting what looked like a knitting needle. 'It is inserted into the womb –'

She took a step backward.

'You're blanching,' he said. 'We've only just begun.' He was taking cruel relish in this.

'No, I think we're quite finished,' Bessie said, turning on her heel and yanking open the door. Already she felt a rush of despair – what would she do now? – but a wedge of sunlight fell into the room, and when she glanced back the doctor looked stricken, throwing up his arm to hide the plate.

'Get out,' he hissed. But she was already out, taking gulps of the rank-smelling air, running down the alley toward the bustle of Mission Street.

On the afternoon of November 9, after the reporter had left Lee's Ferry, Bessie hiked up to an Indian hogan, where the ferryman had told her she might buy a handwoven rug. It was a warm day, the sky clear of clouds, and soon she had pulled off her sweater and cinched it at her waist. She had almost reached the hogan when she heard goats braying nearby. After a clatter of hoofs and two sharp whistles, a little girl came out of the bushes, carrying a stick. She stopped short, eyeing Bessie warily. The goats came along behind, chewing at the brush.

'Hello,' Bessie said, smiling shyly. She held up her hand in greeting, and then felt foolish.

The girl smiled and started up the path. She was beautiful: glossy hair and tough brown legs. Bessie fell in beside her, pretending to be at ease, but quickly ran out of breath. The slope was steep. She stopped to rest and look down at the view. To her surprise, the girl stopped, too. She looked out at the canyon, flaring open beneath them in bands of gold and rust, then looked at Bessie, as if curious.

'It's beautiful,' Bessie said.

'Yes,' the girl said softly.

Bessie startled. 'You speak English?'

The girl shrugged: 'Yes.'

Just the one word then.

The goats had stopped with them, and a few of them butted against Bessie's legs. She reached down and scratched at their coats.

The girl said something and pointed at the animal Bessie had touched. It was a scrawny goat, but it pushed at her hand in a friendly way. A bigger one tried to butt its way in, but the girl gave it a shove.

Then Bessie remembered the orange in her pocket, a gift from the ferryman's wife. She pulled it out and offered it to the girl.

She shook her head.

'We'll share,' Bessie said. She sat on a rock and peeled it quickly, holding out half.

The girl took it and sucked at the tart flesh, then pointed shyly to the peels in Bessie's lap.

'You want them?' Bessie asked. 'They're sour.' She held out the rinds.

The girl offered one to the tiny goat. This caused a small commotion among the animals. The girl bumped them aside with her hips and doled out the peels selectively, always feeding the smallest stock. When the peels were gone, she gestured at her mouth, and then pointed to Bessie.

'I don't understand.'

The girl squatted behind a paunchy goat and slipped her hands between its legs. The animal released a few green pellets, which the girl caught expertly and tossed aside. Then she worked an udder with quick strokes, wringing with one hand and catching the stream in the other. She held up a tiny palmful of milk.

'Oh, I couldn't,' Bessie said, thinking of the droppings.

The girl insisted.

After hesitating a moment, she smiled and bent down to sip. It was warm and rich and smelled faintly of – goat.

The girl smiled approvingly and patted the animal's rump, then licked her sticky palm. The air was dry and quiet. Bessie felt a powerful calm slip over her. Here she was, drinking milk from a stranger's hand, with this immense, unearthly landscape unfolding in front of her. Who knew you could travel so far in one life? It made her think of her mother – no doubt mending at Broida's. And Katherine, her best friend from high school, whose second boy would be – what? – two years old by now. When Bessie had slipped over to her house to say goodbye, the baby was in his high chair, a little king with a spoon. 'I think I've become Mother Hubbard,' Katherine said. 'You must promise to write me fabulous letters.'

Bessie had laughed, and only now heard the muffled note of panic beneath the joke. To think she could have lived and died in that town, having known nothing but the stifling regularity of days: a roast and then dishes, knitting and a pot of tea. When she breathed in the sage and dust and tang of orange peel, it smelled to her like deliverance.

Reith Hyde

On December 17, I took the train east again, this time to Grand Canyon Village, where I was to meet Emery Kolb and a couple of men who were willing to search for Glen and Bessie by boat. The kids were a full week late by then. The day before I had sent a wire from Peach Springs to the village, offering a $1,000 reward to anyone who could bring news of their whereabouts. These two – a railroad brakeman and a local handyman – had sent back a reply expressing interest.

The train was passing through open scrub and stands of pine. Something about the clicking of the rails set my mind adrift. I should have been looking ahead, planning the next step in my search, but instead I kept casting back, mulling over the chance events that had brought Glen and Bessie together. They met on a ship of all places, as if the whole thing had been preordained, and within weeks they were engaged. At the time, I remember thinking it a little rash, but I couldn't say a word, because it had happened the same way to me. I met my wife in a fabric shop in Vancouver. I was a homesteader from up the coast, barely scraping by, and she was the daughter of a wealthy shipping family. She'd had elocution lessons and had been to finishing school. Any other girl in her position wouldn't have given me a second glance. But Maggie said she got just what she wanted. 'You were self-possessed,' she wrote me once, when we had already spent fourteen years on the farm, and had three children, and she had gone back to her mother's for a visit. 'I'll always remember the way you stepped into that shop. You had a purpose about you, and didn't think twice about the genteel atmosphere. I guessed that you were married, on an errand for your wife, but then you started handling the fabric, making choices, and I reconsidered. A wife would have given instructions. This had to be a gift. The shopgirl was chattering to me about the merits of Spanish lace, and I sat on an embroidered chair and watched as you examined bolts of wool. You were a bit of an exotic, I suppose. I was accustomed to men in kidskin gloves and high button shoes, and your coat looked like it had been quite recently lopped from an animal. But if your appearance sparked my curiosity, I think I fell in love with you for the fabrics you chose: burgundy and lavender grey, a soft steel blue. I wanted to be a woman in a dress made of those colors – sensible, calm, unfrivolous – and then you turned around and asked for my opinion.'

Not long after she wrote me that letter – four months to be exact – Maggie would be dead. We were living in Prince Rupert at the time, on the west coast of British Columbia. The wind and rain whipped off the ocean all winter, making a constant pelting at the windows. I had noticed she was pale, but convinced myself the weather had worn her down. When she suggested going to the city to get her strength back, I agreed at once. She'd come back out to the homestead in the spring. I saw her to her father's house, and before I caught the ferry home, stopped at the store on a whim and bought a hundred daffodil bulbs. Back at the farm, I planted them in thick under the southern windows, and told myself, When they bloom, she'll come home.

That December, she fell ill. The doctor said it was cancer, all through her body when he found it. I went back and forth from Prince Rupert to Vancouver as often as I could, walking straight from the ferry to the hospital. Finally the doctor said he couldn't do anything more, and sent her home to her father's house. I hated walking into that place, where I had once been considered too poor to call. It was as if I had to give her back. And her mother still hated me, that was clear. Looked at me like I was killing Maggie with my own hands. They had her set up in her old room, in a big mahogany bed. Her mother made excuses to stay nearby, fluttering around with hot towels and trays of food that Maggie wouldn't touch. She never left us alone. I don't know that if I'd been given the chance I'd have known what to say, but it bothered me that I never had a private conversation with my wife in her last days. Not like our first nights at the homestead, when we lay awake under a pile of quilts, whispering in the dark. Maggie's hands and feet were always chilled, and I'd let her put them against me – cold irons to the fire – astonished that a girl like that could love me at all.

Toward the end she didn't seem to notice when anyone was talking. You could rouse her with a touch, and if you made a special effort, she would listen and make an answer, and then after that she sank back and slept. My poor wife. She was bruised everywhere. Looked like she'd been in a cat fight – all from her mother turning her over in bed. I'd sit there and trace over the veins in her hand, the way they lifted up and over the tendons like vines caught in a rake, and got narrower, and fed down into her fingers. I swear I could see her bones.

She was buried on a Sunday in February 1912. When I brought Glen and Jeanne and Edna home from the funeral, the daffodils I'd planted had started to come up: a hundred green spears forcing through the dirt. The sight almost made me sick, and I was sicker still when the jonquils bloomed and the sweet smell came in the windows. One night when I couldn't sleep, I went out to the barn and got the hoe and started toward those beds, ready to hack them up. But something stopped me. It was a cold night with no wind, and the moon was full. The daffodils were lit up against the house: yellow and white and orange, as perfect as wax flowers. I thought, I've got to learn to live with this, and I put the hoe back in the barn and went to bed.

Glen was twelve years old when his mother got sick. When it was clear she was going to die, I felt terrible for him. He used to buck her off at times – she wanted him to sit beside her, reading by the fire, but he preferred to be outdoors. I'm ashamed to say that I encouraged him in that. I'd hustle him out the door, giving Maggie a quick kiss and telling her I needed him for this or that chore. We'd saddle up the horses and trot by the house and Glen would wave to his mother through the window. Then we'd ride out to check the fences, even though we'd checked them the week before.

Still, he adored his mother. Perhaps more than was good for a boy. I can still picture the way they were together: Maggie with her hand on his shoulder, beaming; him tall and thin, full of his watchful quiet. He got skittish with the way she hovered, but the truth is he would have done anything for her. Because of her, he got to like reading. She'd sit with her crewelwork and laugh when he read things out loud. Slowly he took to books and did passably well in school, but the boy couldn't spell to save his life. That rankled me, I suppose. I learned my spelling in a one-room schoolhouse, every damn word lettered in chalk. It didn't come easy to me – that or the sums – but I was glad for it later. I kept the books for the ranch in big black ledgers and every penny was accounted for. When it came time to write a letter to the bank for a loan, I wrote a first draft, checked it over, changed a word here or there, and then copied the whole thing out on good paper. But my son was too lazy for that. He devoured the magazines Maggie got for him – *Collier's* and *Scribner's*, there were stacks of them everywhere – but it all went into his head and made no difference. When it came time to write a note he would just dash it off. 'Sarry to make you worry,' he wrote me, when he went off on his first river trip. 'S-a-r-r-y.'

When I think about it, that boy had too many people under his thumb. I was certainly no exception. When he was seven or eight, and I was still putting in hay, we'd get up for coffee before dawn – he drank his with lots of milk – and he'd sit there across from me, a little man, dressed up in tiny denims his mother had ordered from a catalog. He mostly kept his thoughts to himself, but I remember one morning he piped up about a dream he'd had the night before: he was on his horse, and when he looked down he saw that he had no legs, his body just disappeared into the flanks.

I didn't say a word, so as not to take anything from his story, but I had had that very dream once. He described certain things about it perfectly. Such as he could see out of both sets of eyes – the horse's and his own – and could turn his two heads in opposite directions, taking in the scenery all around. It seems a strange thing to say about a child, but I admired him.

Then Glen got interested in rivers. That I never understood. I told him if he belonged on a river God would have given him fins, but he just laughed. When his mother died and we moved to Idaho, he started running the Snake, which lay right alongside the ranch. Built a scow out of spare lumber from an old barn and started trying it out on white water. Then he made a run on the Salmon – the River of No Return, they called it – and took his sister with him. Jeanne was a tomboy, not like her mother at all – big-boned, with a big voice. My long-armed gal, I called her. She would yawn and get tangled in the houseplants, tip over the lamps. Looked as angry as a wet cat when she had to put on a dress for church. I'm glad Maggie didn't live to see two of her three kids in a homemade boat in the middle of that river. It nearly made my heart fail to watch them set off. They were everything I had left in the world – except Edna, of course – and to have them plunked down on one roll of the dice . . .

But I have to say Glen knew how to handle a scow. He looked like an old-time ferryman, moving the boat into the center of the current. Like he'd been born to it. And they made it through, in spite of what everyone said.

I suppose there was no avoiding what happened between the three of them – Glen and Bessie and Jeanne. At first Glen had planned to take his sister through the Grand Canyon, and Jeanne was game for it. But then he met Bessie, and the plan changed. Glen couldn't be without his bride, and she was enthusiastic: they'd be the first husband and wife to run the Colorado, and Bessie – with her art school training and knack for poetry – would write an illustrated book. Lindbergh had just crossed the Atlantic. Glen was greatly admiring of that. He read all the newspaper reports and even watched Lindy land in San Francisco when he made his victory lap of the country. God knows how many people out there, seeing the kind of fame it brought him, set about hatching schemes.

At first Jeanne was jealous. There were some scenes early on. She never missed a chance to make Bessie look impractical or frail. But after a while she got over it. She saw Glen had made up his mind. And it helped that Bessie never pushed her claim. She was soft-voiced and modest, yet matter-of-fact. I couldn't help seeing something of Maggie in her, when he first brought her home. It was right there to slap you in the face: same dark hair and fine features, and her, too, always with her nose in a book. I thought, Well, he's got her back.

Glen and Bessie Hyde

They untied from the bank at Lee's Ferry, the gateway to the Grand Canyon, on November 9, 1928, in the midst of light showers. It had taken them three weeks to reach this point, the heart of their journey, and by Glen's calculations, it would take another month to run the two hundred seventy-five miles to the Grand Wash Cliffs, then drift out through the flats to Needles. The ferryman and his wife stood in the drizzle to bid their goodbyes, and waved until the scow moved out of sight.

The rain fell slanting and quick, like dots and dashes of Morse code, and then the sun broke through and lit the drops as they fell. Glen took off his hat and turned his face up to the wet light. The first few miles were smooth. They floated swiftly between tight limestone walls, while cotton-wool clouds massed and parted overhead. The ferryman had warned them about two big rapids ahead, the only ones he'd seen on his forays along the cliffs. 'First there's Badger, then Soap Creek,' he said. 'That one looks like rough sledding.'

They ran a few riffles, then heard the low growl that signaled a run worth scouting. 'This must be Badger Creek,' Bessie said, folding up the map. Glen steered over to the bank, and she jumped out and held the painter while he went down to explore. While she waited, she watched the slow ticking of rain on the rocks, felt the drops slide off the brim of her cap and into her sheepskin collar. When they first arrived at Lee's Ferry, and the hardships of Cataract were fresh in her mind, she had been dreading the return to fast water, but now that they were on their way, she was glad. It was becoming familiar

– the rhythm of their days. Flat-water sections, when they would talk, the runs through modest white water, which hardly fazed her by now. Even the worst rapids – the ones that choked her with fear at first sight – became thrilling in hindsight. The tranquil float through Glen Canyon had been restorative, but another month of that and she would have gone numb to its pleasures. She was starting to see what Glen loved about the difficult stretches – the way danger made everything grow sharp, essential; and the flush of satisfaction when you made it through a big run without mishap.

Glen was coming up the bank – he hadn't been gone long, so the rapid must be easier than the ferryman had led them to believe. As usual, he walked at a brisk, even pace. He wasn't one to dawdle, but he never hurried either. Even with the rain soaking his coat and hat, he moved deliberately among the rocks. She was admiring this – his self-possession – when a strange rustling gathered behind her. She turned just in time to see the river leap into motion upstream, the surface pleating with whitecaps. Then the wind hit her and the painter went taut. She clamped her hands down, but the rope burned through them and flipped free. She shouted for Glen, but he was already sprinting up the bank. His hat blew off, wheeling away. In one fluid motion he stripped off his coat and dove into the water. For a moment the wind stalled and he surfaced within reach of the boat. Then it surged again, pushing the scow downstream along the rocks. Bessie stripped off her coat and followed him, gasping as the water hit her waist. She lit out at a fast crawl, hardly looking up, and then suddenly her wrist slapped down on the rope. She grabbed ahold and dropped her feet – amazed to find bottom. She had leverage, but where was Glen? Then she saw the bow swing around. He was manning the sweeps. Together, pushing and pulling, they brought the scow back to the bank.

It was too cold to go on without drying their clothes, so

they gathered driftwood from under an overhang and started a blaze. Ten in the morning, and they were stark naked and shivering in front of a fire.

'I thought I could hang on,' Bessie said, her teeth chattering. She had felt a flare of anger when the rope slid out of her hands – shocked at the limits of her strength.

'Oh, come on. That was a freakish wind,' Glen said, putting his hands out toward the fire and smiling at the memory. 'I don't think the two of us could have held it together.'

Their clothes were splayed out on sticks beside the fire, limp as drenched scarecrows. For the moment, the rain had stopped, but the canyon was topped by a gray lid. It would take a good hour for their pants to dry in weather like this. Bessie was peeved to lose the morning's momentum, but Glen seemed undisturbed. He turned in front of the fire like a bird on a spit, warming each side by turns.

'We're lucky this happened early,' he said, as if reading her thoughts. 'We should just tie off from now on. Even if we're only stopping for a minute.'

She studied his sinewed back, covered with gooseflesh. For all his physical restlessness, his constant forging ahead, he didn't mind diversion. It was one of those pleasing inconsistencies that drew her in. From their first meeting she had recognized his single-mindedness, the way he wouldn't be put off a goal, so it surprised her to discover that he didn't bridle when the road detoured. But weren't these the keys that turned the locks of love – such moments of surprise. After spending only a week with her, Glen had been barefaced about his hopes: come to Idaho, come with me down the Colorado. Much as she was swayed by this, she held back, sure that when he knew her history, all the threads to be untangled before she was free, he would balk as quickly as he had committed. This was a fear as old as memory. Her father was always spinning plans: he would start a wallpaper business – good taste for the working man – draw the designs himself and hire art students to paint the rolls. But then he'd hit one snag and the dream would unravel. The bank would never lend him the money; he'd never get more than piecemeal work. It would be a week before her mother could coax him off the bottle and into bed. So imagine Bessie's shock when she told Glen the truth – she had been married before, was married still – and he didn't falter. Just booked two train tickets to West Virginia and went with her to confront Earl. He was like a foxhound, nose to the ground, not minding if the scent led him in circles, as long as he didn't lose sight of the prize. And that was how he tackled the river.

When their clothes were dry, they dressed and passed through Badger Creek rapid without trouble. Next came Soap Creek, the one the ferryman had warned them about, and this time they tied the boat securely and scouted together. Just below the ledge, a large rock split the current in two. Vaulting waves filled the channel, lashing over one another and breaking into froth. On the left side, a series of half-submerged boulders littered the path. Glen pointed off to the right. There was a long, clear chute, with only a few obstacles to be dodged at the end. 'There's really just one big turn to make,' he said. 'When I shout, pull to the left of those.'

Within minutes they were out in the current, lining up for their entry. Then over the edge and down the right tongue, and Glen's shout piercing the roar of the waves. They pulled hard on the sweeps, just skirting the rocks, and seesawed into the wash. Another clean run. So far the lessons they'd learned in Cataract were serving them well.

By midafternoon, the clouds overhead tore like cheesecloth, and the sun poured through. Such a relief to be warm. They took their hats off and basked. The water was light cinnamon, the cliffs high and close. It felt as if they were traveling down a long twisting corridor, without any sense of what lay behind the walls. After floating several more miles, they passed a side canyon fronted by a riffle and got caught in the eddy below. 'Maybe it's a sign we're done for the day,' Bessie said. They pulled over and tied off.

Switching into their boots, they hiked up the creek bed, hoping to come out at the top of the cliff, where they might get a look around. The walls of the narrow gulch were polished by grit, moving up in bands of white and pink and mauve. Gone were the fired reds and ochers of Glen Canyon – this was colder, harder stone. High above, the last of the day's sun angled down like a blade. They waded through chains of clear pools. Here and there a pile of boulders choked the stream, and they would squeeze their way between them until they reached a level bench again. Finally they came to a spot they couldn't pass: a long smooth fall of rock, perhaps a hundred feet high. Water spilled down the face, feeding a long smear of moss. It was an eerie green, the color of an old bruise. The canyon rim was nowhere in sight.

The light was starting to fade. They had yet to set up camp, so they headed back down the creek bed. Now that the sun had dropped, the temperature plunged, as if someone switched off a furnace.

'Do you really think we'll be invited to lecture?' Bessie asked.

'I can't see why not,' Glen said. 'People are crazy for records these days. And let's face it, you'll be quite a draw. The men at Lee's Ferry couldn't believe you made it through Cataract.'

'Did you hear what that reporter asked me?' She leapt off a small ledge and landed with a crunch in the gravel.

'No, what?'

'He asked if I had any trouble keeping house on the boat.'

Glen laughed. 'What did you say?'

'I told him you were excellent at ironing, so I hardly had to do a thing.'

Glen smiled and shook his head. 'I hope he knew you were kidding. The newspapers don't specialize in irony.' In the twilight, the limestone had turned the color of dusty plums. 'Well, whatever that fool writes, he was brave to show up,' he said at length. 'That road from the rim can't be easy.'

'I know, I was surprised he took an interest. And it was probably good – hearing the questions he asked. It made me want to take better notes.'

'Do you worry about that?'

'About what?'

'Getting it all down for your book.'

She ran her hand along the polished creek wall, touched that he asked. 'A little. You seem so sure I'll make a good job of it. All based on a few silly poems.'

'It wasn't just the poems. You write great letters,' Glen said, stopping to look at her. He had fallen in love with that face – delicate and curious. But her letters told the story of the person behind it. 'And you're a good talker.'

Bessie waved this off. 'It's easy to talk. But lecturing, I don't know. I used to get terrible stage fright before our school plays. Once I threw up into a top hat backstage. The mayor had to go on bareheaded.'

Glen smiled. 'Did you remember your lines?'

'More or less.'

'Well, then?' He shrugged. 'A little fear keeps you sharp.'

'I suppose you're right. No one ever died of nerves.' They walked on a little, then skirted a small pool, the stones at the bottom as blue as cold milk. 'God, I forgot water is supposed to be clear,' Bessie said. The Colorado was choked with silt. At night, they settled water in a bucket for their morning coffee, but often they were too hungry to wait before cooking their dinner with the thicker stuff.

'I know. We should bring a jug up here,' Glen said. 'That river grit is wearing down my teeth.' He scrambled down the boulder pile damming the stream and waited for Bessie at the bottom. She was fitting her toes and fingers in the cracks, nimble as a spider. He was always amazed at the strength in those wiry limbs. When she reached flat ground, he wrapped his arms around her. 'Any ironing for me back in camp?' he asked, kissing her cold cheek.

She smiled. 'No, but you could make me some of your biscuits.' He was by far the better cook. The one advantage, she thought, of being a motherless child.

'That I can do,' he said, and took her hand for the walk back to the river.

The next day they started with a rough rapid. A massive rock, big as a two-story house, had fallen from the cliff above, narrowing the river like an hourglass. Below this, the current lashed into terrifying breakers, as if in fury at its former confinement. They scouted from the bank, then steered down the tongue and into this confusion, waves crashing over the gunwales, the floorboards grinding over rocks. Glen fought to keep them out of a deep hole, pulling on the sweep handle with all his weight. In the middle of the torrent, with the scow tilted nearly sideways, Bessie lost her footing on the bench. When Glen reached forward to right her, she noticed his sweater, how it was worn through at the elbow. I must remember to mend it, she thought. What a thing to seize on at such a moment. Once they had come out into the wash, she felt a twinge of longing for her mother, the way her love was expressed through a kind of slavish attention to their clothing – hers and her brother's. To look at the way they were dressed, you would never have guessed at the family's meager finances. Mrs. Haley sewed Bill's collars by hand and made Bessie's dresses, the panels perfectly fitted and held together by hidden stitches. What a thankless job, motherhood. All that effort, and if it's done well, if you don't call attention to your labor, it becomes not unlike the best mending – invisible. When she saw her mother again, she'd have to tell her that she knew.

They got through nine more rapids that day, one after another. There seemed to be no letup. The walls were rising on either side, but showed no signs of widening. In between the frequent cataracts, the river sped along. Just when they had reached their limit, exhausted by the furious pace, the river turned a bend and a waterfall appeared on the cliff above. White ropes of water reeled out of the stone, and tangled fern and moss twined down hundreds of feet to the river. They pulled over to the bank, a narrow slope of stone below the cliff, and filled their water buckets from the spring. 'This must be Vasey's Paradise,' Bessie said, consulting the map. There was an island in the center of the river, just as the survey showed, and downriver, on the right-hand shore, a sandbar thick with driftwood. A light rain had started falling. 'I don't know about you, but I'm ready to camp,' Glen said, cocking his head toward the beach.

Bessie didn't look up from the map. 'I think there's a cave just around the bend. We might be able to shelter there.'

Glen rubbed his eyes and sighed. 'The sun's down. I don't like running this close to nightfall.'

'The map hasn't been wrong so far,' she pressed. 'It should be less than a mile.'

'I'm sure there's a cave,' Glen said. 'But you don't know if it's at the waterline. And if we can't stop there, we might end up running a rapid in the dark.'

She was too tired to argue it farther. And he was right to be cautious. If they were swept into a cataract blind, it would be certain disaster. 'Okay,' she said, folding up the map. 'Let's camp here.' They floated a hundred yards to the beach and moored the scow.

That night, after dinner, Bessie looked back at her diary. So far, she had filled only five pages in the notebook, and in places – when they had been in Cataract Canyon, and again here at the start of the Grand – she barely recognized her own handwriting. The letters were huddled on the page, a sign of her preoccupation and fatigue. Suddenly she thought of Miss Carlisle, her fourth-grade teacher, how she walked the aisles with a rubber-tipped pointer, tracing the loops and curves of the Palmer method in the air. If only Miss Carlisle could see her now: crouched on a driftwood log, dirt under her nails, and her notes scrawled in a crabbed hand.

On balance, though, it didn't matter. That was the corrective power of danger. All the petty things fell away like chaff. But even after she gave up worrying who might see the pages – she could always transcribe them later – she could still barely bring herself to make more than a few cursory notes on the day's run. It was especially hard to write when it rained like this. It had taken all her concentration to make it through the miles, to wait out the cold, flat stretches, and then negotiate the rapids. Now she was exhausted, and could think of little to say. She stared at this evening's entry:

Nov. 10, 1928

Ten rapids today. Bad one in morning – big rock in channel. Boat nearly vertical. Nine more in close succession, but we ran them well. Camped now at base of waterfall.

She knew she hadn't committed to paper the true scope of her thoughts – and yet how could she forget any of it? The granular quality of the cliff faces, the gut-wrenching fear that evaporated as they tipped over the first ledge. As tired as she was, she felt a kind of bodily satisfaction at the miles they had passed that day, images she would remember as long as she lived. Her diary was just a set of crib notes – something to remind her of the chronology.

But even as she reassured herself, it was clear she'd already lost hold of certain details. The early miles, just after Lee's Ferry, already seemed like a dream – a montage of low cliffs and beaches, wild patches and then calm, a kind of practice for the furious stretch they had just passed. In the end, if she was called to write about them, she would have to make it up. And what of that? Embellishment was already a tradition in Grand Canyon accounts. John Wesley Powell had done it. The one-armed Civil War veteran collapsed his two trips into one, neglecting to mention that on the second foray he had quit the canyon before the halfway point. Even the Eddy party accounts felt suspiciously fluent in places.

She sat with the small book balanced on her knees, a blanket shielding her from the rain. The fire leapt up steadily in spite of the weather, and Glen smiled at her from across the flames, but said nothing. He had the instinct to keep quiet when she was writing. Just then, the generosity floored her. He had such faith in her abilities. They each had their roles to play, and he managed his with perfect ease – deciding whether to run or line, fixing the boat. She trusted to him everything practical, thinking of herself as the scribe, her only job to fashion a gripping tale, which even a hack could do. She sighed, dried the end of her pencil on her shirt, and resolved to try harder, hoping that later she would recover her perspective. The question was: her perspective on what? The ending shaped the journey. If they survived unscathed, these days would be bathed in a softening light: the hard road, now over, its terrors already difficult to recall. And if they didn't – It was a thought she refused to consider.

She closed her journal and packed away the coffee and flour. They curled up on the box springs, which Glen had kept dry with the oilskin. They were perched high on the beach, the river nattering softly at their feet. There was something strangely pleasing about a mattress in such a wild place. They were tucked under wool blankets, their jackets for pillows, the oilskin as a waterproof quilt. Mercifully, the rain stopped and a narrow band of stars appeared – a runner of pinpricks hemmed in by the cliffs. Bessie fixed on one particular point of light, and tried not to take her eyes off it. Hard to fathom such a distance. And yet the star was real – it burned out there, as sure as she lived.

Then, just as she was watching it – she was certain it was the right one – the star wavered, as if someone had sluiced it with water, then wavered again, and went out.

'Glen,' she whispered.

He didn't stir.

'I just saw a star go out.' It was a trivial thing to wake him for, but she couldn't help herself. She put a hand on his motionless back and felt a pang of loneliness. That star had burned out millions of years ago, and yet its fire had streamed toward her ever since, a long ribbon of light, seen from one end, so it looked tiny, spherical, still. The ribbon had been paid out and paid out through the keyhole of time, until the last length slipped through and she could see the dark behind.

What a dismal thing, to live an unremembered life. At least you had that brief reprieve, during which you persisted for a while in the minds of others – your gestures, the specific sound of your voice, pinned in their memories. But then what? She tried to guess what record she'd leave of herself: a sheaf of poems, this puzzling journal. Even the old sea creatures, sand-wiched into the rock above the river, had left more of them-selves. You could see the shape of what they had been. Back home, in volume H of her father's encyclopedia, was a violet she had pressed for Earl and never delivered, the petals as friable as moth wings. Still, delicate as all that, they would probably outlast her.

All the more reason to finish this trip, and find a way to make it into art. She turned on the box springs, pulled the covers up to her chin. Hadn't she learned, during her first months in San Francisco, not to think of the future late at night? It took practice to know your own mind. Better to sleep now. In the morning she would try to write again.

Bessie's first month in San Francisco had been grim, and then everything turned at once. Earl sent a check for her 'operation,' managing to word the note as coldly as an invoice. Still, he had sent the money without a fuss. Then Greta found the name of another doctor, a decent man who saw Bessie after hours in his spotless examining room. If she hadn't been so woozy from the ether, she might have kissed his hand in gratitude. Greta escorted her home on a streetcar and tucked her into bed. The sheets felt so soft, the mattress nearly liquid beneath her. But when she woke in the morning, a gray fog light at the windows, she felt empty as a husk. She made tea to rinse the taste of anesthetic from her mouth, then fell back in bed and wept, not out of regret – she had never questioned her choice – but out of sorrow at having brought herself to such a crossroads at all. For a few days afterward, her body felt strange, as if some internal weather were shifting. Then she noticed: she was at peace. Wasn't it always this way? Happiness crept up on you, so that one day you turned on the radio, and opened the window for a little breeze, and it became clear: you were inhabiting the world more fully. Small things seemed possible. Taking care in fixing a meal, walking out to sit in a café, even though no one was there to meet you.

She only owned one key – a brass key on a length of cord, which opened the downstairs entry and the lock to her flat – but what satisfaction she felt when she unlatched the apartment door and switched on the light! It was all there waiting for her: the bowl of apples on the counter, the fern growing imperceptibly in the dark. She sat at the tiny kitchen table, still in her coat and hat, and surveyed the room. It was a scene of comforting tawdriness, for it spoke of choices made. And such quiet. Only the faucet dripping into the sink. A spider fingering its way along the underside of a cabinet. When she moved in, she had scrubbed the top of the icebox, washed the curtains in the sink, and wiped the windowsills with vinegar. She kneeled in front of the oven door and rubbed a rag over little clots of food and grease. It was like a slow coming clean of an original surface, the one she saw in fever dreams: covered first with chaotic scribbling, then blank.

Most amazing of all – she wasn't lonely. Walking up the back stairs from taking out the trash, she thought, This wet can stinks, I haven't made love in months. But she didn't mind any of it. There was no one to remember what she had forgotten, no one to ask for things she didn't want. She bought a bag of apples and they lasted a week. She went about her day, shopping for bread and cheese, drawing a little at the window seat, and watched herself with cool amazement.

In the mornings, on the way to school, she would duck into a shop in Chinatown, breathing in the pungent, unfamiliar air – a blend of tea and cloves and mildewed root. She was elated by the strangeness. Dipping her head toward the proprietor (a gesture she thought vaguely Oriental) she browsed amid the dusty aisles. This was nothing like the dull, orderly shelves of the grocery store in Parkersburg, where the tins of scouring powder were lined up like soldiers. This was commerce of another style: a marvelous jumble. Rosewood tables clustered here and there, teetering stacks of sandalwood trunks with elaborate black fittings, lacquered trays of joss sticks. The cramped, scented space made her faint with happiness.

What a surprise then, to find that Oscar Wilde had been there before her – Wilde, who seemed to be of another era altogether – and had marveled at Chinatown, just as she had. She was reading in the art school library, nibbling from a sack of candied ginger (her new vice), when she came across Wilde's description of a tea shop bill: 'It was made out of rice paper, the account being done in India ink as fantastically as if an artist had been etching little birds on a fan.'

Nothing new under the sun.

Still, she persisted with her own account of city life – a haphazard diary, interleaved with drawings, kept in a black sketchbook, the pages rippled by watercolors.

Dec. 12, 1926

Over to Greta's apartment today. Heavy rain all afternoon, my umbrella is still leaking – torn at the stem – but I can't afford another so I stopped on the way and bought a pack of gum, chewed a piece, and gobbed it in the hole. This worked reasonably well, once the cold had hardened it. Lovely afternoon. Greta made soup and we had toast and a pile of figs. I taught her how to make Oolong, the way Mr. Chen showed me, clapping a saucer over the cup to hold back the leaves. It's a little awkward at first, like playing castanets. We talked about poetry. Then more tea and a cigarette and more talk while I sat in her bay window, looking out at the rain. I watched a couple run past with a newspaper over their heads and duck under the eaves across the street. They laughed, shook their hair. The woman tugged the man toward her, deeper under the roof. Watching from a splattered window half a block away, it seemed such a feminine gesture – tenderness mixed with some faint reproach. As if he might stand unwittingly with his shoulder in the gutter spill. But perhaps she was brusque to overcome his chivalry. Perhaps they were new to each other, and he knew full well he was getting drenched, but didn't want to crowd her, and then he got distracted by the rain, its riveting force. You could see it approach – a smooth wall sweeping forward. It spilled over the enormous upright wedge of church on the corner, closed for repair. The workers arrayed over its face on flimsy scaffolding ducked under their tarps. Such an exact and furious rain. Ten feet from us, then five feet, the sticks in the gutter chattering in advance of the wall. It's only rain, I told myself, to loosen the knot of dread in my throat. And then it was upon us, pouring in curtains over the roofs, filling the street with the sound of crumpling paper. They were kissing, under the eaves. Did I say I don't miss being kissed? – I do.

There was only one thing nagging: she hadn't heard from her father in a month. It wasn't like him to go so long between letters. She was about to send a telegram when this arrived:

Dear Bessie,

   I'm afraid that present finances prevent me from continuing your monthly support. I've tried every way to make it work, but orders are down, and your mother has been having a bit of trouble with her eyes. We have faith that you'll manage. With your typing skills and fine energy there will no doubt be plenty of employment. Of course your room is always here. Mother keeps everything fresh. Please buy yourself a Christmas present with the enclosed.

Much love,
Dad

In the envelope were two wrinkled ten-dollar bills.

She went directly to the landlord's office and gave notice – it was important not to dawdle at moments like this. By the end of the day, she had found herself a room in a boardinghouse at the edge of Chinatown, a grim little place with a sagging staircase and mice in the cabinets. Still, it cut her rent in half. The next morning she went through the paper, marking up job listings and walking the streets until her ankles ached.

The eighth notice brought her to a bookshop near the Civic Center, which had advertised for a full-time clerk. It was an orderly little space, with glass bays at the front and oil paintings between the shelves. The owner introduced himself as Mr. Elder, which matched the name painted over the door, and invited her to a small office behind the register. It was a room that seemed to be built of books – crammed shelves rose from floor to ceiling, neat towers collected on the floor.

Mr. Elder offered her a leather chair and remained standing. 'Have you worked in a bookshop before?' he asked. He was heavy-bottomed and jowled, as if he stood in a puddle of extra gravity.

'No, sir. But I worked on my college literary magazine. And my father has a small business – I used to help him with the books.'

'Well, there won't be any accounting required. Just ringing up sales. Perhaps we can come to the point,' he said, smoothing the front of his tweed vest. 'Would you file the *Odyssey* under history or literature?'

'I'd put it in under literature,' Bessie said. 'And file a card in the history shelves.'

Mr. Elder smiled softly. 'This isn't a library. The cards are all up here.' He tapped his temple. 'But I'm sure you'll pick things up quickly. When can you start?'

Her hours would be ten A.M. to four P.M., Monday through Saturday. Mr. Elder let her off early each day and closed the shop himself, so she could make it to drawing class in the evenings. The salary was enough to pay her rent and then some, but she couldn't afford full-time tuition any longer – she had to cut back to one course. Only once this was all settled did she feel a rush of despair. She was on her own now. A tightrope walker without a net.

Thank God she had discovered espresso – not the watery coffee served at college gatherings, but dark Italian brew, ringed by froth. On days when the fog rolled in and she was tired, she walked through North Beach until the nutty sharpness cut the air. After sipping a demitasse at a marble table, she would revive and look forward to class. She even took to buying a paper sack of ground beans to brew up in her room. Hot plates were forbidden in the boardinghouse – Mrs. Whippley, the manager, had lived through the 1906 blaze and was loath to light a fire in the hearth even during the wettest months – but Bessie put a towel at the foot of the door to block the vapors and felt a pleasant sense of insurrection as she sipped. She even carried a small thermos to the bookstore, and while Mr. Elder favored Darjeeling in a porcelain cup, she drank her thick black brew.

'You should be careful with that stuff,' Mr. Elder said. 'You'll give yourself an ulcer.' His face bore a faint scowl, which Bessie read as disapproval.

In fact it was worry. He thought she was looking thin. The months of keeping up with classes and scraping by on bread and cheese and apples had begun to show. Still, she was quick in the stacks, carrying boxes from the storage room and sliding the new titles into place. Running a bookshop was not such a sedentary business as one might imagine. Mr. Elder liked to grouse that he should have gone into an enterprise with a lighter product. Worst of all was the shelving, which required a repetitive sliding aside of volumes that made his wrists swell. He had been relieved to see that Bessie was stronger than she looked, and that – as her first interview had revealed – she was attentive to detail. He began to look forward to her shifts – her modest companionship, her curiosity. When he found out that she was trying her hand at poems, in addition to her studies at the School of Fine Arts, he made her a gift of the new e. e. cummings volume. For himself, Mr. Elder would rather read Eliot – he preferred elegance and rigor to easy music. But cummings suited Miss Haley. She read the book constantly when the shop was empty. Long after she had left his service, after he had chanced across her photograph in the newspapers, he found a scrap of paper on which she had copied out these lines:

the Cambridge ladies who live in furnished souls
are unbeautiful and have comfortable minds

*

On November 11, Glen and Bessie woke late, moving slowly in the chill to roll up the bedding and make coffee, their breath mushrooming into the air. They packed the scow, cinching the crates tight for rough water, and pushed back from the bank. A mile around the bend, an enormous cavern appeared on the left. It was as big as a Greek amphitheater, with an arched ocher roof and a floor of sand sloping down to the river.

'Holy snakes.' Glen looked over at Bessie with eyebrows raised. 'I promise I'll never doubt my navigator again.' They turned to stare at the cavern siding past, deep as a giant's mouth.

They had covered thirty-three miles since they left Lee's Ferry. In the opening neck of the Grand Canyon, the strata had been stacked as flat as sheets of paper, the layers eroded raggedly, like a book with deckled edges. There were hardly any rapids. Then the sandstone had scrolled upward, replaced at the waterline by sheer limestone walls, and the gauntlet of white water had begun. Since the cliffs they now passed were made of the same hard stone, they braced themselves for more close-packed rapids. But for the next two days, the river surprised them: long, smooth sections, broken by falls they often ran without scouting. At sundown on November 12, they came to the confluence of the Little Colorado River. The canyon began to widen – shelves and buttes of reddish stone, shouldering back to the rim. They camped just below the junction, where the bright green flow of the Little Colorado mixed with the brown course they'd been following. It was an easy spot to pick out on the map – a wishbone of water. By Bessie's calculation they had twenty-five miles to go before they reached Phantom Ranch. A rustic resort, built for tourists riding mules down from the rim, it was one of only two places in the whole length of the canyon where they would see people along the river. From Phantom they would hike up to the settlement at the South Rim, where they would send mail and replenish supplies. Lately, they'd been making fifteen miles a day. She figured they would reach the ranch by November 14. Their food stores were starting to run low again, but with only two days to civilization, they splurged on a generous dinner, biscuits and beans and the last can of Reith's pears.

When they set out the next morning, the sky was deep blue, the air cold and crisp. Wind blew down the canyon like breath through a straw, pushing the scow forward and pleating the river ahead of them. Three miles downstream, without warning, the right cliff swerved back, opening into a wide side canyon, bigger than any they'd seen – ridges and spires layering back into the distance. They would have stopped, but their attention was taken up by a rapid ahead – a quick, bouncing ride. It was just as well, because a mile farther on, the real wonder began. The cliffs on either side flared back for miles, each layer of stone rising up, then giving way to the next. It was as if they had been mining in a dark tunnel, able to look only back or ahead, and suddenly they chipped through to an underground cathedral. Both of them pulled their hats off and stared. The Grand Canyon. They had been down in a ditch, the cliffs like blinkers. Only now could they see the majesty of the place.

They steered over to the left bank, just upstream of a large rapid, and decided to lay over for the afternoon. Speed record or no, it would be a crime to pass such a spot. They changed into their boots, packed a knapsack, and set out up a wide valley stretching south toward the rim. They had spent the last five days on the boat or camped on narrow beaches. It was a relief to have room to stride out. Glen quickly detected the thread of a trail, snaking up a talus slope, and they followed to see where it led. The sun burned high overhead, warming the air. Soon they tied their sweaters at their waists. Several hours later, they reached a plateau, a narrow isthmus of stone, with views on all sides. They stretched out in the sun and opened their lunch. Bessie had packed biscuits, leftover from the night before. She spread them on a handkerchief, then dug deep in the knapsack and unearthed a treasure: a jar of Reith's blackberry jam. 'Where'd you get that?' Glen asked. His father's neat lettering on the label caused him a rare flash of sentiment. Reith, who did everything – fixed engines, made jam, trying to be father and mother rolled into one.

'He gave it to me before we set out. Said if it didn't break along the way, it would remind us of home.'

They pried the wax hat from the jar, slathered the biscuits with jam, and washed them down with cold water. Amazing how good it tasted, as if the setting made their senses more acute. Bessie had packed the glass in newsprint, and now, smoothing the months-old sheet, she was stopped by an item at the top of the page: 'Gabfest Gibberer! Irma Barnette, expert swimmer, ex-showgirl, and conversationalist de luxe, wins $1,000 talking marathon.' Such a small event, in such big type. It made her laugh. The triviality, the jaunty tone – from where she sat, it didn't seem to bear on anyone's life. Soon it would be used for some unmentionable point of hygiene.

Glen rolled his sweater into a ball and leaned back against a boulder. Bessie put her head in his lap, both of them quiet, watching the canyon pigments deepen in the afternoon light. To the west, a few anvil clouds slid over the sun. The deflected rays shot down in visible bolts, striking the temples of rock in the distance. Bessie took his hand, warm and chapped. 'Glen?' she asked softly.

'Yeah?'

Her face was suffused with feeling. 'Thank you for bringing me here.'

On November 14, they came to several hair-raising rapids, first Unkar, which they managed to run with some difficulty, and then Hance, a long drop thick with boulders, which had struck such fear in previous river voyagers that Bessie had memorized the name. At first it looked impassable, but Glen finally thought he spotted a route. They would have to make several split-second changes of course, zigzagging between the rocks. To be off by as much as a foot would spell calamity. Glen stood on the shore with Bessie, going over the markers for each turn. 'I'll call them out,' he said. 'But we've got to steer in tandem.' She nodded, her heart in her throat. At last they pulled into the current, lining up for the entry. Once again she discovered that the anticipation was worse than the run. The moment they tilted over the ledge, a surge of resolve came up in her. She bent her knees and gripped the oar handle, every nerve put to use for the task at hand. Over her shoulder, she heard Glen's voice, calling out the cuts – 'Left – hard left! Now right!' – and was amazed to watch the scow follow their command. When they reached the last plunging waves, Glen let out a war whoop and grabbed her up in his arms. They were grinning, watching the tumult recede behind them, the waves leaping up like grasping paws. But they were safe, out of reach. They had shipped a foot of water, but hadn't hit a single rock – a seamless run through one of the toughest rapids the river had to offer.

They hoped to make it to Phantom Ranch by nightfall, and the thought of a hot bath and clean sheets made them hurry. While Glen bailed, Bessie consulted the map. It looked like they were approaching Sockdolager. Bessie remembered a line from an article Clyde Eddy wrote, claiming that the waves in Sockdolager, at low water, measured twenty feet from trough to crest. She had been so riveted, she looked up the word: 'sockdolager: a decisive blow or answer: FINISHER.' It gave her a chill. Glen considered Eddy a showboat, likely to exaggerate, but they'd find out soon enough if he was telling the truth. Already the channel had narrowed and turned glassy, and now it narrowed again and plumes of spray leapt up ahead. They leaned on the sweeps, trying to steer for shore, but the scow kept speeding toward the drop. 'Pull hard!' Glen shouted to Bessie.

'I am!' she called back. When she turned forward again, white arms of froth reached up from the rapid.

Glen threw all his weight against the back sweep handle, muttering under his breath, 'Come on, come on,' and slowly the scow started veering toward the bank. They ground to a halt against a small skirt of rocks, only yards from the rapid. Glen jumped out and tied off to a boulder.

'I'll be right back,' he said, striding along the narrow shore. He quickly dropped below the lip of the falls and out of sight. The roar was deafening. When he came back, moments later, his face was drawn. Bessie watched him carefully.

'Looks like a straight shot,' Glen shouted, untying the bow line.

'Is it bad?'

'Big waves,' he said, giving her a nervous grin.

Bessie pushed the hair from her cheek, plastered there by the mist. 'Why don't we line?'

'Because there's nowhere to line,' Glen said, heaving himself into the scow. 'The walls come right down to the water.' He saw the fear in her face. 'Look, we don't have any choice. We can stay here until we starve or get in the boat and go.'

She stared at him for a beat, then took a shuddering breath. 'All right,' she said. 'Let's get it over with.'

They pushed out into the current, Glen steering for the marker he'd chosen, then dropped over the ledge and into the maelstrom. The line looked good, they were dead on the tongue, boiling forward. Then Bessie heard a furious crack. A split second later, the force shuddered up through her bones. She flew one way and Glen flew the other, like kindling dropped to each side of an ax. When she caught her breath and struggled up from the pile of duffel, her husband was gone and the scow was turning broadside to the current. One good wave, and they'd flip. She grabbed the back sweep and gave it a yank, amazed that the boat slid back into plumb. Lucky stroke. She scanned for Glen. Nothing but roiling brown water on all sides. Then a wave towered up and smashed over her. *Hold on to the sweeps* – she felt her arms nearly yanked from their sockets. *Stay with the boat.* Then she burst into the air again. The scow nosed into a trough, hit another rock, and glanced off, veering toward a terrifying hole. She pulled hard on the sweeps, steering the boat back toward the tongue. Only when she was bucking through the tail waves could she search for him. There was something off to the right – his jacket? – but it rolled over and lifted a branch. The roar of the river was softening. Her eyes darted over the surface. To think she hadn't even called out when he fell.

Now the cry escaped her. Glen! A strange disembodied sound. My God, to be alone in this place.

And then, as if summoned, his head broke the surface, a good forty feet behind the boat. He burst up like a man from the underworld – gasping, wheeling his arms – then sank again. Bessie rushed to the back of the scow and flung the stern line in his direction. The rope unfurled over the water – *please, let it be long enough!* – and landed with a slap. For whole horrible seconds she watched. Nothing but froth. Then she saw the line pull taut and raise his body. He was holding the knotted tail, dragged along by his arms, fighting to twist his face up for a breath. She leaned over the back of the scow and started reeling him in. When he was close enough, she tried to heave him into the boat, but his clothes were soaked and heavy with silt. He was so cold he could hardly move. They struggled for a good ten minutes, Glen too feeble to climb up, Bessie grasping at his coat sleeves – until finally she reached over his back, took hold of his belt, and hauled him in with a sudden burst of strength.

He lay on the mattress with his eyes closed, too tired to speak. She kneeled down beside him, wiping the water from his face, gripping his chest with relief. He was alive and breathing. Safe.

'I thought you were going to leave without me,' he said, teeth chattering. His lips formed a gray smile, but he turned only his eyes toward her, as if his head were caught in ice.

Bessie rubbed frantically at his arms, but it was pointless through his wet clothes. She laid her body down on top of his, and pressed her cheek, flushed from exertion, against his. 'We've got to warm you up,' she said. She stood up and looked around. They were caught in an eddy, circling with a flotilla of driftwood below the rapid. When the scow swung close to the bank again she jumped out and ran up the rocks with the painter, dragging the boat toward shore. Waterlogged, the scow must have weighed half a ton, but she felt as if she could pull the world on a rope. When she had knotted the painter to a rock, she scrambled over the narrow slit of sand, gathering a nest of driftwood. She tried to remember the way Glen made a fire: pile the kindling into a tent, then lean a few logs on top. That done, she waded out to the boat, jackknifed over the side, and pulled the matches from their rubber pouch. 'I'll have the fire going in a second,' she said.

'Let me help you.' He struggled to sit up.

'Just be still,' she said, and then splashed back to the beach and made a fire big enough to roast a horse. She kept throwing on log after log, until she was sure it wouldn't go out.

It was a struggle to get him out of the boat – he seemed to have used all his strength swimming, and now his arms were limp. But once he had stripped off his clothes and baked by the fire, once Bessie had rubbed him over with the wool blanket, chafing color back into his arms and legs and then swaddled him like a child, he seemed to return to himself. She heated a can of beans at the edge of the fire, and looked up to find him staring at her.

'For a minute there I thought I might have bought the farm.' He didn't seem frightened by this, but rather surprised.

'So did I,' she said. The beans were bubbling in the can. She lifted them from the coals with a pair of sticks.

'I should teach you how to use the rifle,' he said. His hair was still plastered over his forehead.

She didn't like what this implied. 'We can't waste bullets on target practice. Besides, look what you can do when you're desperate.' She pointed to the fire. It looked like a flaming haystack, and sent a wide swath of smoke toward the rim. She laughed, remembering how she had scurried around the beach. Now that he was safe, it seemed like slapstick.

But Glen wasn't laughing, he was studying her. 'You ran that rapid on your own,' he said. 'There's one for your book.'

She dipped her head, but couldn't help smiling.

The pleasure was short-lived. A moment later, she looked up and saw clouds sliding over the rim – high and creased, like milk shuddering in a cup. Glen had taught her to recognize them: the ice crystals that blow before a storm. Like any farmer worth his salt, he knew how to read the weather. But lately she had come to think it was a curse: you suffered the cold before it arrived.

He was still shivering when they climbed into bed, so she kept the fire going all night, slipping out to gather wood by the coals' glow and climbing back under the covers to press against him while the flames leapt up against the cliffs. By morning she was exhausted – her arms feather-light, her skin dry as paper. But it was more than the fire that had kept her awake, it was nerves, a new terror that had reared up and couldn't be tamed. They could die in this place. On their honeymoon, for God's sake. And her husband, who she had thought was invincible, was no match for the river at its worst.

Reith Hyde

When I arrived at the South Rim on the 17th of December, there was a telegram waiting from Bessie's father. The governor of West Virginia – Gore, I believe his name was – had pulled some strings and persuaded the army to lend planes for a search. Since Glen and Bessie were eight days overdue, someone finally saw fit to help with their rescue.

I had never met Mr. Haley. The wedding had been quick, and he hadn't come out for it. Bessie had described him as a decorator, which didn't recommend him to me. But when I read his telegram there in the office, I let out a gruff shout – 'Good man!' People turned to stare, but I couldn't help myself. It was such a relief to have someone else on the case, someone capable. I hadn't realized until that moment how much I had been missing my wife, missing the chance to talk to the one person who had just as much at stake. Right then Mr. Haley filled that gap a bit.

I checked into the El Tovar Hotel, perched right on the rim of the canyon. It was the hub of the little settlement there, a fancy tourist place with a restaurant. I knew Bessie and Glen had stayed there, since they'd posted a letter to me on the hotel stationery. When the clerk assigned me my room, I asked if he'd look at the ledgers from the middle of November. Sure enough, after paging back, he came across Glen's signature, dated November 15, 1928. It gave me a chill to see his handwriting, as if he were still upstairs, around the corner, and at any minute I might run into him.

At noon, the two railroad men came to see me – Francy and

Harbin were their names – and right away it was clear there had been some misunderstanding. They were expecting $10,000, plus expenses. I tried to explain: if I sold everything I owned I was hardly worth that much. I told them there must have been a mix-up at the telegraph office – someone added a zero. Harbin got surly, said it was a low trick to bait them that way. Then they went off for a while to talk it over. I had a bad feeling about those two, but I wasn't in a position to be choosy. They were the only ones with a boat at Phantom Ranch – it seems they had salvaged it from some movie-making expedition a few years before – and it would be hard to find anyone else willing to brave the river in the middle of December. Finally they came back and we made a bargain. They would take their boat down from Phantom Ranch to Diamond Creek, almost to the end of the canyon. I'd cover expenses. If they managed to bring back information that led to a rescue, I'd pay them $2,000. They were to make note of any campsites or messages in the sand, and of course, if they found Glen and Bessie, to carry them along.

At the last minute, Park Superintendent Patraw insisted on going along as an observer. I was less than pleased about this – it would be hard to carry enough supplies for three people, let alone five – but I could hardly say no. The canyon was under his jurisdiction. We agreed that when they got to Havasu Canyon, the halfway point of their trip, they would hike up to the Indian village near the rim and telephone me with an update. Harbin estimated the whole trip would take two weeks, at which point I'd meet them at Diamond Creek.

Once that was settled, I walked along the rim to Emery Kolb's place. It had been a few days since we'd spoken on the phone. I was hoping he'd hold true to his promise of assistance. I had heard that he was making a living off his fame as a river runner, taking pictures of tourists and showing motion pictures of his 1911 trip down the Colorado. A man that busy might not have time for a volunteer search. When I knocked on the door a young woman came out to meet me, lifting her hand against the glare. I introduced myself and stated my business.

She said she was Edith Kolb, Emery's daughter, and her father had mentioned I would be coming by. She reminded me a bit of Jeanne, a girl with substance. I asked if her father was in.

Miss Kolb nodded. 'Let me go fetch him.'

Emery Kolb proved to be a stand-up fellow. People talk about his temper and his big head, but he never showed me anything but kindness. That day he dropped his work and offered me lunch. When I told him that the army planes were on their way, and that Francy and Harbin were setting out in the morning from Phantom Ranch, he seemed encouraged.

We decided that it made sense to wait for the pilot's report, but if the scow was spotted past Diamond Creek, Kolb volunteered to search that final stretch of the canyon. 'There's an old boat at Diamond Creek, left by the drilling crew,' he told me. 'We could fix it up enough to get down to Spencer Creek and take it out there.'

We were still discussing this plan when the clerk came over from El Tovar to say there'd been a phone call: the army pilots had arrived at Grand Canyon Airport. We pushed back our plates and drove out to meet them – two officers in uniform, young and spruce. They agreed that if the weather was good, they'd fly over the canyon the next day. Said they could take two passengers. I had never been in an airplane before, and frankly the prospect made me feel half sick, but I decided I had to go. I asked Kolb if he would come along as my second, being as he had a better knowledge of the canyon's landmarks. He leapt at the chance.

The next morning, Kolb and I and the two lieutenants climbed into the plane, a big closed-cockpit outfit with a row of seats on each wall – I guess it was a newfangled model. The pilots fired up the three motors and fiddled with the controls, as cool as if they were fixing breakfast. Then we started roaring down the airstrip, picking up a horrible rate of speed. Just when I thought the wings would break off, I felt a sinking in my gut and looked down to see we'd parted ways with the ground. I could just imagine what Glen would say when he heard the story: his old papa, who couldn't swim and didn't like to motor more than fifteen miles an hour, was the first in the family to go up in an airplane. The things we'll do for our children.

It was cold inside the cabin. Wind whistled in the doors. We were circling up over the mesa, a high pan of brown earth, marked by watercourses and carpets of pine. The landscape looked just like a map – the same beige and green of geography books – only it had startling detail and depth. We were coming up to the Grand Canyon from the south. Already I could make out the road leading up to the El Tovar Hotel, and the cars parked out front like child's toys. It was all rather miraculous, as long as I didn't think about what would happen if the engines stalled out.

Lieutenant Adams buzzed over Grand Canyon Village, then banked and turned west, and a cleft opened in the tabletop below: the banded canyon, fed by side streams, widening and narrowing into the distance. He eased the plane over the rim and pointed the nose toward the string of river at the bottom. As we dove, the canyon seemed to rise up to meet us, widening like a mouth. The river broadened too. Soon I could make out rapids, like ruffles on a shirt. Once we flew over Phantom Ranch, a little cluster of buildings on the right side of the river, Kolb got his bearings. He pressed his face to the window as we flew downstream, the river below turning thin and white, then expanding into calm stretches. Here and there we passed a crescent of beach.

Kolb had a hard time recognizing the rapids from above.

From the air, they looked minuscule and flattened. Hermit, which he said had raised the hair on his neck when he saw it at water level, looked like a harmless riffle. Every now and then we'd pass something unusual – a big island in the middle of the river – and he'd get oriented again. Finally we came to Diamond Creek – Kolb pointed out the big side canyon coming in from the left and the mining shacks near the mouth – and then we banked around a soft curve in the canyon and there was the scow! A neat dark rectangle stalled in an eddy.

'That's it,' I shouted, leaning forward to touch the lieutenant on the shoulder. My heart was in my throat. He nosed up out of the narrow gorge and banked and flew back over again, this time coming at it upstream. Sure enough, there it was, a perfect boxy shadow in the water.

'Can you get any lower?' Kolb yelled to the pilot.

'I can try.' He dove deeper, until the wings seemed nearly to graze the cliffs on either side, and as we roared over the boat, I could make out the individual sweeps, the mattress in the bottom, the neatly lashed pile of duffel. It all looked peaceful, no sign of an upset, but neither one of them was in sight.

Glen and Bessie Hyde

The morning after his swim in Sockdolager, Glen woke up in good spirits. He made Bessie stay in bed while he fixed oatmeal and packed the boat.

'I might need a nail to get this undone,' he said with a wry smile, tugging on the bow line. She had cinched it so many times the knot hung like a lumpy braid.

'I didn't want to lose the boat,' she said, burrowing down in the covers.

Glen squinted up at the clouds. 'I'd let you sleep, but the sky doesn't look good.'

Before they could pack up the rest of the gear, the rain set in – hard, clattering rain that rucked up the surface of the river. Then the wind started howling up the canyon. No point setting out in that kind of weather. They pulled the bed back under an overhang, where it was partly shielded, rigged up the oilskin like a lean-to, and passed a slow day there, reading and talking. They had plenty of kerosene, but their food stores were nearly gone, so they kept warm and full on cups of black coffee.

The next morning, November 15, the sky broke clear, and they set out for Phantom Ranch. Bessie leaned back on the duffel, wrapped in a wool blanket, amazed at how much could change in a day. Her husband safe, the boat intact. Even a faint wind at their back. They ran a small riffle and sped along on flat water for several miles. Then she heard a rapid ahead – a big one, from the sound of it – and her anxiety returned. She kept seeing it all over again: how he'd flown overboard, how small his body had looked among the waves. Just the memory made her stomach weak. But Glen seemed unfazed by his mishap. He scouted quickly and came back to the boat. 'I think we should run it,' he said.

While he was gone, Bessie had consulted the map. 'It looks like a big fall,' she countered. 'I'd like to have a look.'

Glen looked surprised. She had always left the scouting to him. 'All right,' he said grudgingly, stepping into the boat. 'But do it quick. We might lose the weather anytime now.'

She glanced at the sky. 'It looks clear enough to me,' she said, taking her time refolding the map. She could feel his eyes on her as she picked her way along the rocky shore, still slick from the previous day's rain. Flicks of spray arced up ahead. The rocks sloped downward, and she caught a glimpse of the rapid. It was narrow and steep, a roiling chute of water, thick with holes, a near perfect twin to Sockdolager. What made him so sure they could run it? She looked carefully at the rapid's edge. It was ragged with huge boulders, the fast water surging up between them. Lining wouldn't be easy, but it seemed foolhardy not to learn from experience. Shouldn't they be cautious, now that they were six miles from Phantom Ranch? They might crack a plank and have to lay over for repairs. She would hate to spend another night on the river, when a cabin and a warm bed were close at hand. She studied the rapid again. No, Glen was right. Lining would be just as dangerous as running, maybe more. She tried to pick a route. It wasn't familiar – judging the water in advance – but if she had to guess, she'd aim straight for the tongue.

'What do you think?' Glen asked, when she got back to the scow.

'I think it looks like a bad run,' she said, watching his face. 'But lining looks worse.' She was braced for a show of smugness, but he just nodded, his brow creased.

'I thought we'd just go down the tongue,' he said, jumping down to untie the scow. 'Unless you saw another route.'

She watched as he coiled the rope from elbow to wrist, feeling an inward flush of surprise. 'That's what I thought, but it's hard to tell from the shore.'

He tossed the painter into the bow, where it landed with a wet thwack. 'Well, if we're wrong, we'll be wrong together,' he said, giving her a rueful smile.

They pushed off and aimed for the center of the current. The scow went nose first into the waves. Bessie was tense, her body braced for another blow. But they had been right. The boat heaved up the crests and down into the troughs, water lashing over the sides, and in minutes they were sliding into the washout, not having so much as grazed a rock.

'Nice work,' Glen said, when the rapid's roar died behind them.

Bessie nodded, loosening her grip on the sweep, but she was still too nervous to take credit for their luck.

They passed through four small rapids in the next few hours. At noon they spotted a suspension bridge spanning the river, the first man-made crossing since they'd left Lee's Ferry. According to the map, Phantom Ranch was just a short distance downstream, so they moored the boat and set out walking along the right bank, then cut back into the side canyon where the cabins were clustered.

At the front desk, the clerk asked them to sign the register. Bessie took up the pen: Mr. and Mrs. Glen Hyde. Going down the river – November 15, 1928 – in a flat-bottomed boat. Hansen, Idaho.

When the clerk saw the inscription, he began peppering them with questions. A small crowd gathered at the reception desk, most of them turned out in spotless denims, still creased from the store, even the women in slacks and Stetson hats. After a week of struggle and solitude, it was impossible not to swell to this attention. Glen and Bessie exchanged shy glances. It seemed as if they'd done something grand.

When the hubbub died down, they settled on the porch with cups of hot coffee. A stocky young man, in his middle thirties, came up to offer his congratulations. His clothes were fine, but well worn – cuffed trousers, a wool sweater. He was a tourist, clearly, but had enough confidence to forgo the western costume. 'I'm Adolph Sutro,' he said, extending his hand.

Glen shook it. 'Any relation to the famous engineer?'

'He was my grandfather,' Sutro replied.

Bessie looked at Glen in surprise. 'You knew him?'

'Only by reputation,' Glen said. 'He oversaw the draining of the Comstock Lode. Even got a mention in *Roughing It*.'

Sutro looked amused. 'Even Twain couldn't make the old man laugh. He said, "I don't think Sutro minds a joke of mild character any more than a dead man would."' He was always pleased at the chance to twit his grandfather, who cast a looming shadow. The old millionaire used to walk through San Francisco with a purse of gold coins, handing them out to anyone who asked. 'Just no sob stories,' he insisted. 'I prefer a plain request.'

'So what's the purpose of your venture?' Sutro asked.

Glen shrugged. 'Do we need one?'

'I suppose not,' Sutro said, cocking his head. 'Adventure for adventure's sake. I just wondered if you were gathering some scientific data, setting a record, that sort of thing.'

'We're on our honeymoon,' Glen said. 'My wife wanted to see a little of the west. But it looks like she's the first woman to run all of Cataract Canyon, and she's already tackled half the Grand.' He glanced at Bessie and smiled.

'Grit *and* beauty,' Sutro said, taking Bessie's hand and bowing over it. 'You're a lucky man. I must say, though, I'm a little wary of records, having nearly sunk myself in the pursuit.'

'You're a sailor?' Bessie asked.

'Hydroplane pilot.' He pulled a cigar from his vest pocket and clipped it neatly. 'Care for a smoke?' he asked Glen.

Glen declined, waiting for the rest of the story. But Sutro was making a production of lighting his cigar, so Bessie had to prompt him: 'Did you set a record?'

'Set three,' Sutro said, trying to look modest and failing. 'Speed over distance, altitude, weight carried.'

'What year was this?' Glen asked.

'1913. We flew four and a quarter miles in a little under four minutes –' He saw Glen's astonishment at the minuscule numbers and blew out a puff of smoke. 'It was quite an accomplishment at the time.'

'You still fly?' Glen put down his coffee. He took an interest in aviation.

'Only as a passenger. I took a spill in the San Francisco Bay in November of '13. A dear friend of mine got caught up in the wires and nearly drowned. It was an exposition – ten thousand people in the stands. Another pilot broke one of his wings in midair and had a touchy time landing. Not a good show for the sport.' He chuckled and pulled on his cigar. 'After that my family made me promise to give it up. Of course, they didn't protest when I went off to fight the Huns, which was a damn sight more deadly –' He took on a somber look. 'But necessary, of course, absolutely necessary.'

Glen quickened at the mention of the Great War. He never tired of soldiers' stories, perhaps because he had never faced a risk like that – a risk he didn't choose. When the train had pulled out of the station in Twin Falls in 1917, the coaches hung with bunting, half the town turned out to see the boys off. Ladies Aid gave out cakes and pies and cigarettes. Glen sank back into the crowd, feeling like a shirker, even though he had earned his deferment fair and square. Six months before, when the newspapers had first reported the coming draft, the farmers around Twin Falls had been mad as hornets, gathering at the dry goods in little clusters to convince one another of the thing they all agreed on: if every farmer took up a gun, the whole country would starve. And what were we doing tangled up with some foreign belligerents? Glen had stood back, listening to the talk, but the truth was, he was dying to go. Then word came about agricultural deferments. Any rancher or farmer could apply. Reith was fifty-nine – too old to serve. Glen was eighteen. Just over the wire. He had finally decided to apply for a draft card when Reith sat him down in the kitchen one evening, a grave look on his face. He had noticed that Glen hadn't filed the exemption forms. His father hardly ever gave orders or offered advice. He led by example, and he had always given Glen a lot of rope. But now he let it be known – in his stiff, halting way – that he could use his son's help on the ranch. 'I suppose I could hire someone,' Reith said. 'And those East Coast engineers will figure out the irrigating soon enough.'

This was a calculated jab. The Snake River dam project, which had turned the Idaho desert into farmland, put great stock in fancy degrees, but none of the college types had ever done any real irrigating. They drew up elaborate flow predictors and then overwatered, letting the ditches silt up. Glen and a few other men had gone down to the offices to consult on the water management.

Glen couldn't look his father in the eye. 'Casper went down to get his number.' He didn't have to say what a stab of envy this caused in him. It was plain in his face.

But the next day, he drove the Model T to the precinct office and filed the deferment papers. And all that year, until the war's end, Glen followed the newspaper reports from the front with something close to obsession. Half the houses in Twin Falls had gold stars in the windows, the mark of a fallen son. Every time he went into the dry goods, he had to face Byron

Mitchell, only a year ahead of him in school, working the register with his one remaining arm.

Now Glen looked at Sutro with the same bitter fascination. 'Where'd you fight?' he asked.

'Alsace–Lorraine. Machine-gun battalion.'

Bessie sat forward, eager to change the subject. 'You mentioned San Francisco. Are you connected to the Sutro Baths?' She knew how war stories made Glen brood.

'That was the grandfather again,' Sutro said, vaguely peeved.

'I lived in the city for a while,' Bessie said, 'but I never made it out for a visit.'

'They're worth a look. But as sights go, you can't beat this place. And seeing it from a boat – that's the way to do it,' Sutro said. 'I rode a mule down. Terrible idea. They're worse than camels. I was thinking I'd trek along the river for a few days. Get away from this organized tour. One of these mule packers claims he knows the trail. Say, I don't imagine you'd like to take on a passenger?'

Glen glanced at Bessie, gauging her response. She had been stiff since Sockdolager. It might cheer her up to have company. And Sutro seemed like a capable fellow.

It seems that he'd judged her correctly. 'Why not?' she said, giving a light shrug.

Glen turned to Sutro. 'We could take you down as far as Hermit Camp. There's a good trail from there to the rim. The ride will be rough, but the scow's better suited for water than a float plane.'

After they'd finished their coffee, the three of them hiked upstream to examine the scow. When they reached the beach, Glen pulled up short.

'Listen, there's something I forgot.' He turned to Sutro in discomfort.

'What's that?' Sutro asked.

'Our food stores are a bit thin. You're welcome to them, of

course. But you might start thinking you're back at the front.'

Sutro brushed this aside. 'As long as I've got my Cubans and a spot of gin I don't care what I eat.' Then he seemed to reconsider. 'But listen here, I don't want to jeopardize the expedition.'

Glen winced at that phrase, 'the expedition.' Such a pompous ring. 'We've got plenty of grub, if you don't mind lima beans.'

Sutro thrust out his hand. 'Done. Besides, a two-day fast ought to do me good.' He patted his gut.

Bessie and Glen agreed to meet him at the scow on November 17, and they began packing for their trip to the rim. They'd spend two nights in the swank hotel at the top – a splurge that would cost them a quarter of their cash – and buy some much-needed supplies. Glen got out his razor and brush and shaved on a rock near the water's edge, rinsing the blade in the river. Bessie dug out her purse, buried deep in the duffel, and packed a few toiletries and clothes in a satchel. It was a long climb – eight miles of switchbacks – so to keep their pack light, they took only one change of shirt each.

At one o'clock, they cinched the oilskin over the scow, protecting their gear against rain, then crossed the suspension bridge and started onto the Kaibab Trail. The blue weather had been a fluke. As they worked their way out of the canyon, an armada of bulging clouds passed overhead, letting loose rain and then – as they gained elevation – flurries of snow. Still, their spirits were high. They could see for miles in each direction. The cliffs shifted with the changing light. Bessie's heels rubbed in her knee-high boots, but after a few miles the pain disappeared and her legs felt strong. The trail zigzagged up the face. At every tenth turn she'd stop and look down. First the river shrank to a narrow stream, then it dropped out of view. What a relief. Now she could admire the layered gulf yawning beneath her. Who would believe a river could have carved such a gash in the earth? They were two moving specks, making their way up the stairstepping cliffs, their progress no more significant than the stirring of two dust motes in a vast room.

The snow turned from flurries into gusts, then settled into a gently falling curtain. Drifts built up along the trail. Even though they were slogging up a stretch of relentless switchbacks, their hearts pumping at full strength, the cold nipped at their faces and hands. At least it's dry cold, Bessie told herself. And there's the top. But as fast as they climbed, the rim receded ahead of them. Only as they gained the top of one sheer wall could they see the next, set farther back.

The light was turning gray, and Bessie was starting to worry about frostbite – they hadn't brought blankets or a stove – when they stepped onto the plateau. Thank God. They squinted through the flurries for the hotel. It was supposed to be right at the top of the trail.

Nothing. That is, nothing but stands of piñon and slabs of snow-dusted rock. The trail seemed to continue, so they followed it and came to a road. Still no sign of a building. It was dark now, and the snow was still falling.

'Did we make a wrong turn?' Bessie asked, tucking her hands under her arms.

'How could we? That trail was like a highway. The hotel must be right around here.'

They peered up and down the road.

'My gut says it's left,' Glen said, turning toward the east.

'Wait, let's think.' Bessie called up the map in her head. 'The Bright Angel Trail took off downstream of the Kaibab. And they both lead to the hotel, so I say we head right.'

'Last time I doubted you, I had to eat crow,' Glen said, shifting the satchel from one shoulder to the other. 'Just lead me to the nearest steak.'

Bessie smiled in the darkness. For so long she had relied on his judgment, at least in regards to the boat and the river. She had always had faith in her opinions of people and art and the sensory world – the things that mattered to her. But she deferred to him in the realm of action. And because her job was to record that action, she had fallen into the strange belief that it couldn't alter her, that she couldn't die – it would mean the story would stop. But when he had flown over the side in Sockdolager, and she had had to fish him out, that dream had dissolved. She saw he was fallible. And that she had been half asleep. The funny thing was, something had shifted in him, too. She had expected more of a fight. How often did you tip the scales in a marriage without causing a fuss? But he must have been tired of his role, always deciding for the both of them, always soothing her fears. Now he seemed happy to confer with her, and at times to yield.

They set off briskly, leaning into the wind. Half an hour later they were still on an empty road, cutting a trough through the snow. Perhaps she'd been hasty, plowing ahead into the dark. Just then a soft churring cut the quiet. Two cones of light swung over the trees. A car pulled up beside them, and a man leaned over from the driver's side. 'Where are you headed?'

'El Tovar Hotel,' Glen said.

'It's about three miles farther on. Why don't you hop in?'

Bessie had never been so grateful for a ride, in fact for the sight of an automobile – they'd seen nothing but boats and mules for a month. The driver chatted with them in the warmth and darkness of the car. He seemed to Bessie, in his shadowed outline, like a model of human kindness. Twenty minutes later, he dropped them in front of the hotel, a massive split-log building, with the peaked roof and scalloped trim of a Swiss chalet. They knocked the snow off their boots and went inside.

So strange to find that the world had gone on without you. They had spent twenty-eight days on the river, but it felt easily twice that. Bessie picked up a newspaper in the lobby and glanced at the date: November 7, 1928. A week old. According to the headline, Hoover had won the presidency, beating Smith by a mile. She had forgotten it was an election year – her first chance to vote. And now, in her exhaustion, it was only of passing interest. She was too absorbed by the change in their surroundings – from an old box spring tucked under a cliff to a dark, snug lodge. A fire blazed in the stone hearth, making her cheeks flush and her nose run. Deer and elk stuck their heads through the walls. Glen booked a room, a double with a private bath – it was off-season and the rates were halved. They washed up, changed into clean shirts, and went straight to the dining room.

Glen started with a flank steak. Halfway through he ordered another. Bessie split open a baked potato and dropped a slab of butter in the crease. Sour cream. Hot coffee. And to eat sitting up at a proper table, with salt and clear water at hand's reach. She watched other patrons rushing through their meals – oblivious to their good fortune – and made an effort to lower her fork between bites.

But none of this compared to the bath she took later – the hot water loosening her by inches, until she was warm to the marrow. When she came out, wrapped in soft towels, Glen was reading the discarded paper from the lobby. 'Did you see this?' he asked her. 'The Republicans won again. My father must be in a foul mood.'

'I'd have thought he'd vote Republican,' Bessie said, rubbing a towel over her hair. Reith Hyde even bore a resemblance to Silent Cal – lean and reserved, an avid fisherman.

'He'd rather chop off his leg than back Coolidge's man. Not after he vetoed the farm relief bills. Hoover calling himself the Prosperity President – that got a big laugh around Twin Falls. Have a look around here, they said. We've got more apples than God, and prices are down in the gutter.'

'But everyone's going on about the boom,' she said. 'I'd have thought –'

He shook his head. 'We all cranked up for the war effort and then got left high and dry. My father's still paying off a note from the '21 harvest.'

Bessie sat on the edge of the bed and stared. Glen never talked about politics – or money, for that matter. She had assumed the ranch was doing well. It certainly didn't have the air of a failing concern, and Mr. Hyde conveyed no anxiety about costs. The machinery was well maintained, the orchards thick with fruit. She had spent that summer and early fall fancying herself a character in a Willa Cather novel, so caught up in the symbolic bounty of the harvest she had forgotten to ask what price it fetched.

That night they each wrote letters home, painting their trip in pastel tones, making assurances that the worst was behind them, and posted them at the front desk. In the morning, they had breakfast in the hotel – eggs, bacon, toast, oatmeal, coffee with cream – and then walked a hundred yards along the rim to Emery Kolb's studio, hoping to find him home. There were wooden sidewalks leading to his door, and yucca plants dotted among the rocks. The studio was set just below the rim, a log and shingle building notched over the canyon. Under the eaves, a banner read:

Kolb Bros.
Shooting the Rapids of the Colorado River Canyons in Motion Pictures

They knocked on the door and introduced themselves. Said they had come down the river by boat and wanted to pay their respects. Kolb's wife, Blanche, greeted them warmly. 'Emery's delivering some photographs to a hotel guest. He'll be back in a moment.' She invited them to sit in the parlor. Navajo rugs were scattered over the dark wood floors. Framed photos of the canyon covered the walls. 'Emery's work,' Blanche said proudly, and invited them to look. The rest of the decor tried to civilize the setting: wicker furniture, rose-patterned wallpaper, lace curtains. It all looked fragile and strange, juxtaposed against the spires and buttes out the windows.

Soon Kolb came in and introduced himself. 'I understand you're trying to follow in my footsteps,' he said, his chin tipped in the air. He was wiry and bow-legged, with a high-pitched voice.

'We'd be lucky to do as well,' Glen said.

'Luck has nothing to do with it,' Kolb said. Then he softened a little. 'So what'd you think of Hance?'

'We did all right there. Bessie's getting a little tired of the cold, but the scow's holding up.'

'Any upsets?' Kolb said, eyeing him warily. He was an incorrigible boaster, but disliked it in others.

'Not yet. We've both gone over the side a few times. But the boat is so heavy it does all right without us.'

Just then a young woman, perhaps twenty, came striding into the room. She had wind-chapped cheeks and thick hair cut into a bob. Emery introduced her as his daughter. 'Edith was the first white child to live year-round at the rim,' he said. 'She rode a mule down into the canyon before she could walk.'

Bessie watched Kolb with curiosity. A man like that seemed certain to have wanted a son, but she read nothing but pride in his face.

'These two are going down the river in a flat-bottomed scow,' Kolb said, nodding at Bessie and Glen.

'Oh, I envy you. What an adventure,' Edith said. When her father and uncle made their first trip down the Colorado, she and her mother had spent many nights with a telescope trained on the canyon floor, hoping for a signal fire. 'It's easier to leave than be left.'

'Edith got the jump on you, though,' Kolb said to Bessie,

putting a hand on his daughter's shoulder. 'First woman to shoot a Colorado River rapid.'

His daughter laughed. 'As a passenger, mind you.'

'Which one was it?' Bessie asked, guessing a riffle.

'Hance,' Edith said. 'I went down on a mule to meet Papa on the survey trip in '23 and one of the boatmen offered to give me a thrill ride.'

'Gave *me* a thrill, is what it did,' Kolb put in. 'Damn fellow nosed it straight into a hole. I thought for sure she'd be knocked off. I went running for the water and then the boat punched through the back wave and there was my girl, clinging to the bow like a wet cat.'

Edith smiled down at the carpet.

'She was grinning, just like that,' Kolb said, hooking a thumb in her direction. 'Wanted to try it again.'

'Well, if you made it through Hance, you could probably manage any of them,' Bessie said, her voice full of admiration. She was surprised to find that she wasn't jealous of Edith's feat. In fact, it was a comfort to meet someone – another woman, at that – who had a small inkling of what they'd been through. Of course, it was easy to be generous in the face of such a mild threat. Edith had only been through a single rapid.

Together the four of them moved toward the picture window in the living room, a polished pane of glass opening out on the view. The cliff dropped away beneath the house, stairstepping down a vertical mile to the river, then rose up in banded red layers to the North Rim, twelve miles away. There was nothing to compare it to, the sensation of standing at the lip of that massive cavern. The sight of the ocean might come to mind, but that was a baffling vastness – you could squint at the horizon, try to guess how far it was, but it was an abstraction, like trying to imagine the distance to the moon. The canyon dwarfed, but it could be measured by the eye. You could see the far rim, you could imagine yourself standing on the other side, and yet the yawning expanse of air in front of you brought a disorienting humbleness, a kind of pull, so you rocked forward a little toward its emptiness, then teetered back in relief.

Glen stared down toward the bottom, where small turns of the river could be seen between the sheer inner walls. 'It looks like a creek from here,' he said.

'That's what the Spaniards thought,' Kolb said. 'Cárdenas sent some of his men down to fetch water. They came back three days later, nearly dead of thirst. Hadn't come anywhere near the river.'

Glen smiled – he loved that kind of lore – then moved closer to the glass, hands in his coat pockets. 'What I'd give to wake up to this every morning,' he said softly, looking over at Bessie for confirmation. She nodded, out of politeness to Kolb, but she didn't agree. It was one thing to visit such a stark, overpowering place, another to live with it day after day. She preferred the comforting scale of the Hyde ranch: the rows of apple trees skirting the house, and the kitchen gardens spread out neatly beneath the windows. Just the thought gave her a pang.

'Well, if you finish your trip, I'll have to make sure no one lets you have any land nearby,' Kolb said.

Glen cocked his head in puzzlement.

'You'd be horning in on my business,' Kolb explained. 'I've been told I'm pretty charming, but I can't compare with your wife here.' He was smiling, but Bessie caught the tinge of envy in the remark.

Just then Mrs. Kolb appeared in the doorway. 'Lunch is ready,' she said, smoothing her hands on a blue apron.

Glen turned quickly from the window. 'Oh, I'm sorry to have kept you from your meal, Mr. Kolb.' He held out his hand. 'I can't thank you enough –'

Kolb waved him off. 'Save that for later. We haven't fed you yet.'

'We don't want to impose,' Bessie said, glancing at Mrs. Kolb. 'We're happy to eat in the hotel.'

Kolb made a derisive snort. 'They're making a killing over there. Charging a buck for a twenty-cent steak. Save your money for supplies.'

'The table is already set,' Mrs. Kolb added, smiling from the doorway. 'We'd be delighted if you'd stay.' Before they could protest further, she untied her apron and led them to the dining room, where Edith was pouring glasses of cold sugared tea.

The food was modest but delicious: chicken pot pie, the crust shattering under the fork, creamed corn. Kolb talked a little of river lore, his wife and daughter listening with affection.

At length, the talk turned to the proposed dam. 'I suppose you've heard those fools in Congress have finally brought it to the table,' Kolb said.

Glen shook his head. 'We've been away from the papers.'

'They're going to authorize the dam. Six years after they signed the river compact, the thing is finally going through. The states kept fighting about water rights, but now it looks like they've got all the votes.'

Glen shot Bessie a look. 'Have they decided on the site?'

'Down in Boulder Canyon.'

'Where's that?' Bessie asked.

'Southeast of Las Vegas,' Kolb said. 'It's a narrow section, but it'll still be the biggest high dam in the world. Some people say when it's finished and the river starts backing up, it'll put half the rapids of the Grand underwater.'

Edith put down her tea and leaned toward Bessie. 'You may be the last expedition to run that section,' she said, her face flushing with excitement. 'Wouldn't that be a thrill?' She glanced at her father and saw how his face had soured.

Kolb picked up his fork. 'Well, you've made it through some

rough water. But there's worse ahead.' He was quiet for the rest of lunch. When the dishes were cleared, he pulled out a set of maps and gave Glen tips about the rapids downstream.

Bessie tried not to listen to their talk. How could things get worse? It didn't seem possible. She distracted herself by studying Kolb's photos. One in particular caught her eye: a broad archway of stone, spanning a canyon. It looked impressive enough, until she noticed a minute human figure on top – the size of an ant on a doughnut. She moved to the next picture. A rapid with notched cliffs on either side. The river looked sepia-toned, as if the water itself were old. Only when she spotted the tiny nose of a boat, piercing a white-capped wave, did she get the proper sense of scale.

She glanced back at Glen and Mr. Kolb, bent over the maps. 'Then there are the three big ones,' Kolb was saying. 'Lava Falls, Separation, and Lava Cliff. Worse than anything upstream. And in low water like this the rocks will be mean.' He went on for some time, explaining routes and pitfalls in his squeaky voice. 'But of course things could have changed since we saw them. You'd best scout well and then cinch up your life preservers.'

Glen was quiet.

'You have got life preservers,' Kolb said.

'Haven't needed them so far,' Glen said. 'We're both good swimmers.'

'I don't care how well you swim, you ought to wear them. I've got a few lying around I could loan you.'

'You're very kind, but we'll be taking out at Needles and heading straight back to Idaho for Christmas. No way to return them.'

Kolb tried to talk him into carrying an inner tube. 'You could tie a rope around it – use it as a life ring.' But no amount of cajoling could change Glen's mind. He found Kolb an odd character: cocksure but cautious. Certainly he was the real thing – an experienced riverman – but Glen didn't share his stubborn faith in life preservers. They violated his deepest beliefs about how to stay alive on a river. Cap Guleke had once told Glen the story of a mining engineer who rode along on a stretch of the Salmon in a newfangled vest, against Guleke's advice. The man flew overboard in the first bad rapid, and though they searched the river for two hours, they couldn't find him. When they got into camp that evening, Guleke waded out to unload some gear and the bloated engineer bobbed up between his legs. His life vest had snagged on a nail, and they had dragged him under the scow for fifteen miles. Only when they pulled into the shallows did his body scrape free.

Kolb and everybody else could say what they liked – Glen would follow his instincts. You wanted nothing to hang you up, nothing to constrict your arms. In a thick cork vest, you couldn't swim worth a damn – you could only wait for the current to carry you to shore. Guleke called them 'custom-fit coffins,' and that was the only thing to be said for a vest. It would bring your body up eventually, and give the relatives something to bury. Glen preferred to be clear from the start: if you went in, the only thing that would save you was a fast Australian crawl.

He reached out and shook Kolb's hand, surprised at the strength in the man's tiny grip. 'I'm grateful for all your advice,' he said. 'Don't know quite how to thank you.'

'Just send me a postcard from Needles,' Kolb said gruffly.

Glen glanced around for Bessie, thinking he'd find her chatting with Kolb's daughter. Instead she was standing in a corner of the living room, listening intently, her face fixed with some emotion he couldn't read.

They walked back along the planked pathway, past the stunning views of the canyon, but Bessie hardly turned to look. She was stiff, her head ringing with Kolb's warnings.

'What's wrong?' Glen asked, when they got back to their hotel room. Her mood seemed to have turned so quickly.

'I thought you said we were over the worst water.' She unbuttoned her jacket and threw it on the bed.

'I never said it got easier.' He was working to keep his voice calm. 'Just more of the same. Nothing we can't handle.'

She had been pacing the room. Now she stopped, arms strapped across her chest. 'That's not what I gather. I heard you two talking.'

Glen's eyes flashed. 'Don't you think Kolb has his own agenda here?'

'What do you mean?'

'I'm saying he has reasons to make it sound worse than it is. You saw his face when Edith said we'd be the last ones through before the dam. The man's jealous. He's got his little outfit going here, hero of the canyon and all that, and he doesn't want anyone to come along and foul it up.'

Bessie watched him for a long beat, half incredulous. 'You're always sure you know better than everyone else. Don't you ever take advice?'

Glen winced inwardly. His father had always accused him of being mulish. And the truth was, Kolb's caution had reminded him of Reith's – caused an old, familiar chafe. 'I hear people out,' he said, unable to keep the bite out of his voice. 'I just consider the source.'

'Well, consider this,' Bessie said, her face darkening. 'I'm your wife, and I think we should stop here.'

Glen glared at her, his jaw tight, then went to the window and looked out. She could feel the seconds ticking past, the silence between them tightening like a wire. How could he turn his back at a moment like this! She stood planted in the middle of the room, waiting for an answer. Her whole body shook, the muscles jumping with anger or fear, she couldn't tell.

When it was clear he wasn't going to speak, Bessie wheeled into the bathroom and locked the door. She ran herself a bath, sitting on the toilet while the water poured. Even in her fury, the room was comforting: the frosted glass sconce over the sink, the warm pine floor and clawfoot tub. She didn't want to give it up. Didn't want to go back to that freezing river. When the bath was full, she undressed, tossing her clothes to the floor, then sank into the steaming water. Her legs were sore from the previous day's climb. Her battered fingers, split from the cold and the silty water, ached and stung. She slid down the slick porcelain, turned the taps closed with her feet, and started to cry.

She had come as close to begging as her pride would allow, and still he wouldn't budge. She could hardly face it: that he wanted something more than her happiness. Her knees surfaced, sending waves sloshing against the sides of the tub. She wiped her cheeks. Why on earth wouldn't he quit? The answer came easily: because he'd dreamed of the trip for years. He couldn't let go of it. In that moment, it occurred to her that Earl must have seen her in this same light: full of selfish drives, ready to sweep aside anything that stood in her way. Perhaps now she should be the one to bend. She could return to Twin Falls, let Glen finish the trip by himself.

It sounded reasonable, but her heart rebelled. What kind of a man sends his wife home alone from their honeymoon? A grim thought forced its way to the front of her mind. Glen had hatched his idea for the trip before he met her. That was all well enough, but was it the reason he married her? The river had been run by eighty-odd men, but never by a woman. And though Jeanne had been willing, a brother-sister team didn't have nearly the ring of a pair of young newlyweds. She twisted away from the thought: that he could be so mercenary, and she so blind. God, if she was right, there was no other choice. She would have to give him up.

She sank down until the water covered her ears. She could hear the knocking of the pipes, the buzz of voices from the room below. She wanted to stay there forever, muffled and warm, her hair drifting like seaweed. Of course, she might be misjudging him. She was certainly assuming the worst. And if she left Glen, where would she go? Back to San Francisco? To Parkersburg? It all sounded dismal. Starting over again – she didn't know if she could stand it. She had been fighting for so long – years, in fact, ever since she left Earl – to have some kind of independence. And while she didn't regret any of it, the struggle had come at a cost. She was tired. She wanted – was it so much to ask? – someone to depend on. Much as she feared what lay ahead on the river, Glen's company, the very fact of being near him, made her feel safe.

She lay in the water until her fingers were furrowed, then stepped out and patted dry with a towel. When she came out of the bathroom, Glen was lying on his back, staring at the ceiling. Looking at him, she felt a mixture of awe and bitterness. Awe at his calm and self-sufficiency. Bitterness because he made her judge herself as wanting. She went and sat on the edge of the empty bed, already thinking of how she would toss and turn that night, her nerves too frayed for sleep.

Glen rolled onto his side, facing her. He took in her heat-flushed face, her eyes shining and sad, a little red at the rims. She reached up to rub at them. That dear, familiar hand. When they first met, he had fallen in love with her fingers, small and neat and capable, with their pared nails and ink-stained calluses. It seemed so long ago. Now her skin was raw and split, the pink flesh showing in the cracks. What had he done? The same thing his father did. Dragged the woman he loved into a place she wasn't suited for.

'Bess,' he said, reaching across the gap between the beds. 'We can stop here.'

She dropped her hand and stared at him, her eyes flooding.

'I don't want you to be afraid,' he went on, his voice low. 'I'm sorry you've been afraid. I think I just got carried away with the idea.'

'The idea of what?' she asked softly. She wanted to hear him say it.

'Finishing. Setting the record, I guess.'

She pressed her lips together, trying to stop them from quivering. It was as if he had finally reached the sliver in her heart: his single-mindedness, which she had started to feel had little to do with her.

Glen slid his legs over the edge of the bed and sat up. 'Listen,' he said, hands slack between his knees. 'I love you.' He stopped there for a moment, his throat cinched up, feeling foolish. What on earth had been wrong with him? It wasn't so hard to speak of it. 'I want you to be happy. We'll stay here a few more nights, so you can rest. Then we'll take the train home.'

At the word *home*, she felt as if a great weight were lifting from her, the weight she'd been carrying since she reached over the edge of the scow and pulled her waterlogged husband to safety. She went to lie on the bed, resting her head in his lap. 'I never thought it would be this hard,' she said, taking his hand. She turned up to look at him. 'I hope you don't think I'm a coward.'

He ran a chapped palm over her cheek. 'I think you're tough as nails. Plenty of grown men walked away from the Colorado before they even saw any fast water. Now why don't you get some sleep.' He pulled the quilt up over her legs. 'I'll wake you for supper.'

'Where are you going?'

'I thought I'd go for a walk,' he said. 'Maybe take a few pictures.'

'All right,' she said. The hot bath and the flood of emotion had left her drained. But after Glen gave her a kiss and shut the door softly behind him, she found that she couldn't sleep.

She got up and went to the window, which looked down on the turnaround in front of the hotel. Tourists in fur coats were waiting with their trunks, ready to be taken to the railroad station. In a few days, she'd be standing there herself. But first, she and Glen would have to hike back down to the river to gather their valuables. Perhaps they could even get a little money for the scow. Someone might want to use it to ferry driftwood across the river. Then again, no one else seemed to know how to steer the damn thing. That thought – of their particular skill, their attachment to the boat that had served them so well – launched a small wave of regret. If they did quit and go home by rail, she would be indistinguishable from the other tourists, marveling at the views out the train windows. No one would take note of their departure. No one would know what they had done. She had passed eighty-seven miles of the Grand Canyon – some of the roughest water in the whole country – but the hardships they had faced so far would never merit a mention.

Now that she felt she had a choice, the thought of going on began to beckon. Hadn't she vowed to do the things she feared most? It was like scrubbing the moss from your heart. She had been afraid of so many things: defying Earl, setting out west on her own. But when they were done, she had found that for a time her lesser fears shrank back. She could say: I've faced worse than this.

When Glen came back from his walk, he found her dressed and sitting on the edge of the bed. 'Are you all right?' he asked. There was a strange glint in her eye.

'I've changed my mind,' she said.

His stomach dropped. She was leaving him. He looked around to see if she'd packed her things.

'I've been thinking, while you were gone. I want to keep going.'

He exhaled sharply, a gust of anxiety and relief. 'Are you

sure?' He set the camera down on the bed and studied her. 'You're not doing this for my sake?'

She took his hand in both of hers. 'No, for myself. Or for both of us, I guess. As long as we're in it together.'

That night they ate another hearty meal at the hotel, and wrote a second set of letters to their families. 'We're heading downriver again tomorrow,' Bessie wrote, 'well fed and rested. If the weather doesn't hold us up, we'll reach Needles by December 9.'

At sunrise the next morning, November 17, Blanche and Edith Kolb pulled up in front of the El Tovar in a Model T, Edith at the wheel, Mrs. Kolb in the backseat, looking elegant in a wide-brimmed hat. They rattled along the edge of the South Rim, back toward the head of the Kaibab Trail. One of the windows was stuck down, and a sharp wind filled the cab. There was haze over the plateau to the east. The sun burned through it – a sun with no edges, only a slowly coalescing pool of brightness. Snow piled at the sides of the road.

Bessie stared at Edith in the glare. What a comfort to meet a woman who seemed at home in this wild place, who drove like a man but dressed with style. She glanced down at Edith's shoes – the soft leather and narrow heels – and thought of her favorite shop in San Francisco, the windows framed by velvet, each pair of shoes on its own rosewood stand. She used to slip in before her drawing class, walking amid the baskets of cut flowers, the polished tables, admiring the kidskin boots. Not that she could afford any of them.

'I wonder if I'll ever wear pretty shoes again,' she mused.

Edith wouldn't meet her eye. 'Of course you will,' she said, her hair writhing in the breeze. 'And then you'll wish for a good pair of boots.' She put the flivver into first gear and pulled in at the trailhead.

Glen jumped out and grabbed their satchel from the back,

eager to strike out. He'd arranged for fresh supplies to be hauled down to the river – not as much as he'd like, prices were steep at the rim, but enough to see them through if they were careful. He wanted to arrive in time to meet the mules.

'You ready?' he asked, opening the door for his wife.

Bessie gave Edith a peck on the cheek. 'Thanks so much for the ride.'

Blanche Kolb moved up to the front seat and looked at them gravely. 'I pray the good Lord's watching over you,' she said.

Edith, embarrassed by the grim tone, put a hand on her mother's arm.

'That's all right,' Glen said, smiling gently. 'We all need a little watching over.' And with a wave they set off down the trail.

Reith Hyde

Once we spotted the scow, with no sign of them in it, the plan to take a makeshift boat down from Diamond Creek became doubly urgent. Kolb and I drove from Peach Springs down a rutted road toward the river, and when that petered out, we hiked the rest of the way and camped at the beach. Kolb found the abandoned boat and started fixing it up. He was a good carpenter, clearly knew what he was doing, but the boat was a mess. He put in bulkheads and a bit of decking. Ran a lifeline all around. We used scrap lumber from an old shack, left over from a drilling operation.

On December 23, Emery's brother, Ellsworth, hiked down to meet us. He had read about the rescue effort in the papers and had taken a train out from Los Angeles to help. Ellsworth was an easygoing fellow, taller and quieter than his brother. I gathered he had been the one to write the book about their 1911 trip. He deferred to Emery on everything regarding the boat, and managed to tease him a little in the bargain. Not that I really minded Kolb's swagger. Not after all he was doing on my behalf. I kept offering to pay for his time, but he waved me off – even looked a little insulted. After the disagreeable business with Francy and Harbin, he restored some of my faith in humankind. Of course, it didn't take much. I was so torn up with worry, anyone who did me a good turn then had my everlasting gratitude.

While the two of them were working, I hiked upstream along the river. I checked each beach over carefully, but I didn't see tracks or signs of a fire. Finally I came to a sheer cliff and couldn't see any way around it. Heading back past a small side canyon, I heard a dull rumble and glanced up, half expecting to see a wall of mud and boulders bearing down. It was only a small rock slide, skidding down a cliff. The weather was still clear, but Kolb said it had been raining at the rim for weeks.

I thought of Glen and Bessie, riding the river in the pouring rain. They hadn't packed a tent and must have been huddling under overhangs. But for now the good weather was holding. It was a relief to think that even if they had been cut off from their supplies, they were at least sleeping dry. Glen could start a fire from tinder. I remembered he had said that if they ran into trouble he would stick to the river. The foolish thing was to set off into the canyons where you'd die of thirst. Warmth and water – assuming they had those two things, they could last quite a while. They might be hungry when we found them, but we'd find them alive.

When I got back to the campsite, the boat was nearly finished. I was tempted to go along, but decided it was better if I went back up to the rim, where I could wait for Francy and Harbin's phone call. In a few days, I'd hike down to meet the Kolbs at Spencer Canyon.

The next morning, December 24, the Kolb brothers launched, Emery at the oars. The boat took on water like a sieve. Five feet from the beach, Ellsworth was already bailing. 'I knew I'd come in handy,' he said.

Emery grinned and stroked into the channel. 'If we're not out in two days, go ahead and eat our share of the Christmas turkey,' he said. Then the current caught the boat and they were off.

Glen and Bessie Hyde

They set a brisk pace down the trail, making the knee-jarring descent toward the river. With every switchback, every drop in elevation, Glen's spirits rose. Once he got started on a trip, he didn't like to stop. Running a river straight through, you fell into a rhythm, and if you rested too long, your timing got thrown off. He watched his wife, striding ahead of him, and tried to gauge her mood from the set of her shoulders. He had been ready to leave the river on her behalf, but when she changed her mind, he was elated. Quitting might sound good in the short run, but later it would begin to gnaw. This wasn't the kind of trip you tried twice. He would be the first to say they'd survived the three hundred-odd miles from Green River on their skill and their wits, but you couldn't deny the element of luck. The scow was in perfect shape; they were making record time. Best to do it right the first time and be done.

As they worked their way down from one plateau to the next, the stone changing from cream to peach to rust, he went over his talk with Emery Kolb, committing to memory the pointers on the big rapids ahead. By noon, they reached the river. The mule packer was waiting at the ranch. Glen was disappointed to see how little their cash had bought them. It fit easily on the backs of two mules: a ten-pound sack of flour, coffee, sugar, and salt, a crate full of canned meat and beans. As they were loading the food into the scow, Sutro came striding along the bank, carrying a soft suitcase. He was wearing tweed knee pants and looked like an overgrown Boy Scout, grinning and waving his hat.

Glen wondered if inviting him had been such a good idea, but Bessie seemed pleased with the company. Sutro greeted her with elaborate courtesy, and his unfamiliarity with the boat – he got stuck climbing over the high side and ripped his tweeds – made her smile.

As soon as Sutro's bag was secured with a loop of rope, they headed downriver. Things started well enough. They slid through the riffle at the mouth of Bright Angel Creek – a fast, easy ride. But quickly they lost momentum. The wind was running against them. Glen turned the scow sideways and began to row, but it was slow going. When a big gust billowed up-canyon, the boat would stop completely, as if halted by an unseen hand.

'That looks like a hard pull,' Sutro said.

Glen shrugged. 'Keeps you warm,' he said, gritting a smile.

Sutro offered to have a go, and after a few more strokes Glen obliged, stepping aside.

After that they took turns, each of them rowing until their palms cramped up, inching toward the second rapid, another pillowy ride, according to Kolb. When they heard it, Glen stood up on the cross plank for a good view. The waves were good-sized, but it looked like a clean run, and they barreled through without scouting. Heaving through the last trough, Bessie caught sight of Sutro, pale and wide-eyed, and his fear caused her mild surprise. It had been weeks since a run like that had fazed her. Wait till he saw waves the size of houses.

When they hit quiet water again, Sutro pulled a camera from his valise. 'Mind taking one for the scrapbook?' he asked Glen.

It was an expensive machine – full of settings and levers – and after he'd explained its workings, Sutro posed in the stern with a serious face.

'The Brooding Skipper,' Glen said from behind the lens.

Sutro laughed and tipped up the brim of his golf cap. He struck a jauntier pose, fists perched on his hips, and the buttons on his cardigan gapped. Glen pressed the shutter. No one would take Sutro for a pioneer aviator, a war hero. He had gold spectacles hooked over his leafy ears. A soft gut. Looked more like a greengrocer.

They rowed hard through a mile-long calm stretch. Here the walls were dark and close. The strata heaved perpendicular and slid straight down into the river. It looked like a great violence had been done to the stone, but of course it was done slowly, the violence of millennia. Soon they heard an escalating roar. Up ahead, the river dropped away cleanly, as if it poured over the edge of a shelf.

'Probably Horn Creek,' Glen said, steering for the bank.

Sutro sat up and peered downriver. 'Is this a mean one?'

'Mean enough,' Glen said. He saw Bessie stiffen.

They tied off the scow and went down to investigate. It was a short, furious stretch of water, studded with boulders. But the biggest obstacle was at the entry: a big rock in the center of the channel, splitting the tongue in two and forcing them into the hazards downstream. Glen crouched down to water level, climbed to the top of a rubble slope for a better view, then scrambled back to the beach.

'Quite a few rocks,' he said.

'A few?' Bessie said. 'They're thick as tombstones.'

He frowned – he had hoped she'd left her gloom at the rim – but finally conceded. 'We'll line it. Shouldn't be too hard with the three of us.'

When Sutro heard that they wouldn't be facing the waves, he looked relieved.

Three hours later, when they had lugged the most important duffel to the bottom of the rapid, slid and scrambled through the frigid water, and nearly lost the scow to the current, he didn't look so pleased. It was four o'clock – the sun had disappeared over the rim hours before – and nearly freezing in the shade.

They reloaded the boat and floated for another two miles, drenched and shivering. When Glen heard another rapid approaching, he pulled up at the head. 'We'll run this one in the morning,' he said.

After they'd pulled out the bedding and made a fire, Glen asked their passenger what he thought.

Sutro shrugged and cleaned the silt from his spectacles. 'I daresay I've seen worse,' he said.

Bessie and Glen exchanged a look. They both had seen him crouched down during that first run, his hands twisted in the ropes.

'We'll have to let you steer through the next one,' Glen said.

But that evening, around the fire, Sutro redeemed himself by telling stories. He had studied aviation with the Wright brothers at their factory in Dayton. Just took a train out to Ohio and asked for a job. Orville offered to take him for a joyride, and when he didn't flinch, they hired him on. Then the war started and he went to the front. One month in the trenches, and he got a bayonet wound. 'We both stuck each other, and then stood there staring, waiting to see who dropped dead.' He recovered in a field hospital. On his first day back at the front he was tossed six feet in the air by a Boche shell. 'One of the boys said I did two aerial back flips. I was knocked unconscious and came to expecting to be short a limb. Imagine my shock when I did an inventory and found nary a scratch.'

Apparently the war records in Washington reported him dead three times. 'First I was listed as killed in action, then I died of disease,' he said. 'I'm not sure what got me the third time.' The State of California even offered his family the Golden Scroll, handed out in honor of the war dead. He wrote a telegram to the governor saying that, under the circumstances, he'd decline.

The firelight flickered on his broad face. 'I don't know about you two, but talk makes me thirsty.' He walked off into the darkness and returned with his valise. 'Alligator,' he said, when he saw Glen staring. 'Only good use for the damn animals.' He pulled out a square leather case and flipped open the lid. Inside were a shaker, swizzle stick, and flask, held in place by buckled straps. 'My picnic kit,' he said. 'Pity we don't have ice.'

When Glen saw Sutro's fear of the river, he had started to wonder why the fellow asked to go along. Now he had a glimmer of an answer. Sutro wanted a taste of his old adventuring days. It must have been years since he'd taken such a chance. It would certainly afford him better bragging rights than a hunting trip in the Dakotas, where the game was flushed out by the guides. He could just see Sutro describing the rapids in some oak-paneled men's club, adding a detail there, a flourish here.

Now Glen and Bessie looked on, half amazed, as their passenger shook up three martinis. Sutro struck an avuncular pose, even though he was at most thirty-five. He was young, and yet somehow already staid. The high tone, the golf cap, the valise. He tried to give them the feeling he'd lived – and yet Glen had ignored his boasting at first. The war gave him legitimacy, the air of a difficult secret, perhaps things that couldn't be spoken of. He hinted at this, between the stories and jokes – the turf he wouldn't venture into. It tempered Glen's scorn. They had been born only seven years apart, but the war had opened a gulf between them as wide as the canyon above.

They sipped the gin from dented camp cups, and Sutro refilled them. After a while, the liquor loosened Glen's tongue.

'Did you visit the Kolb studio at the South Rim?' he asked Sutro.

'I did. Paid my fifty cents to watch his film of the rapids. Not exactly MGM quality, but there were a few thrilling moments.'

'We're hoping to go on the vaudeville circuit when this is done. Bessie is going to write an illustrated book.'

'Is that so?' Sutro said, looking her over. 'Do you have any training?'

'I went to art school for a while,' she said softly. She wasn't used to drinking. Her tongue felt thick.

'I feel as if I've seen quite a few books about the canyon,' Sutro said. 'Kolb certainly has captured the market with his volume. He would hardly let me out the door before I sprang for a copy. Are you sure you'll be able to find a publisher?'

'If we set two records we will,' Glen said. He didn't like the way Sutro had sized Bessie up. 'First woman down the canyon. And we're on target for a speed record. Besides, the press seems to follow any old craze – flagpole sitters, marathon dancing. Did you hear what they offered Lindbergh to do vaudeville? Two lectures a day for a month – a hundred grand.'

Sutro arched an eyebrow. 'That's not exactly easy money. You try flying solo across the pond.'

'Well, then, look at Peaches,' Glen said. 'Sorority girl marries old pervert, gets chased around her bedroom on all fours, and they pay her eight thousand dollars a week on the two-a-day.' His face was warm from the gin, he was blathering – what did it matter. He looked down into his cup. 'I'm sure we'll have a few offers.'

Sutro drained the last of his drink. 'I always took my cue from Emerson: "My life is for itself, and not for display."'

Bessie had been listening quietly. Now she flushed and picked up the supper pans. 'I'd better wash these before they stick.'

Glen saw her dismay, but he refused to be squelched. Sutro had his fortune. Who was he to say they shouldn't get theirs? Glen had been too polite to mention it back at Phantom Ranch, but he knew about the Sutro tunnel because it was the biggest boondoggle in mining history. Hundreds of men had died digging it. By the time it was done, the silver had been tapped out. At least he and Bessie were risking their own necks. And for all they'd weathered, they might as well get their due.

Down at the riverbank, Bessie was scrubbing the pans with wet sand, her fingers numb from the cold. She shared Glen's hopes, but hearing him speak of them out loud, with a near stranger, made the whole enterprise seem vulgar. Then again, she couldn't believe that man had the gall to throw Emerson at her husband – and misquote him, no less. Pompous idiot. Greta would have known what to do with him. Suddenly she felt a tug of longing for her friend. It had been six months since they'd lost track of each other. What she would give to peer down into the moonlit water and catch a glimpse of her now.

Greta Grandstedt was a lucky girl. She gathered good fortune like windfall plums. Jobs, apartments, trips to the spas in Calistoga with benevolent friends – they all tumbled into her lap. Her stories often began with the phrase 'This chance came up,' but she told them without pride, in fact with a kind of mild amazement. If she took no credit for her enviable fortune, she also didn't worry about whether it would continue. And life, in turn, didn't give her much to worry about. Well, that was not quite true. Her parents had dropped dead in the influenza epidemic. She went to her grandmother's for the weekend, and when she came home they were gone. That was how she told the story: lightly, and without emphasis. At least they had left her a small inheritance – that must have soothed. She would never be out on the street.

Later, when they knew each other better, Bessie was surprised she hadn't guessed Greta's ambitions from the start. She had an ingenue's soft, almost weightless blond hair, but her features were sharp: angled eyes and full lips that had appealing wrinkles set into them – not the eerily smooth lips of a china doll, but a more textured, human kind of lips, seamed by their fullness, given to pressing together over a thought. Sometimes Bessie felt guilty at the way she floated along in her friend's wake – but why not? Greta gave her confidence. We all have our character, to be sure, but we can work with what we're given. At least that's what Bessie believed. Even at times in which everything, outside us and within, worked to make a certain outcome likely, there was always the possibility of surprise – of human change. And it might only be a few degrees' turn of the compass, but the results could be catastrophic, or marvelous. She thought of it like a musical range: you were given your key, but it could be stretched, with practice. And if being in Greta's company pulled her in useful ways, where was the harm in that? What harm in admiring someone enough to strive a little in their eyes?

Bessie's admirations were, of course, rooted in specifics. She, too, had once dreamed of being an actress – in high school she'd performed in a few melodramas. It had all been too silly to know if she was any good, but it struck her that acting had an advantage over being a painter or a poet: when you made people feel something – made them gasp or laugh – you got to feel it back. What a fabulous skill. Greta, however, was not particularly in command of it. Bessie had once seen her perform at a small theater off Market Street. Even in the heat of an emotional scene, her friend gave the impression of trying on the character like an ill-fitting coat. Her face looked as if it were made to register fine shades of feeling, but in fact she never lost a certain woodenness when saying her lines – as if she were reading from some far-off, blurry page. Everyone's consensus was that Greta would do very well in Hollywood. She had some marvelous stills taken – her face tilted up, smooth as eggshell – and sent them off to her agent in Los Angeles.

That evening, after the play, they went out for supper at a nearby steak house and Greta announced her plan: Mr. Maxwell had landed meetings at a few studios. She would move to Hollywood at the end of September.

'Oh, Greta, that's marvelous,' Bessie said, trying to hide her disappointment. 'Will you take the train down?'

'Trains are so dull. I thought I'd take a steamer.' She closed her menu. 'Did you hear they've started a regular airplane service to Los Angeles? Maddux Air, it's called, which I think is just perfect. Sounds mad to me. And who can afford it?'

'Movie stars, I suppose,' Bessie said. 'When you become one, you'll have to fly me down for your premiere.'

Greta leaned forward in her chair. 'You should come with me.'

At first, Bessie thought her friend was joking, but she should have known better. Greta always preferred impulse to fore-thought. 'What on earth would I do down there?' she asked, buttering her bread. Greta insisted on paying for their suppers out. She was ashamed at how much she relied on it.

'What everyone else is doing,' Greta said. 'Write scenarios.'

'But I don't know a thing about motion pictures.'

'You could learn. And it's a perfect time to break in, with the talkies coming. It'll have to be about wit, not slapstick – the things people say. Someone has to think up all those lines.'

Bessie smiled. Greta loved to talk, loved to hold forth in her musical voice. 'And I can't think of anyone I'd rather hear deliver them,' she said. At that moment she meant it. Greta was no Barrymore, but what extravagant faith. It was like watching an airplane lift off.

'Oh, don't bow out like that,' Greta said. 'You're resource-ful. You could illustrate posters, paint sets.' As she gestured, a little rhinestone bracelet slipped at her wrist. 'You just have to behave as if you can do it, then people will believe you.'

At that moment the waiter arrived and the subject was dropped, but over the coming days Bessie would admit to herself that Greta was right. She couldn't work in a bookshop all her life. She wanted to make a living out of art. There were mornings when the sight of an orange segment, sutured with white threads, made her rush to take up the pen. Everything was shining with extra meaning, and she wanted to take that feeling and strain it through herself, to make something of it – but what? The orange already was there. What could she make of it but a hostage of her own longing?

Perhaps that was her problem – looking at orange slices. She had no subject. Jack London tramped off into the snow. Upton Sinclair lived alongside the meatpackers. And recently a fellow art student had told her that Genêt, whose 'Letters from Paris' she devoured in *The New Yorker*, was really an American woman named Janet Flanner, who had left her husband and moved to the Left Bank. Now Bessie walked to her rooming-house window and stared once again at the view it described: the corner of Mr. Chen's produce stall, with its slowly changing array of vegetables and fruits, the newsprint and cornhusks in the gutter. It was like a diorama box – a fixed illustration of life, not life in motion. She had stared at this particular swath of wall and street and its passing foot traffic for months, until finally nothing that went on there was of consequence. She had summoned up the courage for one great upheaval in her life, and now, as if she had learned nothing from the effort, she clung to the spot where she had landed.

Full of resolve, she pulled on her new leather coat, hip-length with a shearling collar – purchased with an unexpected check from her father – and walked to Greta's apartment. No one was home, so she left a note:

9/12/27

Book a double berth. I'm coming with you.

Your stowaway,

B.

On the way home, she stopped on Mott Street and picked up a loaf of bread and some soft Italian cheese.

'Maybe your husband would like a little pastrami?' the shop-keeper prodded.

'If I had a husband, he likely would,' she said.

'Yes, who needs a husband?' He laughed. 'You are young!'

Back out on the street, her dinner in a paper bag, Bessie felt that old familiar happiness at the moist air, the lights and noises from the shops. When she first arrived, she was electri-fied to be out by herself, walking in a strange city after dark. The streets seemed to pulse with purpose, nothing like the sleepy elm-lined avenues of Parkersburg, deserted at night. Here office clerks hurried home, their hats pulled down against the wind. A man sold the evening paper from his pouch, trilling like a songbird, the same phrase over and over. Chinese boys in knickers pulled in crates of produce for the night, as resolute as little men. It all thrilled her. But after a while she had become numb to these scenes. A bunch of flappers straight out of a Chester drawing would crowd past her, a herd of flashing skirts and beads and hennaed hair, trailing smoke and laughter, off to whisper a password through some grated door, and she'd feel as lonely as a schoolmarm. But now that she had decided to leave, the old pleasures were returned to her. She wandered back toward her apartment, buzzing with new plans.

That night, she sorted through her drawings. There was no telling what kind of lodging they might find; it seemed prudent to pack light. She paged through her old sketchbooks, spread her watercolors of the Presidio across the floor. She could see that she had learned something in the previous year. But in the end it all fell short. So much imitation. There were only three sketches that showed any kind of life. She stowed these in a paper folder and tied them with string. Her manuscript, 'Wandering Leaves,' went along with them, though she felt even more disappointed with the poems than she did with the pictures. Even her verses in praise of adventure sat primly on the page. It was an awful thing: to see where you had failed. But if not for these moments of brutal clarity, how to improve?

In the morning, Bessie woke in confusion. Where was she? Then she heard the growl of a rapid and it all flooded back. Glen's foolish talk of the night before, and Sutro making him look like a rube. Their passenger had already tied his bedroll and was down at the river, taking pictures. She ran a hand through her hair and sand spilled onto her folded coat. Only one day back on the river, and already the sand was everywhere – in her clothes, their food, the sheets. Everything they cooked had a telltale grit. She rose and helped Glen make cowboy coffee and eggs, bought at the rim and cradled in sawdust. Still her mood didn't improve. She was making a note in her diary – Nov. 18 – when Glen asked her if she'd pack the stove and dishes. She shot him a look. 'Why don't you get the dishes. I'll get the rifle.'

He looked bemused. 'All right.' He was always happy in the morning.

When they were settled in the scow, Sutro leaned over and gave Glen a wink. 'What ever happened to the days when men were men, and women were nervous?' he whispered. He must have overheard her remark.

Glen gave him a cold stare. 'We're both nervous.' The fool would be too, if he had any sense. He'd met plenty of men like Sutro, men who got around ranchers and started quoting Will Rogers and making jokes about geldings. But what would he make of Reith, who could bake a perfect berry pie – crimped edges, pinwheel slits for the steam – and sewed flawless stitches through the thinnest bit of shirting? His father never acted shy about any of that. He never made silly pronouncements about a man's role. It was city-bred men like Sutro who wore their manhood like a badge – sheepish when they had to hold a wife's purse, useless with a mixing spoon.

They were out into the current now, and nosing toward the rapid. Sutro assumed his rigid pose, crouched down between the thwarts like a wrestler. The waves came over the gunwales. Bessie lost hold of the sweep for a moment, jarring them off course, but a moment later she caught it again and they finished the run without trouble. Less than a mile later, they heard another rumble – this time louder than before.

'I think this must be Monument Creek,' Bessie said, getting out the map.

Glen nodded. 'Kolb mentioned it.' His face was set, remembering the warning.

Monument was a rocky mess. The current made a long left-hand curve, ripped by huge waves, then split in half at the head of a rocky island. They might have tried to line the first section, but Glen didn't like the thought of working side by side with Sutro for another day. So they loaded back into the scow and pulled into the river. The trick was not to get driven against the sheer right-hand wall. And then to make the cut to the left of the island.

'Where should I stand?' Sutro asked Glen, as they caught the current. Now that he'd seen the size of the waves, his bluster had disappeared.

'Don't stand, sit,' Glen barked, pulling hard on the stern sweep. Bessie was on the bow. He watched for the boulder he had chosen from the shore and then cut hard for the entry, down along the left edge of the tongue. The waves were curling toward the right, forcing them toward the cliff. 'Hard left!' he shouted to Bessie. No sooner had he got the words out than a wave rose up, twice the height of the scow – they seemed to be riding through a tunnel of water – and slammed down on them, heavy as a load of bricks. But when he looked up, Bessie was still on the front sweep, her hat brim bent down by the avalanche. Good girl.

They nosed into another trough and punched through the wave at the back, then made the left turn at the head of the island and seesawed through the washout. Sutro got up from the floor, his sweater soaked through.

'You all right?' Glen asked.

He nodded, his glasses askew.

'That was the last big one you'll see,' Bessie said. And she was right. After passing through a small riffle, they heard the growl of Hermit Creek and pulled over to the left. They landed just above the rapid and tied off to a boulder. Sutro grabbed his valise and jumped onto the beach, the relief plain in his face.

Hermit was another tourist trail, with a lodge at the rim and a rustic camp just above the river. Now, looking up, Bessie saw a group of people picking their way through the rocks: women in long wool skirts and straw boaters, some of them pausing to wave. She felt a stab of envy. Oh, to have clean hair, clean nails, to be on a holiday – safe. Of course, she had committed to going on, but it was torture to pass another civilized outpost so soon. It weakened her resolve.

Once they were close enough to be heard over the roar, one of the women pressed forward. 'They told us at the rim that you might pass by during our stay,' she said – a stout woman in a pleated blouse. She thrust out a gloved hand. 'Mrs. George Van Norten. Such a pleasure to meet you.'

Bessie felt her chapped fingers taken up firmly. The other women pooled behind the matron, nodding hellos. There was something odd in their expressions. She reached up to smooth her hair – I must look a sight. The women tracked the gesture.

Then one of them spoke: 'We're so in awe, Mrs. Hyde. Just to think of going down that river –' She broke off with a shiver.

So that was it: they admired her. She was too tired to enjoy the irony.

Together they walked up from the beach to a cluster of cabins, set on a ridge beside a line of wind-whipped trees. Bessie took a peek inside: woodstoves, mattresses on metal camp beds, a bit of rough-hewn wooden furniture. It looked like heaven. Mrs. Van Norten had appointed herself their guide. 'You must see the lodge at the top of the trail,' she told Bessie. 'They call it Hermit's Rest. There's a delightful stone room with chopped willow furniture, bear rugs, Indian weavings everywhere. It looks positively prehistoric.'

Bessie cast a glance in Glen's direction. He wasn't listening. 'I'm afraid we don't have time for a trip to the rim,' she said.

'Of course not!' Mrs. Van Norten exclaimed. 'What was I thinking? I'm quite sure your campsites have twice the atmosphere.'

They sat down for lunch with the other tourists. For an hour Bessie slipped into a pleasant lull. The sun fell into the dining room, a big pitched hall with long tables. They were surrounded by a bubble of attention – the cook making a show of heaping their plates, the chairs around them angled in. When the guests peppered them with questions, Sutro had the grace to defer. 'You'd have to ask the captain here,' he said, gesturing toward Glen. 'I was only along for the ride.' But their respite would be brief. As soon as they finished eating, Glen pushed back his chair.

Bessie took him aside. 'What about spending a night here? We could get a good night's sleep and start early in the morning.'

'I think we'd better keep going,' he said gently. It was just noon. They'd made only five miles the day before, on account of the headwind. 'I wrote to Reith saying we'd be out by the ninth of December, and at this rate we'll be cutting it close.'

Of course, he was right. Her family was waiting, just the

same. She had already wrapped their Christmas presents – jars of apple butter with watercolor labels, a sketch of the orchards, a steer skull for Bill – and left them with Jeanne. Given the slow holiday mail, she didn't think she'd be out in time to post them. But if the package arrived before she sent word from Needles, it would be a grim Christmas in the Haley house. In his last letter, sent to Green River, her father had written: 'As for my wish list, I want only one thing: a telegram, saying you are home safe.'

They decided to wait while the cook packed them roast beef sandwiches. Then they'd try to make a few more miles before nightfall.

Bessie wandered along the stony ridge between the cabins and came across Sutro, smoking a cigar. Now that they were parting ways, he seemed almost dear. She looked down the slope at the other tourists – the men playing horseshoes in their dude ranch clothes, the women taking photographs of the river. At least Sutro had an inkling of what it could do.

In a moment of impulse, Bessie put a hand on his sleeve. 'Do you think we're foolish to go on?'

But before he could answer, Glen rounded the corner with two waxed-paper boxes. 'Sandwiches are ready,' he said.

Sutro freed his arm. 'There's our man,' he said, a little too heartily. 'Time for a cigar before you go?'

Glen shook his head. 'No, thanks.' He had just broken away from Mrs. Van Norten, who had cornered him by the kitchen and told a meandering story of her boat trip down the Nile. 'Are you ready?' he asked Bessie. For a moment they stared at each other.

'You can't leave yet,' Sutro said, breaking the awkward silence. 'I've got to get a last photograph.' He hurried off to find his camera.

It seemed to take him an eternity to decide on the right background. Finally he had them pose in front of the cabins, lunch cartons at their feet, and spent a long time adjusting the aperture. 'Must have sand in the works,' he said, blowing on the lens. 'Just a minute, let me try again.'

Glen sighed impatiently.

'I hope I've got the light right,' Sutro said, glancing over his shoulder at the rim.

It wasn't until they were untying the scow and saying good-bye that his stalling made sense. The canyon filled with a rhythmic clopping. A mule train pulled into camp. Sutro rushed up and spoke to the packer – a skinny man dressed in denim – and the fellow herded two animals down to the river. They were laden with crates of supplies: flour and coffee and canned fruit, two smoked hams, a dozen eggs.

'To replace the provisions I ate,' Sutro said, as the mule packer hoisted the food into the scow.

'You hardly ate all that,' Bessie said with a laugh.

Glen took off his hat and shook Sutro's hand, feeling sheepish at how he'd misjudged him. 'I don't know what to say –' He looked down at his boots.

'I won't hear a word,' Sutro said, slapping him on the shoulder. 'Just send me a postcard from Needles.'

By now a crowd had gathered – all the tourists from the camp, the cook and the mule packer – waiting to see them run Hermit. One of the men gave a cheer. Others burst into applause as they pried free of the bank. They looked so at ease, two lean figures, stepping over the pile of duffel, hopping up on the thwarts and waving. As if they were boating on a pond. Then they turned and steered toward the tongue, and the scow pitched down over the ledge. They both dropped into a crouch, gripping hard on the sweeps. When they hit the bottom a wave curled up and buried the front end of the scow, but they burst through, made a pivot to the right, and passed a big hole in the center of the run. Wild cries went up from the onlookers, but Sutro was quiet. He was thinking of the way Bessie looked through the camera lens: her calves startlingly thin in their lace-up boots, her face direct and darkened by worry, still asking the question he hadn't been willing to answer: Are we foolish to go on?

Mrs. Van Norten stood beside him, waving her gloves as the scow pitched through the tail waves. Already it looked tiny between the cliffs. 'What a marvelous adventure,' the matron said with satisfaction. 'Don't you wish you were going along?'

'As a matter of fact, I don't,' Sutro said, his eyes trained on the boat.

'Really? You strike me as the courageous type.'

He studied the end of his cigar. 'I've always held that it's better to be a live coward than a dead hero.'

Mrs. Van Norten laughed. 'Well, when your friends see photographs of you shooting the rapids, I daresay no one will call you a coward.'

'I didn't take any pictures,' Sutro said.

'No pictures?' She looked ready to swat him with her glove. 'Why on earth not?'

He turned to face her. 'I was too damn scared.'

Reith Hyde

I had set all sorts of efforts in motion, but in the meantime, I was going half crazy, having little to do. The Indians were tracking on the mesas. Francy and Harbin and Patraw were working their way downriver. The Kolbs were going after the scow. When I got back to the El Tovar Hotel, on December 26, there was a reporter out on the porch, waiting for me. The ashtray at his elbow was brimming with butts, so I guess he'd been there awhile. 'I'm Tom Keene, Associated Press,' he said and stuck out his hand. 'I was hoping to talk to you for a few minutes.'

There had been quite a few articles written about the search in the two weeks Glen and Bessie had been missing, all of them full of inaccuracies. We were getting the San Francisco and Denver papers by rail, and when I sent the clippings to Jeanne, she was furious. They made Glen and Bessie out to be 'thrill seekers.' Made it seem like they'd never been on a boat before – honeymooners on a lark. As if they stepped onto this barge in their wedding clothes and got washed downstream. Straight out of *Perils of Pauline*. But readers ate that stuff up, and the newspapers knew it. They always had to jazz things up, as if the plain facts weren't enough. And so we had the composograph, pasting Valentino's face onto another man's corpse. Melodrama and speculation. They even spelled Glen's name wrong, with two n's instead of one.

I looked this fellow over, trying to size him up. He looked decent. Maybe if I talked, he'd set some of the story straight. 'All right,' I said. 'Just as long as you put that out.' I nodded at his cigarette.

He began by asking simple questions – how long had they been overdue and so forth. I was tired of recounting the facts, but I obliged. Then he asked what I thought of my son taking his bride down the canyon.

Taking his bride. I looked across at the building opposite, a replica of an Indian house, designed by a woman architect, I'd been told. Red rock and chinked windows, and stick ladders leaning against the walls. It looked like a fort, snug and tight and perfectly matched to the cliffs. Not like this tourist hotel, stuck up on the rim like a big gingerbread house. No wonder the suffragettes had taken to the streets. No one gave them credit for having any sense.

I told the reporter to try another question.

'Did you beg your son not to make the trip?'

Beg him? I rubbed my aching knee, and waited for my blood to simmer down. No matter what I said, the story would come out the way they liked.

Just then the phone rang inside, and the desk clerk came out to the porch. 'It's for you, Mr. Hyde,' she said, and if I was not mistaken she threw me an anxious look. She was in her middle forties, with flinty eyes and a soft mouth. I had been eating all my meals in the restaurant. She knew why I was there.

I excused myself and went to the telephone, trying to keep my hands steady.

It was Harbin, the cocky one, calling from the Indian village at Supai.

'Did you find them?' I asked, forcing myself to take a breath.

He said no, but they'd been seeing their footprints and fire rings all along, and marks where the scow had been moored. The river was dropping, so the damp sand held it all pretty clear.

The clerk stopped pretending to be busy and watched my face.

I told Harbin that the planes had come just after they'd set out, that we'd found the scow downstream of Diamond Creek.

He swore under his breath.

'That doesn't mean they aren't between you and Diamond,' I told him. 'The scow could have gone a long way on its own.'

He grumbled for a while, said they'd been having a miserable time. Apparently the park superintendent had been asked to leave at Bass Cable, twenty miles downstream from Phantom. 'He was nothing but dead weight,' Harbin said. I said I thought it strange that Mr. Patraw hadn't come to see me at the hotel – he should have been back by then. 'Probably got lost – he's an idiot,' Harbin said.

I urged him to make haste downriver. I was worried that Glen might give up waiting for a boat rescue and try to hike out. Kolb had said it was nearly impossible to reach the rim without a good trail. I didn't want them getting stuck on some high bench, away from food and water.

Harbin mentioned the money again.

'Yes, well, bring me news of their whereabouts and I'll put the check through,' I told him.

It had taken them a week to get that far – he figured it would be another week to Diamond Creek, where we agreed to meet.

'Don't bother showing up without any whiskey,' he said, before hanging up. It must have been cold down on the river. Still, I didn't like his tone.

'In it for the profit,' I muttered to myself.

When I turned around, the reporter was there, pen in hand.

Glen and Bessie Hyde

The crowd on the bank at Hermit grew smaller and smaller. Finally Bessie turned forward and pulled her collar up against the wind. She was determined not to watch them disappear. The breeze was blowing hard in her face, the scow barely moving. Glen was quiet, looking down at the current, trying to decide, no doubt, if he should turn broadside and row. They were deep in the heart of the Inner Gorge, where the river made its deepest cut. Boiled black stone shot straight out of the water and rose up two thousand feet, blocking the sun. At some point, in nearly every Colorado River account, the canyon was likened to a prison, and now Bessie understood why. She shuddered, and cast a backward glance in spite of herself. The river must have veered – there was nothing but dark cliffs, the boat opening a rent in the water.

They had only gone a mile when a rhythmic thudding filled the air. Boucher Rapid – the mule packer had mentioned it. They pulled over to scout. It wasn't as bad as Hermit or Monument – just a long, choppy run – but halfway through they got clipped by a big wave and took on a foot of water before righting themselves. Close shave. Glen caught the eddy at the bottom and started to bail.

'Maybe we should stop here,' he said. The wind was beginning to howl. Bessie was bent over, resting her forehead on the sweep.

She turned to look at him. 'On my account?'

He glanced away. 'Can't make much progress in this wind anyway.'

That evening, as they made camp, she kept thinking of Mr. Sutro. What was he doing now? Eating steak and potatoes, sleeping on one of those dry camp beds. In the morning, he would ride a mule to the rim, up into the cold desert sun. She couldn't help feeling she'd missed her chance.

Sitting in front of the blazing fire, she felt flushed and then chilled. She pulled a blanket over her knees and tried to eat some of the food Glen prepared, but her heart wasn't in it.

'I think I'll turn in early,' she said, trying to keep her voice light. She crawled into bed and dropped off immediately, the wind blowing her hair back against the mattress.

That night she dreamed she was in her parents' house, circling the rooms at dusk, admiring the wide porch, the strength and solidness of the walls. The house was safe, immovable, a pivot. But even in the dream, she knew she was still on the river, that she would have to go back and find her way out in daylight, in fact. It was a strange lucidity. If she stayed in that house, if she didn't wake up in a sandy bed by the river, it could only mean one thing: she was dead. So she forced herself to float out the door, over the pitched roofs, across the plains and mountains, until she was following the river again. From above, she could see what she had missed in the tumult below. The river wasn't moving – it was a long fluid sculpture, the waves remaining in the same places for years, the water evaporating and raining down. She slid along its length, until she saw their camp – the ring of cinders from the night's fire, the boat scuffed onto the sand. It looked like a dollhouse toy, at the base of those towering cliffs, nothing you would trust your life to. But when she opened her eyes, she saw that it was all real, that she had not woken from a nightmare, but into one.

She sat up among the blankets, hair tangled, puffy hammocks under her eyes. Glen was dressed and shaved, and had already packed up the stove. He brought a bowl of oatmeal to the bed. 'Did you sleep well?'

'What time is it?' she asked.

'Around ten.'

'God.' She wiped the sleep from her eyes and started to get up.

'Why don't you eat there. It's warmer.'

She shook her head and took the oatmeal to a log by the cold fire. 'Are you in a rush to get going?' she asked peevishly, pushing her spoon through the lukewarm oats.

Glen looked uncomfortable. 'Not if you need more time.'

He was being careful, treading thin, but his politeness only made her chafe. 'No, I slept too long as it is. I just thought I could have a cup of coffee before we left.'

'Sorry,' he said. 'You know how I hate to sit still.' He had been up for hours, trying not to wake her, and packing the boat had given him something to do. He tried a quick grin. 'I'll get the pot boiling again.'

She dropped her half-finished bowl on a rock, the spoon clattering. 'Don't bother. Let's just go.'

Glen stared at her, his face turning cold. 'What are you so steamed about?'

She watched a muscle working in his jaw, feeling a sudden fury well up. She was angry at having to fear for her life, but she didn't know how to speak of it. Instead she bridled at petty things: that he woke early while she slept, that he catered to her, that they were down in this pit, where the sun never reached. 'This place depresses me,' she said, staring at the slick, black cliffs.

He sighed and picked up her bowl, flinging the cold oats into the sand. 'Then why the hell did you want to keep going?'

There it was – a match to the tinder. The truth was, she was furious with herself. How had she ended up in this mess? Because she wanted to be what he saw in her. She had kept up a brave front as long as she could, but now it was starting to wear thin. She didn't want to live in constant fear. She looked over at Glen, holding the dirty bowl and spoon. She had never considered herself good at masking emotion, but he didn't seem to register her terror. It was as if, not feeling fear himself, he could hardly recognize it in another. That blindness made her question everything else. Did he have any idea what he was doing? Would the scow hold up in the big water downstream? She had the feeling that she had linked her fate to a reckless man. 'Because I'm stupid,' she said harshly, the words ringing off the cliffs.

'Jesus!' Glen looked at her in disbelief. He stalked off toward the river, then threw the bowl down and came back. 'You know what? This is my fault.' The veins stood out in his neck. 'I shouldn't have listened to you back there. We should have quit. But it's too late now. There's nothing to do but get through this, as quick as we can.'

Bessie didn't answer. She didn't trust herself to speak. She squinted up at the cliffs, then went to the bed and yanked the covers off, wadding them into a ball. Together they pulled the mattress into the boat, hardly speaking, and pushed off into the current.

In the course of the morning, Glen shot several rapids he might have lined, in order to save her strength. Where once she might have argued for caution, she now only nodded and left the choice to him. He worked both sweeps on his own and got them through another bad run while she crouched down on the duffel. The scow was so familiar to him now: the way it would catch an eddy, the amount of play in the sweeps, how quickly he could steer it to shore in a certain current. He sometimes imagined it was an extension of his body – a big flat foot he slid over the river. By three o'clock he had run only four miles, but Bessie looked miserable. He decided to make camp for the afternoon and hoped the wind would die down in the morning.

*

Once the steamer pulled out of port in San Francisco, and Greta made sure their trunks had been delivered to the cabin, Bessie went for a stroll on the deck. The ship was sliding past Alcatraz, past sailboats and Japanese freighters, and through the dull-green-and-gold hills and out to sea. Bessie walked along the landward deck as they passed the Sutro Baths, an indoor natatorium, filled with heated seawater pools. In all her time in San Francisco, she had never been to visit – it seemed so far away. Now it struck her as a pity. She would have liked to make a sketch of it. The mullioned glass roof against the cliffs.

The steamer was heading south. When she looked back, the entrance to the bay had disappeared, as if the hills had slid shut behind them. Mr. Elder once had told her that storm-chased Spaniards had passed that slot for years, missing its narrow mouth in the fog. But this was a September night, and the ocean was clear to the horizon. She rounded the stern and started up the opposite deck. The sun had dropped low. The sea was a hammered pan of coppery blue. Passengers had taken to the decks to promenade: women in mink stoles with cheeks rouged by the wind, gentlemen in raccoon coats and flapping scarves. How honeyed they looked, how rich. Every day the papers were filled with marriage announcements for this heiress, that wealthy capitalist, and the markets up, up, up. Where did all the money come from? Perhaps these were the daughters of steel magnates, the bond traders – what was the phrase? – long on margin. No, she was probably wrong. You had to know a world in order to read it. But at least she could admire the trappings: cashmere, kidskin, Russian mink. Couples and trios flashed past, all of them headed the opposite way, circling the bridge like a giant engine belt – for a moment, she imagined that their very momentum drove the steam from the stacks.

She stopped at the rail. All this appraisal made her shy. Her clothes had been fine for art school. In fact it was a kind of uniform – the long wool skirt and leather coat – but now she felt shabby. She turned her back on the other passengers and watched slabs of water fall away from the ship. It was like a giant plow, turning up wedges of sea. She was thinking this, and then she looked up and noticed a tall young man, leaning farther down the rail. He was wearing a coat with a sheepskin collar and pants gone shiny at the knees. He was clearly not from the city – the cut of his clothes gave him away – but there was something sure in the way he held himself. The sun was making a fiery path in the water, and the parading passengers all turned to comment on the show. But he was facing the people, as if that were the real display, his elbows tucked back on the rail, an alert, bemused expression on his face. Suddenly he turned to Bessie and gave her a smile, as if they knew each other and were sharing a private joke.

She looked down at the water, started to walk on, then paused beside him, her heart thudding. 'Do you have the time?'

His face was calm. 'I'm afraid I don't carry a watch,' he said.

She hadn't counted on that. But he was looking at her attentively, and it made her bold. 'How do you keep from missing appointments?'

He shrugged. 'I don't have many. But I guess I have a rough feel for the time.'

'Well, then. What is it now?'

He smiled at her for a long beat, then glanced back at the sun. 'I'd say about five. But that's cheating. I know what time we sailed.'

Bessie pushed back her coat sleeve and checked her watch. 'Close. It's five-fifteen.'

He laughed softly and shoved his hands in his pockets. 'Well, then,' he said, 'I guess I'm on time for our appointment.' Just like that, they started to stroll down the deck.

'Are you from San Francisco?' he asked.

'West Virginia.'

'What brought you out here?'

'I was enrolled in art school in the city.'

'Staying with relatives?'

'No, thank goodness.'

He laughed. 'Well, aren't you plucky.'

'Now that's a word I'd never apply to myself,' Bessie said, smiling. 'I'd be inclined to say *nervous*.'

He looked unconvinced.

'What about you – where are you from?' she asked, eager to change the subject.

He was from Idaho, he said, a rancher. He and his father owned orchards. Suddenly he stood still. 'I forgot to introduce myself. I'm Glen Hyde.'

'Bessie Haley,' she said, not sure whether to put out her hand.

They smiled, facing each other for a moment, then kept walking.

'What brought you out from Idaho?' she asked.

'Lindbergh,' Glen said. 'Well, apples and Lindbergh. I had to meet with our buyers anyway, but I read he was making a stop in San Francisco, and I decided to go watch him land.'

Bessie had read about Lindbergh's visit – there was little else in the *Examiner* for days – but when the parade moved through town, she had stayed in her room, making a sketch of the people streaming through the streets. They seemed pulled by an unseen force – children stumbling at the end of their mothers' arms, men clapping their hats down as they ran. Lindbergh was supposed to be an average fellow, a Swede, a midwesterner, humble and well-spoken, if the papers could be believed. Who knew we were a nation so desperate for modesty? But then wasn't that what appealed to her about this young man, the reason she had been drawn to him? It was a winning recipe: modesty and confidence combined.

'I heard there were half a million people at the parade,' she said. Suddenly she was sorry she hadn't gone.

'I've never seen anything like it,' Glen said. 'They tore down the fence and rushed onto the tarmac. He had to circle the field a dozen times before they could clear a space for him to land.'

'Did you see him up close?' she asked.

'No, but a fellow loaned me his binoculars and I could pick him out a little. People were trying to swarm the plane. Once they got it into the hangar they whisked him away. It was like a battle maneuver. A whole regiment of infantrymen lined up on either side of the hangar door. They drove him right down between the rows, through a hole in the fence, and straight onto the highway. He was halfway to the city before the crowd even knew he was gone.'

Glen had shown up two hours before Lindbergh's arrival and found a seat in the stands. It was cold there, beside the bay. Wind whistled through the bleachers. He had packed a thermos of coffee, and when he offered a swig to the man shivering next to him, he found out that the fellow had flown the St. Louis–Chicago mail run around the same time Lindbergh did.

'I never would have guessed he'd be the one to do it,' the man told him. 'He wasn't a daredevil. There were other pilots quicker to hang their balls in the breeze.'

While they waited, both of them keeping an eye on the northward skies, the man told Glen stories. 'It was a small enough world,' he said. 'Tales got around about this or that scrape. Everybody played it down, of course. But more than most of us, Slim – that's what we called him, no one called him Lindy – he never bragged about his crack-ups. Said he didn't want to give flying a bad name. But of course word got around anyway.'

'Word about what?' Glen asked.

'Oh, you know. We all had near misses. Half the time you were fixing the planes in the air.' The man made a quick scan for the *St. Louis*, squinting against the misty light. Nothing but a wall of clouds to the north.

'He may not be able to land,' Glen said, glaring at the sky.

'Oh, he'll land,' the other fellow said. Just then they both heard a faint droning and looked up. A small speck, getting larger. 'What'd I tell you,' the pilot said, slapping his knee. 'That's got to be him.'

Glen paused on the steamer deck, suddenly stalled in his story. They had come alongside two lifeboats lashed to the stern, and he drifted over to them instinctively, checking their width and keel.

'It was the strangest thing,' he said to Bessie. 'It'd been raining all morning, and then the minute he landed, the sky opened up and a big bolt of sun came through – lit up the plane. You could hear people gasp.'

'I wonder what that's like,' she said softly, trying to imagine that sunbeam on her shoulders. She meant – to have such faith in yourself. To sit with nothing between you and a long fall except a sheet of painted cotton.

Glen thought she was referring to fame. That's what the sunbeam meant to him. He ran one hand along the side of the lifeboat. It was a bit flat-bottomed for heavy seas. When he spoke, his voice was far away. 'It seems like wherever you are, that's the center of things.' He went quiet, his mind drifting back to the airfield. 'When they were driving him away, there were sirens, people shouting, leaning on their horns. And then the minute he left, the place went quiet. You could hear the noise following him up the highway. I was planning to bum a ride into the city, but the minute he was gone, those cars started pulling away. Next thing I knew, it was just me and a few of the maintenance men, going around picking up litter.'

They stepped over to the railing. The sun had gone down,

and the decks had emptied, all the passengers dressing for supper. Music slipped through the doors of the dining room – Schubert sawed out by a string quartet. Over the players' labored bowing came laughter and the plink of china. A burly man in a silk waistcoat pushed open the nearest door and steered a woman through – her face was flushed, she was clearly in need of air. Their exit let loose a waft of smells: roast meat, coffee, buttered rolls.

'Am I keeping you?' Glen asked Bessie, nodding toward the dining room.

'I suppose I should go change,' she said, and didn't move. She had the sudden urge to run her hand through his hair. It looked like it would be cold, and soft as a baby's. She leaned closer, so their coat sleeves met. Apart from the brush of a toll collector's fingers or Greta's elbow linked through hers on the street, she hadn't been touched in months.

'Excuse me –' A man approached, holding up a dead cigarette. 'My matches blew overboard. Do you mind?' Glen produced a lighter from his coat and cupped his hands.

'Beautiful evening, isn't it,' the man said, blowing out a plume of smoke.

Bessie watched Glen with curiosity. No watch, but a lighter. 'Do you smoke?' she asked him.

'No, but I find a lighter comes in handy.'

'A fellow who thinks of others,' the gentleman put in, lifting his cigarette. He tipped his hat and moved on.

Months later, Glen would tell her how he savored these interruptions. He knew that if they were alone he would reach for her, but for now they had a bit of pointless conversation, and a few strangers between them to prolong the suspense.

After the gentleman had gone, they stared at each other in a moment of charged silence. Then Bessie heard someone call her name. It was Greta, all in cream: long sweater, long pearls, skirt flashing over her knees.

'There you are!' she cried, coming toward them. 'I was begin-ning to think you'd gone overboard.' She gave Glen an apprais-ing glance.

'Greta, this is Glen Hyde,' Bessie said, heat coloring her cheeks. 'And this is Greta Grandstedt. We're going to room together in Los Angeles.'

Greta gave him a brief, brilliant smile. 'Well, I hate to drag you away,' she said to Bessie, 'but we're about to miss supper.'

'Of course,' Bessie said. She turned to Glen, suddenly shy. 'Very nice to meet you.' He nodded intently and didn't smile. When they reached the swinging doors, she looked back. He was leaning against the rail, watching her.

It was November 19, the second night since they'd dropped Sutro off, and they were camped on a beach with a mass of driftwood piled up on the sand. While Glen unloaded the mattress and made a fire, Bessie sat with her back against the cliff, a blanket over her knees. The morning's argument had left them brittle. With nothing better to do, Glen looked around through the camera lens. After considering several shots, he snapped her picture – a tiny figure in a sea of bleached logs.

Something about her posture reminded him of Jeanne, lean-ing back against a pine at the Prince Rupert homestead – she must have been seven or so. 'Glen?' his sister had asked. 'What if you were an Indian, and I was an Indian from another tribe?'

He had felt a small stab of love, watching her wipe the bangs out of her eyes. 'I'd take your scalp,' he said.

That winter their mother had died. When his father came home with the news, he wanted to bawl, but he was afraid if he started he would never stop. He knew it was nothing anyone should hear. Certainly not his father, who was busy hammer-ing new latches on the sheds. Or his older sister, Edna, who wept and wailed as if someone were touching her with a brand.

Only Jeanne remained herself. She snuffled in a stiff-backed kitchen chair, watching his every move.

'Glennie?' she asked.

He froze in dread. That had been his mother's job: answering all their questions in her amused, liquid voice. He couldn't believe she was gone.

'Where they put her, will Mother have the books she likes?'

He turned away. 'Of course, silly. They have a huge library in heaven. Every book ever written. Even the bad ones.' Then he lit a fire in the stove and cooked half a dozen eggs, sliding them onto her plate one after another – the yolks quivering, the fringes crisp – and as long as she ate she seemed happy.

Now he put the camera away and settled on his haunches by the fire, stirring a can of pork and beans. 'You'll feel better when you get some hot food in you,' he told Bessie softly.

She was grateful to him for breaking the ice, but could hardly muster her thanks. Fear had deadened her. It might turn out all right in the end, but meanwhile these were days of her life, passed in this miserable way. Without warning, tears welled up.

'What's wrong, Bess?' Glen asked.

'I don't know,' she said. 'Sometimes I come to these feelings and I just can't say.'

'What feelings?' he asked, treading thin.

Bessie wiped her eyes and didn't answer.

'Now you've started in – you might as well finish.'

'I just don't think I'm cut out for this,' Bessie said, waving a hand at the cliffs. 'I keep counting the miles –'

'You don't have to be frightened,' he said.

She looked away, down the shadowed river. Anyone who wasn't frightened of this place would be a fool.

'Look,' he said. 'We're making record time. We can be out of here in a week – ten days at most. The boat is holding up better than we hoped.'

She gave him a leaden stare. 'I'm not worried about the boat.'

Glen stuck his hands out in front of the fire and inspected them. His knuckles were scraped raw from rope and rocks. One nail was black. 'I thought you wanted to make this trip,' he said, shoving his fists in his pockets. 'Now all of a sudden you're angry you came.'

'Angry. Is that what you think?'

He didn't hazard another guess.

'I'm afraid,' she said softly. 'I don't think we're going to make it.'

Glen's expression smoothed. 'Sure we will. We're cut out for this.'

She searched his face. 'Do you really believe that?' she asked, suddenly curious.

'That we'll make it? Yes, I do.'

'No, do you believe in fate?'

He shrugged. 'I think we go when we're meant to.'

'I don't,' she said. 'I think it's about the choices we make.' She pulled the blanket tighter and leaned her head against the cliff. 'The trouble is, we choose as much by what we don't see as what we see.'

That struck him as true. He thought their trip would come out all right because it was bold. He had faith in boldness. It took a lot to snuff out a life. Now he looked at his wife and had the feeling that her fears might be enough to sink them both.

She seemed to read his thoughts. 'We've all got limits, haven't we?'

'Sure. But if we fix on them, we'll never make a move.' He turned back to the river, giving her a moment to settle herself. Then something high on the wall caught his eye. 'Hey, is that a cave up there?'

Bessie glanced up. 'Where?' she asked, wiping her cheeks.

What a welcome distraction, after such talk – the particulars of the world.

'Might be an Indian ruin.'

She had read about these houses, cut into the cliffs. So high the river would never reach them. The thought of other people in this place – no matter how long ago – brought her momentary comfort.

As Greta and Bessie dressed in their cabin, the seas began to pick up. Standing straight required a soft pressure, first on one leg and then the other. Bessie heard a long scrape, then a clatter, then a scrape again, and traced it to the closet, where the hangers slid back and forth on the bar. Dress was formal. She borrowed a gown from her friend: a black beaded sheath that slipped over her hips, heavy and cool. Greta was wearing cream chiffon and she looked stunning – pale scoop of skin, bright cheeks, her hair marcelled by the wind. Bessie watched her push a curl behind her ear, and felt, as she often did, a wordless appreciation. What a constellation of chance had shaped that face. She borrowed Greta's compact, sliding the velvet puff over her nose and forehead, then helped fasten a choker of pearls at her throat.

'I like your hair short,' Greta said. 'You look like Louise Brooks.' She drew a comb through Bessie's dark bob, smoothing it against her cheek, then faced her in the glass. 'We look like two sides of a woodcut,' she said.

'Illustrating what?' Bessie smiled. 'Virtue and vice? I think I'm miscast.'

'But haven't you heard? The villains wear white these days.'

They locked eyes in the mirror and laughed.

Walking down the narrow corridors to the dining room, they listed a little, as if drunk. 'We'll have to go dancing after dinner,' Greta said. 'We can slump into the gentlemen's arms and claim it's the ship.'

Bessie smiled gently. 'I'm afraid I'll be in bed by then.' She glanced down the hallway at a cluster of men, all stout and gray, waiting for their wives. She couldn't imagine her rancher friend on the dance floor.

They were shown to their table – a poor one, near the galley – and an elderly Englishman rose to greet them. His coarse, wavy hair was combed from one ear to the other, and a single curl had popped free like a broken mattress coil. 'Ladies,' he said, making a deep bow.

'This must be the stray's table,' Greta whispered to Bessie, flashing the old man her glittering smile. In a few moments, however, with the swift efficiency of a surgeon locating a tumor, she discovered that he knew something about the financing of movies, and soon they were locked in conversation.

Bessie scanned the room. Women in satin, diamonds glinting in the folds of their necks. Men in black cutaways. So strange to be lifted up, for the price of her passage, into a world more refined than she had ever moved through on land.

Just then, a figure appeared across the table, breaking her reverie. 'May I sit down?'

It was Glen, wearing a dark suit.

She broke into a smile. 'Please do.'

Greta noted his arrival and cocked her head. 'Mr. Hyde. Fate seems to keep throwing us together.'

He glanced gratefully at the maître d'. 'It does seem that way.' Then with a quiet nod in the Englishman's direction, he took his seat.

The meal was seven courses, each served with the precision of oiled machinery. Bessie smiled at Glen across the table, and he smiled back, but they hardly spoke. There seemed to be no need of it. Perhaps she sensed then what she would later confirm: he was only talkative when they were alone. A more sociable girl might have found it a liability, but Bessie didn't mind. It made her feel privileged, as if she held the key to a private room.

By the time the entrée had arrived, the ship was plowing through heavy seas. The iced tea swung back and forth in their glasses. Glen sliced his roast beef, looking unconcerned. By dessert, the steamer had settled into a deep roll. Cherries Jubilee. The waiters walked uphill from the galley, as if canted into a stiff wind, flames leaping up from the plates. Bessie started to worry. The boat leaned to one side, hung there, then started back again. My God, this stupid dress. Heavy as chain mail, narrow at the knee. Perfect for drowning. She imagined ripping the thing up the side, in front of the astonished stewards, and leaping into a lifeboat. Of course, it was the dress and heels that earned her the right to go first.

After the meal, Greta went off to find the ballroom, while Glen and Bessie lingered over coffee.

'Would you like to take a walk?' Glen asked.

'I'd love to.' She was feeling cloistered in the swaying dining room.

Out on the deck the wind was howling, and they could hardly hear themselves speak. Glen insisted she wear his coat. 'Come this way,' he said, leading her toward the stern. When they turned the corner at the back of the boat, the air turned still. There was a teak bench against the wall. They sat down in the lee of the storm, watching the foaming sea. Bessie wrapped his coat tighter, feeling the smooth lining against her arms. 'It's peaceful here,' Bessie said.

'As long as you're not seasick. Then you'd rather be in the bow.'

'No,' she said. 'I'm happy.' She stared at him for a moment, amazed at how bold the words sounded, then took a deep breath and ran her fingers through his hair. It was not cold, as she had expected, but smooth and warm and worked through with brilliantine that smelled of cloves.

What she remembered later was the look of relaxed wonderment on his face. He behaved as if this were the most natural thing in the world – to kiss a stranger you had met only hours before. He showed no awkwardness or fear. Just leaned in and cupped her cheek in his hand.

When she felt nearly dizzy, she drew back and studied him. 'How do you know so much about boats?' she asked.

He shrugged. 'I grew up on rivers. Started doing a little floating in my teens.' Then he told her about his plan to run the Green and the Colorado. His sister was going with him. They would leave the next fall.

'What does your mother think?' Bessie asked, and then felt silly. The question made her sound young.

'My mother's dead,' he said, matter-of-factly.

'Oh, I'm sorry.'

He reached down and pulled a piece of thread from her cuff. 'That's all right,' he said. 'It was a long time ago.'

'What about your father?'

'Very much alive.'

'Is he opposed to the trip?'

'He knows I can manage myself.'

She sighed. 'My mother would collapse if I even suggested a trip like that. She doesn't keep her worries to herself.' In fact, her mother had made a specialty of a certain kind of anecdote: the horrible, true stories of how the venturesome met their end. Out of these tales, Bessie had inherited a vision of the world as her mother saw it – a world full of dangers and a seeping morbid atmosphere. 'It's catching, you know. That kind of talk.'

'Well, I guess you weren't listening.'

Bessie faced him squarely. 'Oh, I did listen.'

He smiled. 'Then what are you doing here? Traveling alone from one big city to another at – what, twenty-one?'

'I'll be twenty-two in December.'

'All right, twenty-two then.' He took one of her hands, making gooseflesh spring up. 'You could have been shanghaied down at the docks. Any minute now we could go the way of the *Titanic*.' He was teasing, but there was an honest question beneath the joke.

She thought awhile before answering. 'I guess I finally realized that my mother had never seen much of the world, so she couldn't be an authority on how to live in it.' She thought of that moment, toward the end of her senior year of high school. Eighteen years old and seated for her class photo, looking out at the perfect quarter turn, when Earl Helmick, next up in the alphabet, caught her eye and smiled as the flashbulb popped. It was a measure of how tame she was that, in the blaze of light, stolid Earl looked like a risk to her.

'So what did you do?'

'I moved out here to study art,' Bessie said, brushing aside the time intervening. 'That's my idea of adventure. And it's true you can't make a living at it.' She looked at his face – the long straight nose and firm lips – and tried to imagine him on a seething river. 'Aren't you afraid to die?' she asked.

He looked out at the gunmetal waves. She couldn't read his expression. 'To be honest, I don't think about it much.'

Later that night, when Bessie slipped back to her cabin, Greta was fast asleep, wearing a silk eyeshade, her face slathered in cream. She would sail into Los Angeles dewy and unlined. And in the morning, when the ship's whistle sounded their entry into port and the two of them stepped onto the deck, Glen appeared beside them. As they filed down the gangplank toward the wharves, Greta chattered away, oblivious to the looks cast between her friend and this young rancher. San Pedro was a dingy port town – flat-roofed buildings, sailors in uniform, gulls crying overhead – but Bessie didn't care. Love is another country. She noticed that Glen didn't offer to carry her satchel, but instead put a hand on her back as they steered through the crowds.

Later, after they had loaded their trunks into a cab and found a hotel, Greta rushed off to meet with her agent. Glen and Bessie, glad to be alone, went downstairs to the coffee shop and ordered lunch.

'I should find a telegraph office,' Glen said, sipping his coffee. 'Let my father know when I'm heading back.'

'When is that?'

'I'm meeting with the fruit buyer tomorrow.'

Bessie's heart sank. 'Anybody special waiting at home?' She tried to sound careless.

'My dog,' he said with a half smile.

She sighed, thinking of her father's kennels – the frantic wagging and panting, the sour breath. 'What kind of dog?' she asked politely, guessing a fox terrier. Against her will, she had learned all the breeds.

'Black,' Glen said.

She stared for a beat, then burst out laughing.

Glen leaned back in his chair and studied her. 'Do you have any of your poems with you?'

'A few.'

'Can I have a look?'

She smiled. 'I must warn you, they're terrible.'

'Don't say that,' he said, a brotherly chiding in his voice. 'There's no point tearing yourself down.' He put out his hand.

She pulled the sheaf of onionskin from the satchel at her feet and handed it over. He was right. She had done the best she could. And while she knew they were lacking, a small flare of hope lit within her. Perhaps he might catch a glimpse of her in those lines.

Glen put down his coffee mug and tipped the pages toward the window. They were plain poems – he liked that. You could tell what they were about, and they didn't try to rhyme. They were as modest as she was, a bit hesitant in places, but they made clear pictures. He could see her in her city apartment, rationing her smokes, watching ships pull out of the bay and wishing for adventure. Yes, her poems were all right, even if they could use a little perking up. It made him think of Reith, tending his lima beans, how he would go down the row, batting the plants with a light hand. Once, Glen had asked him what he was doing. 'Makes them grow,' his father said with a shrug. Perhaps it was true of people, too – they needed a little jostling to thrive.

He looked at Bessie, sitting across from him, pretty, small-boned, dressed like an aviatrix. Pretending not to be nervous. Suddenly he wished she was coming along on the river.

That afternoon, they walked to a nearby telegraph office, and Glen pulled a blank form from the box and scrawled a few lines.

'You didn't fret much over the wording,' Bessie said, leaning close. 'Let me see.' She could barely make out his angled capitals: 9/21/27 HOME IN A WEEK. MET A GIRL.

Bessie laughed. 'He'll think you've found a brothel.'

'No, he won't,' Glen said, looking at her steadily. 'He'll think I fell in love.'

The color welled up in her face, but she didn't look away. 'And have you?'

He didn't answer, but bent down, in plain view of the clerk, and kissed her. Then he pulled a fresh form from the box. 'You're the poet,' he said. 'What do you suggest?'

Bessie took the pencil from his hand and wrote: FRUIT BUYER ILL. MUST WAIT FOR APPT.

Glen smiled. 'That's not poetry, that's a lie.'

'Emily Dickinson calls it "truth told slant,"' she said. Then she folded up his first draft and put it in the pocket of her dress.

*

The next morning, November 20, the river had dropped by a foot – it had been dropping steadily during their run, making the rocks jut up and the rapids harder to navigate. Glen woke her with a cup of coffee, but even after drinking it, Bessie could hardly get out of bed. 'I must have a touch of flu,' she said. They decided to lay over for a day. She got out her diary and made an entry: 'Tues, Nov. 20. Camped all day as I didn't feel well.' That was done. After breakfast it began to rain. Heavy, straight rain that pocked the beach. Glen pulled the mattress under the shelter of a bush, but still the drops came through.

Suddenly Bessie remembered a strange afternoon in San Francisco, about a week before she set out on the steamer with Greta. The city had been soaked by an unseasonable storm. She was walking home through Chinatown, her umbrella sagging in the drizzle, when she saw a thread of blood running through the gutter. Bright arterial red, pooling up behind a blockage of dead leaves. Someone's been stabbed, she thought, amazed by her calm. She followed the thread up an alleyway, her steps quickening. Perhaps she could be of help. She walked with eyes cast down, examining the flow. It was certainly blood, thinning to pink in places like paint dissolving in a glass. Up ahead was a wooden fence, jogged back from the alley. The body must be there, set back out of view. Her heels clicked on the wet pavement, faster now, her umbrella tipped back and half forgotten, and then she reached the source of the blood and stopped short. It was a mass of chicken heads, tossed like broken statuary in the dirt. What she felt, she was ashamed to admit, was disappointment. She walked slowly back to the street, past the fish stalls and men crouched under sodden newspapers.

Huddled now under a dripping bush, the memory made her sheepish. There I was, longing for drama. And look where it got me.

It rained into the night, ticking through the brambles and slapping the oilskin. But when she woke in the morning the drizzle had stopped, and above her a spiderweb stretched across the brush. She hadn't noticed it the day before – and might well have blundered through it – but now it was a gleaming marvel, a starburst of black beads against the sky. For some reason the sight made her mood lift.

She went down to the river and splashed her face, then used the small mirror from their toiletry kit to run a comb through her hair. When she got back up to the campsite, Glen was waiting with biscuits and eggs.

'Feeling better?' he asked, handing her a fork.

'Much.' She sat on a boulder and started to eat, savoring the taste.

'We can wait another day if you like,' Glen said.

'No, I'm ready to get going.' She smeared the last of Reith's jam on her biscuit. 'Did you see that spiderweb by the bed?'

'I did,' he said, looking up in surprise. It was a good sign – that she had attention for such things.

'It looks abandoned,' she said. 'But the web is so perfect, it can't be old.'

'He was minding the trip wire.'

She cocked her head in puzzlement.

'I've seen that kind before. They don't wait in the middle of the web like most orb weavers, they sit on a nearby branch, one leg on a supporting thread. When a bug gets caught, the spider feels it jangle and rushes in for the kill.'

Bessie smiled at him. 'How do you know that?'

'I once wrote a school paper on spiders. Sat around watching them for hours. It was Reith's idea. I think he was hoping I'd learn a little patience.'

'And did it work?'

He laughed. 'What do you think?' She must have seen his

relief at getting back on the river. He'd had nothing to do while Bessie slept, and the high walls and rain had started to wear on him. There was only one cure for his restlessness – keep moving. It was a fault, but one he couldn't shake. A certain impatience. A need for change. Of course, he admired people who could sit still, tending to a long task. His wife, for one. She would spend a whole afternoon filling in one corner of a painting, dabbing, mixing pigment, stepping back, applying the brush again. It soothed him to watch her, just as he loved to watch the way she ate – cutting small pieces of food, putting her fork down between bites. It was part of what drew him to her: the very traits they didn't share.

They packed the boat after breakfast and made twelve miles by noon. The wind had died down, the river kept rushing along. They tackled rapid after rapid without a hitch. Stop, scout, pick a line, and then hurry back to the boat while their confidence held. They had their rhythm back. At one o'clock they stopped to eat a hot lunch. Bessie got out her notebook. It was a luxury to record so many rapids – the familiar pleasure of crossing chores off a list. When Glen asked if she wanted to make camp for the night, she shook her head. Every mile they passed was one less mile between them and home.

Still, once they were again gliding swiftly between the narrow walls, patches of mist coming forward suddenly like tissue blown in the face, she felt a spasm of dread. If only she knew what lay ahead. She felt as if she were dangling over a cliff, unsure if she'd lose her grip or be pulled up to safety. That state in between was almost unbearable. To suffer or to be glad – they each had their clarities. Not like this strange limbo, in which she was unsure of the proper attitude toward her future – hope or foreboding – and to choose the wrong one seemed like being mocked by the fates. But it was silly, really, this impulse for closure. Childish. That was the whole point of being alive – seeing how it turned out. She looked down the river, at the mist carded like wool on the rocks. This was what her husband believed: death gave life its suspense.

The day before Glen left for Idaho, they took a streetcar out to Ocean Beach, carrying a blanket and picnic lunch. When they'd spread out their things, they stripped down and went for a swim.

Bessie waded through the surf, her bathing costume pulling at her legs, then dove into the waves. Glen followed, watching her brisk overhand stroke.

'Where did you learn to swim?' he asked, when they were out beyond the breakers.

'I grew up on the Ohio River,' she said, backstroking lightly, the water lapping over her shoulders. 'And then I had women's athletics in college. Swimming races, that sort of thing.' She dunked her head and came up again. 'They thought exercise would keep us out of trouble.'

'And did it work?'

'Of course not.' She grinned at him.

'What were your vices?' Glen was upright in the water, keeping afloat with smooth strokes.

'Oh, I was pretty tame,' she said with a laugh, not wanting to follow this thread. She started swimming toward the beach. 'If you give me a head start, I'll race you to the beach.'

'Done,' Glen said. He counted to ten as she stroked in neatly and caught a swell. He had been a champion of the distance races in Twin Falls, and he didn't want to hurt her pride, but when he started in he was surprised to find he had to work a little to catch up. Together they caught a foamy breaker and slid up the beach, laughing as they came to their blanket.

When they had toweled off and were lying facedown, the sun warming their backs, Glen told Bessie the story of his trip down the Salmon River with Jeanne. Wild white water. High cliffs. And the two of them learning, day by day, how to navigate the scow.

'She's hoping to come with me on the Colorado,' he said.

'Hoping?' she asked. 'I thought it was already decided.'

He rolled over to his side and faced her. 'Lately I've had another idea.'

'What's that?' She had her head on one arm, her cheeks flushed from the swim, and for a moment Glen was stopped short by her beauty.

'I thought you could come with me.'

She started to laugh. 'But I hardly know port from starboard.'

He shrugged. '*Left* and *right* usually work fine.'

Bessie saw his expression – the boyish shyness – and realized he was serious. 'I'm sorry to laugh,' she said, sitting up, her face softening. 'I'm honored to be invited.'

'But you won't go.' His disappointment was plain.

'It's nothing to do with you. I'd love to –' She broke off, unable to finish a sentence with that much hope in it. 'It's just that I'm not much of an outdoors woman.'

'Jeanne didn't know a thing about rivers before we set out on the Salmon. I bet you'd learn as quickly as she did. Maybe quicker, with your smarts.'

She studied him, the salt drying in his lashes, the steady look in his eyes. For a moment, it filled her with amazement: he thought she was brave. She had never met his sister, but she could picture her, and no doubt having grown up with such a hardy woman had shaped his views. Still, that vision of a strapping, ruddy girl started a trickle of doubts.

'It isn't just a matter of smarts, though, is it? It sounds like rough work.'

He took one of her hands. 'It can be,' Glen said. 'But I bet you're tough for your size.'

Bessie sighed. 'To be honest, I've never felt my size suited me.' She'd come to anticipate the words people would use to describe her: 'petite,' 'just a slip of a thing.' How many times had she overheard someone say that she would weigh so-and-so many pounds 'soaking wet.' The comments chafed. We don't choose our bodies, after all.

'Then maybe it's time to put that to rest,' Glen said, rubbing the callus on her middle finger, thickened by brush handles and pens. He had always believed that strength was a matter of will. And it was true: her hands, when measured on their own, didn't look frail. They were capable hands – only in miniature. 'Besides, it won't be all work. The Grand Canyon is supposed to be one of the most spectacular places on earth. And you'd be the first woman to see all of it.'

'I've heard it's beautiful,' Bessie said softly. She had a sudden image of them, drifting between reddened cliffs. 'You know, I've never even seen a photograph. Only those paintings by Moran.'

Glen quickened. 'You'd be surprised how little most people know about the place. If you come along, you could write a book about it.'

She smiled. They'd only known each other a week, and already he was weaving her into his plans. Earl had done that, but his vision involved some rounded-off, agreeable version of herself: wife, mother. This man, nearly a stranger, made her feel she had something more to offer.

Still, she had moved quickly before and regretted it. If Glen was decent, he would wait for her. 'Can I think about it?' she asked. 'I feel I haven't really given Hollywood a chance. Not that I've been having much luck so far.' She had called a few studios, asking if there were openings for set painters, but she'd never gotten past a receptionist.

'It's too hard to break in here. Nobody knows you,' Glen said. 'You have to go out in the world and do something. Something original. Then they'll come to you.'

'But haven't people written about the canyon already?'

'There are a handful of books, some pretty good. But none by a woman.'

Bessie cocked her head, feeling contrary. 'Why don't you write one yourself?'

'Have you seen me spell?'

She laughed. 'Is it that bad?'

'I can get you down the river, but I couldn't string two sentences together that anyone would want to read. I sent quite a few English teachers into despair.'

She studied his lean, chiseled face. How quickly he had collided with her life, just standing there at the ship's rail, as if he were waiting. Strange as it was, she felt flooded with a sense of rightness and purpose, as if she could already see how it would be: she would live through his courage, just as he would live in her inventiveness, her emotion.

On the 27th of September, 1927, Bessie walked home from the railroad station alone. It was four miles to the apartment she now shared with Greta, but she wouldn't allow herself the luxury of a cab. Not if her savings were to last till she found employment. Besides, the walk would do her good. She wanted to savor the mixed-up aching feeling of seeing Glen off. When the whistle blew, he had kissed her, palms on the small of her back. He was a full foot taller than she was, so he had to bend over, like a tulip on a thin stem. 'I'd better go,' he said, pulling upright. She nodded, and watched as he boarded the car – one, two steps. Then suddenly he came back and kissed her again. 'This is awful,' he said, grinning. 'Why don't you come with me?'

'As what?' she said.

'As yourself,' he said. The whistle blew again.

'I can't,' she said. 'I just got here. Greta will think I'm trying to rival her impulsiveness.'

He smiled. 'All right. I'll have to wear you down slowly. I'll write the first letter on the train.' He cupped her cheek one last time and mounted the stairs.

Bessie waved through the window and then waited on the platform until the last car turned the bend. When she finally started home, she felt empty, as if someone had pulled a stopper and left her hollow. A dry wind stirred the dust in the gutters and made her hair fly up. With Glen gone, Los Angeles seemed suddenly bleak – a fortress city. How would she find a job? Just the prospect made her worry. The streets were broad and nearly empty. There was a gold, grainy cast to the light. A Packard passed by – a gleaming length of chrome and cream, with a coiffed head in the back window. She watched it glide through the intersection, feet aching in her thin soles. All that talk of storming the studios with her good sense and her art school portfolio – now that she was here, it seemed hopeless. She had a vision of sitting in a waiting room, in her good suit, the hours ticking by as one brash man after another came and went.

When she got back to the apartment, Greta was there, reclining in a new leather chair. 'What do you think?' she asked, running a pale hand over the seat.

'It's beautiful,' Bessie said dully. 'Where did you get it?'

'I found this marvelous shop nearby. The fellow gave me a discount.' She lifted her chin. 'It's amazing what people will do if you ask.'

Bessie slipped off her shoes. Just then, Greta's bravado made her tired. 'Well, it depends on who's doing the asking,' she said, kneading the balls of her feet.

Greta studied her. 'Are you all right?'

'I'm fine.'

'You look tired. Come here and rest.' She drew Bessie over to the club chair and made her sit. 'We'll have to take turns until we can afford another one. Isn't the leather delicious?'

Bessie nodded, tilting her head back against the buttery grain.

Greta sat on a stuffed arm. 'Where have you been all morning?'

'I saw Glen to the train,' Bessie said. She was embarrassed to feel tears well up.

'Oh, sweetheart,' Greta sighed. 'I'm sorry.' She brushed a slip of hair behind Bessie's ear. 'I hate saying goodbye at train stations. After the war, you feel they're never coming back.' She was quiet for a moment. 'You know what you need?' She whisked into the kitchen, where Bessie heard the clink of glasses and ice. Leave it to Greta to find a bootlegger within two weeks of arriving in town. In a moment she was back, carrying two jelly glasses, the bottom halves frosted with cold. 'We'll have to invest in some proper stemware,' she said, handing one to Bessie. 'Meanwhile, I propose a toast: to all the fish in the sea!'

Bessie took a sip and felt the warmth unfurl down her throat. She looked at Greta over the rim of her glass. 'I think I've found the fish I'm looking for,' she said. She was surprised at the firmness in her voice.

Greta looked startled. 'That rancher?'

'He has a name,' Bessie said.

'I know his name. I just thought –' She broke off. 'These things happen on ships. The fresh air, the sea. You get carried away.'

'It started like that,' Bessie said. 'But this is different. I can't explain it.'

Greta set her glass on the floor. 'Bessie, you know I appreciate romance as much as the next girl. And I hate to be a damper, but I think you can do better.'

She looked so sober. For a moment, Bessie faltered. Glen wasn't at all the type of man she'd thought she'd end up with. She had imagined someone from the city, another artist perhaps, wry and sophisticated. But when she thought of him, all those reservations melted away. He was smart, and frank, and had quick judgment – a kind of plainspoken confidence in his own way of looking at things. They had gone to the museum at Exhibition Park during the week of his stay – a show of Picasso, Kandinsky, and Klee – and she was surprised at how often he paused in front of a painting she thought especially fine. He just didn't have any pretensions, that was all. She stared up at Greta, saw the knowing glint in her eye, and found herself rallying to Glen's side.

'What's that look?' Greta asked. All of a sudden her eyes widened. 'You didn't make love to him, did you?'

'Of course not,' Bessie said, taking another sip of cold gin. 'Not that I wasn't tempted. But I try not to make the same mistakes twice.'

Greta looked relieved. 'Why don't you come out with me tonight? I got the password to this speakeasy – all the movie people go there. We'll find you a date with some polish. And a little money. Or are you too bohemian for that?'

Bessie looked amused. 'I think I'll stay home. I've got some things to think through.'

'Thinking is overrated,' Greta said. 'You need to have fun.' She picked up her glass and downed the gin in a gulp. Then she put a Louis Armstrong record on the phonograph and pulled Bessie out of the chair. 'See, you just need practice,' she said, laughing and taking the lead. As they slid across the floor, Greta dropped her voice to a false baritone. 'So, you're an artist. How marvelous. I have a little bungalow in the hills where I could set you up.'

Bessie drew back, resting her hands on Greta's silky shoulders. 'I've tried that already,' she said softly. Armstrong's horn wailed in the background.

'Tried what?' Greta's voice was her own again.

'Letting someone take care of me.' She thought of Earl, his

Babbitt-like fixation with solidity and success. 'It felt like having a pillow pressed over my face.'

Greta sighed. 'What do you want then?'

Bessie didn't answer, just shrugged and drew her friend close, stepping lightly across the floor. But over Greta's shoulder, through the jazz and the blur of the gin, she started to smile, because it was clear to her after all. She wanted to do the things she feared, to feel the bite of experience, to be seasoned and unfrivolous and strong. When Glen wrote her – and she was sure he would – she already knew what her answer would be.

Reith Hyde

When Emery Kolb stepped ashore at Spencer Canyon on December 28, he had a canvas sack in his hand and he was walking quickly. I could barely stand it, watching him come toward me.

'We found her diary,' he said. 'And the camera. All their gear was in the boat, neat as a pin. There was no upset, that's for sure.'

I almost tore the bag out of his hands. The first thing I did was take out that diary and sit down on a rock to read. It's a pretty pathetic document. For a literary person, she sure didn't have much to say. In November, when I was waiting for them back at the ranch, I often wondered how much she was recording along the way, but when I read her notebook, I realized – very little. She must have been deathly afraid.

One entry read: 'Thurs, Nov. 22–18 rapids. High walls on right between 17 and 18. 18th rapid bad. Got caught in eddy. Glen stayed up with boat all night.'

That was it. No mention of the scenery, not a word on what they were thinking. Here and there I came to an entry that made me heartsick: 'Camped all day as I didn't feel well.' The thought of them down there, where the sun hardly shines, with her ill and him mooning around on a narrow beach with nothing to do –

Then I looked up and saw Glen coming up the beach, rifle over his shoulder. I jumped to my feet – *Sweet Jesus!* – and rushed toward him. He stopped in his tracks, looking confused, and I realized my mistake. It was Ellsworth Kolb. He saw my face and started blushing.

'It was quite cold, sir. I thought you wouldn't mind me wearing his jacket.'

So Glen didn't have his coat. Or his rifle. I'll confess I lost a little hope right there.

But once I got over my shock, I got out the USGS maps and her notebook and tried to calculate their last position. The final entry was dated Friday, November 30. At that point the diary was nothing but a series of slashes and O's. On Tuesday, November 27, she had written 'Hot Springs,' beneath an upright slash. And then: 'Did wash.' Emery Kolb said that had to be Lava Falls, forty-five miles upstream – a huge rapid, one of the toughest in that stretch. That gave me a milestone to work from.

The Kolbs were exhausted from their run. They had lined most of the rapids, not wanting to risk them in the flimsy boat. The weather had been so cold their beds froze solid, so we got them into dry clothes and made a meal. As soon as they had some hot food, they dropped off to sleep. One thing was nagging me, though. Emery had said that when they found the scow it was caught fast, the painter pulled taut into the water. After they gathered up the important effects, they cut the rope, hoping it would float on its own down to Spencer Creek, but it quickly got jammed up in some rocks, and they left it there. At dinner, Ellsworth had turned sober and said they might have been hasty to cut the line – there might have been a body at the other end. That got me stewing. But once they were all in bed, I got up and took a rope from the jerry-built boat and put a single knot in the end. It was a gibbous moon, the canyon lit up silver, and I went down to the river and threw the rope into the current. It slapped down and sank, and I walked along the bank, dragging it like a troll line. Sure enough it soon snagged on something, and no matter how hard I tried, I couldn't yank it free. That put me at ease. Glen had told me he always put a knot at the end of his ropes, sometimes more than one – if a gust came along, and the rope burned through your hands, the knot would stop it. So that must have been what was holding the scow.

I sat up the rest of the night by the fire, making notes and consulting the maps. In the morning, I was satisfied. There was no way they could have gone the forty-five miles from Lava Falls to Diamond Creek in three days. They had to be upstream. And that meant Harbin and Francy would find them.

Glen and Bessie Hyde

On November 21, 1928, Bessie and Glen ran sixteen rapids, half of them in a cold drizzle that soaked their hats and made the boat planks slick under their feet. Making camp on the beach that evening, the walls dark and close, Bessie thought of a motion picture she and Glen had seen in Los Angeles, during their first, sunstruck week together. It was a melodrama, *Children of Divorce*. They had been shown to seats near the back, just as the lights were dimmed. Clara Bow and Gary Cooper play a wild couple who marry on a drunken spree, and in the months after, pay the price for their impulsiveness. In the shifting glow from the projector, Bessie caught a glimpse of Glen's face: he was alert, but unfazed. Not at all caught up in the plot. In a strange way she admired him for this. Up on the screen, the heroine was in an impossible jam. She has had a child with her new husband, and wakes up one morning to find that she is trapped in a loveless marriage. Bessie saw all this, and she was pinned by its satisfying and painful truth. It was as if she were watching her life with Earl, the life she would have led had she not made her escape, and to see it made her heart hurry and her palms sweat. At the crux of the action, when Clara Bow is about to drink poison – out of her quite believable fear of living any longer in her misery – Bessie couldn't hide her sympathies, and she wept. The poor girl was succumbing to her worst faults. It was a decision that arose out of everything she had been – it had the momentum of her whole character behind it, and could scarcely be stopped.

In the darkness, after the applause had dwindled, Glen became aware of her quiet sniffling and leaned toward her.

'Are you crying?' he asked, putting a hand on her shoulder. She could see that he was touched, even if he didn't share her sentiment. 'I'd offer you my handkerchief,' he said. 'But the way it looks, you might cry harder.' She laughed under her breath, feeling that pleasant smudging of pathos into humor.

Now, on the rain-pocked beach, she reminded Glen of the film.

'What made you think of that?' he asked.

'I don't know. It was something about that final scene. When she goes to the window, and sees the streetlights snuffed out, and it's the final straw.' She glanced up at the darkening cliffs. 'I guess I was thinking about how fear falls apart in the daylight.'

Glen shrugged. 'I always feel better after I've slept.'

'It's more than just rest, though, isn't it?' Bessie countered, her voice rising. 'It's about all the differences between night and day.' She thought back to her first nights in San Francisco, how her room felt like a cell, the moonlight branding the wall. She lay very still, listening to shouts that grew louder and then trailed off, muttering in the hallway. The smell of tobacco slid under the door. A shadow warped the ceiling. She froze under the covers, furious at being trapped by her terror. Only in the morning, when the sun restored the four corners of the room, was she able to breathe easily again.

She looked over at Glen, his face calm as he pulled the stove out of the boat. 'You take things so literally,' she said. Though she tried for a note of scorn, what she felt was closer to despair. Sometimes they couldn't speak of the simplest things. She wheeled around, desperate to prove her point. 'What about this?' She picked up a stone from the pile of cobble. 'It's ancient, right? A piece of the past. But the river dug it up and now it's part of the present.'

'I'd say it's a rock,' Glen said, acid in his voice, 'and I can't believe we're arguing about it.' He went back to the scow for the food. He didn't say anything more, but she could tell he was angry. There was a vindictive swiftness to his gestures. The way he grabbed a sack of their dwindling provisions and tossed it on the sand, filled the water buckets and carried them up the beach, taking small quick steps, his arms pulled taut. It was all aimed toward her for making him feel coarse.

Bessie watched him, still holding the rock in her palm, feeling its satisfying grit. If Glen couldn't fathom ambivalence – the way your mind could face off over two separate desires – then how could he understand her? Growing up in the Haley household, amid the atmosphere of stale desires, she had learned that we don't always choose the things we want most.

But if she was making a veiled plea, Glen didn't hear it. He had bent to pour kerosene in the stove. Bessie felt the heft of the stone in her hand. For a brief moment she imagined giving in to her fury. The dull thwack that would end the argument.

Glen looked up and saw the glint in her eye. 'Christ! Are you ready to brain me over a damn movie?' For a moment he looked furious, then he started to laugh. 'For crying out loud, Bessie.' He came over to where she stood. 'I may be literal, but I'm not nuts,' he said, prying the rock out of her hand.

She looked down. 'I'm sorry,' she said. 'I don't know what's gotten into me.' At least he had the grace to take it lightly.

They were quiet through dinner and went to bed early, a wide margin between them on the mattress. 'You're not going to strangle me in my sleep, are you?' Glen muttered, wadding up his coat for a pillow. He stared at her in the near darkness, trying to look serious, but it was no use, they both started to laugh. 'God, this has been some trip,' Glen said, wiping his eyes. 'Raining all the time. My wife going crazy.' He lay back and stared at the charcoal sky. 'Maybe I am simple,' he said softly. 'But sometimes I think it's a curse to be too smart.'

In the morning, they woke curled around each other, a habit now for conserving warmth. Glen kissed her hair before peeling out into the cold. He was like quicksilver – never holding a grudge.

'Stay there,' he said, tucking the blanket down around her back. 'I'll get the stove going.'

When they had finished breakfast and were ready to shove off, Bessie noticed the rock, sitting alone next to their footprints in the sand. The river might well have carried it to that spot, but she knew that it hadn't. It bore the mark of her foolishness. She glanced over to see that Glen wasn't looking and then tossed it into the river. How had all this started? It wasn't over a movie. It was over wanting him to see things her way. But now it was daylight, and her fury had dissolved. Even a good marriage has its loneliness, she thought, and went down to the waiting boat.

In the months after Glen returned to Twin Falls, they courted through letters, a less than perfect medium, given his laziness with a pen. But there were things that needed to be said, things that Bessie found easier without the distraction of his presence: 'I feel terrible not to have told you this sooner, but I didn't know where to begin. I had a college sweetheart, a boy from my hometown, and on a whim, one summer, we eloped. It was a foolish thing, too complicated to explain. I haven't seen him in more than a year. Still, I thought you should know.'

Bessie dropped the letter in the mail and couldn't sleep for days.

'Do you love him?' Glen wrote back.

'I feel nothing toward him,' she wrote. 'If anything, I'm angry with myself. I knew it was a mistake, but I just didn't have the nerve to back out.'

In the next letter, Glen sent money for the train fare, and she went to visit him at the ranch in Twin Falls. After a week together, a week of long walks through the high desert, and nights in which they were compelled, out of respect for Glen's father, to sleep in separate beds, they made their decision: they would go to West Virginia and ask Earl to grant her a divorce. It would have to be done discreetly, though. She had never told her parents the truth about her marriage.

They made the trip in October 1927 – the same journey Bessie had made the summer before, now run in reverse. When the train hissed to a stop and they stepped onto the platform in Parkersburg, the familiar air of her hometown in autumn rushed up at her: a mixture of maple and soot. A few men stood outside the ticket window, in tweed suits and polished shoes, newspapers tucked under their elbows. If they had been plucked from their surroundings, if there were no birches and maples flaring bronze and gold behind them, she still would have known they were easterners. They glanced at Bessie and Glen without showing the slightest sign of interest, and yet she knew that a minute cataloguing of their appearance had gone on in that glance. Within an hour, everyone in town would know they had arrived. She followed the men's gaze, trying to see Glen with a stranger's eyes. He did look out of place: pants pooling slightly around his boot tops, his hat brim a touch too wide.

'You call this October weather?' he said, shrugging off his jacket and slinging it over one shoulder.

Bessie had the irrational wish that he'd folded it over his arm.

'Which way to your house?' he asked, picking up their suit-cases, ready to start walking.

'Dad said he'd pick us up,' she said. 'Let's give him a minute.' Just then she saw a Ford coming up the street. When it pulled over to the curb, her brother, Bill, stepped out.

'Sorry I'm late. Dad's indisposed.' He gave Glen a curt nod and introduced himself.

On the drive home, Bill was quiet. Bessie stared at the white house fronts, the neatly spaced trees. It had been more than a year since she'd seen the leaves change. In San Francisco, the eucalyptus silvered and fell, but it was nothing like this. The elms cast down skirts of yellow on the lawns, vivid at the trunk and blurring outward like shadows. 'Everything looks the same,' she said.

Bill pulled up in front of the Haley home and set the brake. 'Well, it's not,' he said sharply. 'I don't know what Dad has told you, but things haven't been going well around here.'

Bessie lowered her chin. 'I got that feeling, here and there, from his letters.'

Bill was quiet for a moment. 'There've been a lot of rumors since you left.' He started to say something else, then thought the better of it, and jumped out to get their bags.

When they stepped into the house, Bessie could feel the pressure in the air. The curtains were drawn, the rooms quiet. In his letters, her father had seemed less than pleased by her plan to visit with Glen. Now she understood. In his strangled way, he'd been trying to warn her off. It was a matter of propriety, no doubt. All of Parkersburg had known she and Earl were sweethearts, and even if their marriage had remained a secret, no one could fail to notice that she'd left town in a hurry. A year later, she was returning, with a handsome stranger in tow. Tongues would wag. Her father, who relied on the town matrons for business, feared the slightest whiff of damning gossip.

'Where's Mother?' she asked.

Bill looked at the floor. 'She's upstairs. Headache,' he said. 'I'll take your bag up to your room.' He left Glen's suitcase in the hallway.

Bessie found her father in the dining room. He sat alone at

the polished table, glass in front of him, eyes rimmed red. She kissed his cheek and felt the rasp of whiskers, which alarmed her – he never went without a shave.

Glen followed her in and introduced himself.

'You're from Idaho, I understand,' Mr. Haley said vaguely. He made it sound like Antarctica.

'Yes, sir,' Glen said.

'That's a long way to come,' said Mr. Haley. He took a slow swig of his drink.

There was an awkward silence.

'Well, your daughter is worth it,' Glen said. He cleared his throat. 'We're planning to get married, and I only thought it right to meet you first.'

Mr. Haley stared at him and shook his head. 'You don't need my permission for that. My daughter has always done what she pleased.' He rose, pulled his smock from a nail by the kitchen door, and went out to check the dogs.

Glen slept that night on a cot in Bill's room. The next morning, a Saturday, he and Bessie planned to walk the three blocks to the Helmick house, but before they had finished breakfast, there was a knock at the front door. Mr. and Mrs. Haley were still upstairs, so Bill went to answer it. Bessie couldn't make out what he was saying, but she heard the muffled shock in his voice. She patted her mouth and went out to the hallway. There was Earl, standing at the doorstep in a dark suit, his face scrubbed and tight.

Bill excused himself and left them alone. After an awkward greeting, they went into the living room. Bessie sat on the sofa. Earl stood rigidly by the fireplace.

'I understand you've brought a visitor,' Earl said, hands shoved in his pockets.

'Yes, I have,' Bessie said.

'And were you planning to introduce me?'

'As a matter of fact, I was,' she said evenly, trying to keep from compounding the hurt. But one look at Earl's face and her eyes veered away. He was more than hurt. He was furious.

'You've really got nerve, you know that? I've been waiting for you, letting you get all this out of your system –'

Glen was standing in the doorway.

Bessie stood up. 'Earl, this is Glen Hyde.'

Earl looked him up and down. 'I don't know what the hell you think you're doing here,' he said.

Glen studied him for a moment. 'Look, what's gone on between you two is none of my business,' he said. 'We're only asking that you release Bessie, so we can all get on with our lives.'

Earl's eyes blazed. 'She seems to be quite good at ridding herself of unwanted obligations – or maybe you don't know about that.'

Bessie began to shake. Her father was right. This was a terrible mistake.

Glen pressed on. 'She wants a divorce,' he said, his voice level as a tabletop. There it was.

Earl flushed to the roots of his hair. 'Well, that's too damn bad.'

Just then Mr. Haley appeared in the doorway. His eyes were bloodshot, but he was clean-shaven and dressed with his usual care. 'What's all this?' he asked Bessie. 'What's everyone shouting about?'

The three of them fell silent.

Mr. Haley looked at them in turn, taking it all in. Something flared in his face. He pulled back his cuff and checked his watch. 'Mr. Helmick,' he said, winding the stem, 'I'm surprised to see you here, given the estimation in which you hold our family.'

'I've come here to claim my wife,' Earl said, gripping the mantelpiece, as if someone might try to tear him away.

'This is ridiculous,' said Bessie. 'I don't know what you're talking about.'

'Your wife?' Mr. Haley said, his boldness dissolving. He turned to Bessie in confusion.

She tried to keep calm, but it was no use, the blood was banging in her temples. 'I want you out of my sight!' she shouted at Earl.

'I'm not leaving,' Earl said. 'I have my rights. You're my wife and you're coming with me.'

Mr. Haley looked stunned. Beads of sweat sprang up on his forehead. He seemed to wither inside his suit.

Glen stepped into the breach. 'What exactly do you plan to do,' he asked Earl, 'keep her locked in the house?' The color had come up in his face, but his voice was light. 'You can't keep a woman like a pet. She'll just run off and leave you again.'

Earl looked around at the three of them, then jerked forward, sending a china figurine crashing to the floor. They all froze, staring at the shattered pieces. For a moment, no one breathed. Then Earl kicked one of the shards, sending it skittering across the polished wood, and rushed out of the house.

As soon as the door slammed, Bessie sank into the sofa. Glen sat beside her. When she looked up, her face was dry, her eyes wide and fixed. 'What are we going to do?' she whispered.

'Go ahead without him. You can file for divorce in Nevada.'

'Nevada?' She'd never set foot in the state. In her shock, she could hardly place it.

'They just cut the residency requirement to three months. There are towns over the border from Twin Falls where we could set you up.'

Three months. It sounded like an eternity. She searched Glen's face, amazed – and a little bewildered – by his presence of mind. But it was that same cool head that allowed him to stand up for her. He was the only one unruffled by Earl's rage.

When she reached for his hand, the skin was dry and warm.

Later that night, he would come to her room – not tiptoeing, without offering an explanation when Bessie's brother sat up in bed to watch him leave. He didn't care what they thought: it was all in the open now. He found Bessie awake, as he had expected, and slid in beside her on the narrow bed. 'I'm sorry for how things went today,' he said. He lifted his arm so she could curl into the crook. 'We won't be able to marry as quick as we'd like, but I can stand the wait if you can.'

'It's not the waiting,' Bessie whispered, her breath warming his shirt. 'It's Earl. He frightens me.'

Glen laughed softly. 'Don't worry about Earl. That boy's a peacock. All show. Besides, if he ever tries to bother you again, I'll knock his bowtie into the back of his throat. I would have come at him a little, just to see him flinch, but I didn't want your father to think you were marrying a thug.'

Bessie looked up at Glen's profile, clean as a stencil in the shadowed room. Once again, she was glad for his restraint. When they had stood up from the couch, her poor father was watching them, his face brimming over with worry.

The rapids were coming thick and fast. The more difficult the river, the more determined Glen became. He took particular care in scouting – checking the water from several angles while Bessie waited in the boat, repeating the markers out loud to himself – then steered them through what looked like a hurricane-whipped sea. Avalanches of muddy water came over the sides. It didn't seem right to call them waves – *wave* implied something softer – this was water as dead weight, dropped like a load of gravel on their backs. But one by one, they pulled through the miles.

They were in Middle Granite Gorge, the canyon narrow and dark. The boat drifted at the bottom like a match in a gutter. There were few beaches cutting the channel, few places to line.

At times, they heard the roar of a rapid in the distance and knew they would have to run it blind. Now they came toward one such drop. Glen stood on tiptoe at the front of the scow, taking a quick look at the water, then he pulled quickly for his entry and hoped for the best. They tipped over the edge and hit a rock with such force it made Bessie bite her tongue, then swerved right into the thundering hole they desperately needed to miss. The scow went nose down, then pitched up a nearly vertical reverse wave and burst through, the bow raked out in the air, a wall of water crashing over them. Within seconds they were riding out the sloppy skirt, the water agitating around them like clothes in a washer. They bailed the scow and kept going.

By midafternoon, Bessie had marked ten rapids in her notebook. They were heading roughly west. The sun, angled at its winter low, never reached the bottom of the canyon. In the morning it struck high on the right-hand wall, slid down the cliffs as the day wore on, and then back up again. She stood on the thwart, staring up at that band of sunlit stone. What she would give to be standing in its glow.

But Glen was probably right: there was nothing to do but press forward. She was too fixed on what might go wrong. Since they left Hermit Creek, she had slipped into the habit of looking at their actions in the light of 'last things.' The last chair she sat on. Mr. Sutro, the last man to see them alive. These phrases bloomed in her mind like picture captions, giving her a chill. Not good to think of yourself as a character in a story, when the story wasn't finished. She shook herself to break the thought.

'You cold?' Glen asked, glancing back at her.

'I'm all right,' she said, but she was glad when he dropped his sweep and gathered her up, blowing warm breath into her collar.

They were still locked together when they floated around a

turn and saw, off to the left, a wide sandy beach with an overhanging cliff.

'What do you say we stop for a hot lunch?' Glen said.

As he worked the scow over to the sand, tears welled up in her eyes. She stumbled up the bank – a miracle, this pile of fine stuff in the middle of a sheer channel – and turned back to look at the scow. From a distance, it looked strange, a big raft with a mound of baggage, the long clunky sweeps. To think she'd lived on it for a month. She could hardly believe the miles she had passed on that thing, clinging for her life – through churning walls of water, the boat lifted almost vertical and then slammed down like a piece of bark – there was no point trying to describe it. Now Glen was looking around for a place to tie it off. The sand only supported a few wisps of shrub. Finally he knotted a spare rope to the bow line and tied this to a rock high on the beach.

After they'd eaten lunch, Glen went down to the boat and came back with their toiletry kit, the leather marked with water stains. He rummaged through a side pocket, vials clinking, and pulled out a pouch of tobacco.

'Where'd you get that?' Bessie asked.

'At the dry goods in Green River. I know you like one now and then.' He tossed her the pouch and watched as she rolled a smoke, the paper fluttering in the wind.

'I'm out of practice,' she said, crimping the ends and holding the thing up.

Glen, sprawled on the sand beside her, cocked his head at her handiwork. 'What the hell, roll me one.'

She looked at him in surprise. He was so moderate in most things, any show of vice seemed endearing. She licked another cigarette closed and placed the lumpy pair on her palm. 'You get to choose,' she said. 'That was always Greta's rule. Promotes good rolling.'

He struck his lighter for the two of them and they sat quietly for a while, watching the smoke billow downstream. Glen held his cigarette like a dead bug – pinched between thumb and forefinger. He squinted, took a big draw, and burst into hacking coughs.

'Easy,' Bessie said, laughing. 'Take little puffs.'

He coughed again and wiped his eyes. 'I always liked the idea of them.'

Bessie flicked the ash beside one knee and pulled the smoke into her mouth. She liked having something to keep in her fingers, and the way the tobacco lifted through her like a familiar wave, leaving her a little dizzy, a little belled open. So easy to mistake recognition for pleasure. Suddenly she was glad for the sand, light as peat, which sank under her heels, and for this spot – a roof cut from stone. She felt herself soften, and the world seemed to soften in kind: the gentle breeze, the light high on the cliff opposite coming to a rosy peak. Glen was lazing beside her in the sand – he never lazed – arms cocked beneath his head, his coat thrown open to the sheepskin lining. She leaned over and gave him a kiss. Beyond him, the river looked gentle, dependable – only a soft chop unfolding down the center – but it was the oily motion of a confidence man, turning cards over one at a time: you were just waiting for the sleight of hand. She stubbed out her cigarette and felt the rasp in her throat. The wind fell still, and in the quiet, she could hear a growl from downstream. How quickly her dread returned.

Two miles farther on, her fear would prove justified. They came to a nasty rapid – Glen spent longer than usual scouting from the bank – and finally decided to run it. They made a good entry, but veered slightly off their line in the second half, and when they reached the washout, got pulled into a massive eddy on the left. At first they weren't alarmed – this happened all the time. You rode upstream along the bank, let yourself circle out toward the center of the river, and then used the sweeps to pry yourself free of the whirlpool. But this time they couldn't catch the main current again. The boat was like a wooden toy, circling a bathtub drain – there was no resisting the water's pull. They went around and around, waiting for the right moment, then yanking hard on the sweeps, but it was no use. Finally the sky overhead turned a deep electric blue. It was clear that even if they could clear the eddy, they wouldn't want to. Not safe to run in the dark. Ordinarily, they would just pull over to the shore and camp, but there was no place to land on this side of the river, not even a cobble pile. They circled next to a sheer cliff. Across the river was a perfectly good place to camp, but there was no way to reach it. They would have to spend the night in the boat.

Glen declared this with a shrug, but his jaw was set tight. Eddies were unpredictable as weather. After holding a boat fast for hours, they might suddenly let it go. He would have to stay awake, in case the current shifted and they were set loose on the river.

Night fell. It was such a strange feeling, to be drifting, unmoored, in the dark, that Bessie couldn't sleep. To pass the time, she started to sing, first 'Frankie and Johnny,' then 'Am I Blue?' Scraps of tunes her mother sang while sewing. Odd how they stayed with you.

'How do you know all those words?' Glen asked.

She shrugged. 'I don't know. It's the first thing I listen to in a song.'

He started to hum a few bars of some sentimental country tune. 'What's that one called?'

' "The Cowboy's Lament," ' Bessie said.

'See, I couldn't sing a line of it to save my life.' A thumbnail moon had come up, casting a faint light over the river. He put his arm around her. 'We're a good team,' he said. 'You watch the map, I'll watch the river.'

They were quiet for a while, listening to the shudder of the rapid and the slap of water on the boat planks. At times, if Bessie closed her eyes, she could scarcely believe she was at the bottom of a mile-deep desert canyon. Before she left West Virginia, all she had known of this countryside had come from books and silent movies.

'Did you ever see *Go West*?' she asked Glen. She had been so convinced by that scenery: sandy wastes, gullied mountains in the distance, bowlegged ranchers in chaps and leather vests. And Buster Keaton, bug-eyed with loneliness, jumping off a freight train from the east and asking, 'Do you need any cow-boys today?'

Then she had made her own westward journey, the plains unfurling out the train window, and finally the Rockies loom-ing ahead, the biggest mountains she'd ever seen. She tried to describe it to Glen, how it changed her whole idea of the country in which she lived, and as she talked, she felt him listening. His curiosity was like a shaft of light making its way down through leagues of water, fraying and opening so her thoughts rose up in answer, silky and strong. She had no more idea than he did where the story was leading, but with him listening like that she felt sure it would end up somewhere. She thought suddenly of a blind man she had watched navigate Columbus Avenue with a metal-tipped cane. He built the street one yard at a time, patient, refusing to panic, tapping and pausing and correcting his course.

She pointed up to the rim, a line of jagged black, as if someone had torn away half the stars. 'The train passed north of here, but I missed the desert entirely.'

'What were you, buried in a book?'

'I was retching in the toilet.'

He stood up and flashed a torch over the river. They were still circling. 'Reith swears that a slice of cold apple under the tongue cures motion sickness.'

'You know I don't get motion-sick.'

Glen paused for a moment, casting the beam of light over the cliff like a jittery eye. 'Of course, anyone who takes an apple grower's word on that would be foolish.'

'If I had a weak stomach,' she said, 'this boat would have ruined me.' Suddenly she knew where the story was heading, the point she had been moving toward. Perhaps he did too. 'I was sick before I stepped on the train.'

Glen turned off the torch, plunging them into darkness. 'Are you hungry? All of a sudden I'm hungry. I could make flapjacks here in the boat.'

'No, thanks,' she said, and shook her head. The memory of that old nausea had made her mouth flood with spit. For a few minutes she listened as he rustled through the food crates, then she sat up and put a hand on his back. 'Glen?'

He turned around.

'There's something I have to tell you.'

He didn't move for a moment. Then she heard him take a deep breath. 'What is it?'

She forced herself to look at him. 'I was pregnant, before I met you. It was Earl's. And when I went to San Francisco –'

'You don't have to say it,' he put in quietly.

She stopped, taking his reticence for shame. 'I should be able to say it.' Her voice was shaking. 'If I had the nerve to do it, I should be able to speak of it.'

He touched her arm. 'You did what you did,' he said. 'There's no need to answer to me about it.'

She sat very still, taking this in. 'I've wanted to tell you for a long time,' she said. 'I was afraid you'd be ashamed of me.'

'Ashamed?' He leaned forward to study her in the dim light. 'You know I'm not the righteous type. We all do what we have to to get by.'

'You don't think of me as "a woman with a past"?' She tried to sound wry, but in fact she was amazed: he didn't seem concerned with what had come before him.

'Everybody has a past. I prefer to think about the future,' he said. He looked away, down the river. The purling of water filled in the silence. 'Sometimes I think about us having kids.'

'You do?' It was the first he'd spoken of it. She was moved by the thought, and by his studied nonchalance in raising it. A child of their own. Even as the vision tempted her, she felt hemmed in. 'If we do go on a lecture tour, what would we do with a baby?'

'I don't know. We'd have to wait till after, I suppose.' He turned back toward her and put his hands on her knees. 'I don't know why, but I always picture a girl. Wiry and smart, with little brown hands. She'd have Reith whipped.'

Bessie smiled. 'She'd have all of us whipped.'

'Well, we have time to think about it,' Glen said. He looked away again, his expression lost in the darkness. Then he got Bessie to hold the torch, and while the scow spun in circles at the base of the cliff, he lit the stove and made pancakes.

Reith Hyde

Emery Kolb had recovered their camera from the boat. Thankfully, it didn't seem to be waterlogged. After we got back to the South Rim, he was anxious to develop the pictures – thinking they might offer some clues as to Glen and Bessie's last camp. He was touchy about his equipment, said the darkroom was cramped, but finally agreed to let me watch. What a strange science, full of strange terms: the stop bath, the fixer. To me, the words rang wrong, because nothing got fixed, not in the sense of set to rights, not even in the sense of being held down for good. They snapped those pictures, and floated on between the walls, not knowing what lay ahead.

In the first frame, the two of them stood in the scow – someone else was holding the camera, so it must have been taken from the bank at Green River – and the image was so sharp it seemed I could reach out and touch the fur on her collar. They were smiling, at ease. Of course it was natural to be hopeful – the journey hadn't started. Next were several shots of the river, muddy and rough. Kolb said they could have been anywhere. A few frames later, a photograph of Glen climbing a rough-hewn ladder, nailed together out of logs and planks. He was at the top, having reached a sandstone bench, wearing his high leather boots. Kolb thought he spotted an old Indian dwelling on the cliff behind him. His hair was slicked back, and he was clean-shaven. He looked serious, handsome. They must have stopped to look at the ruins. I could make out Bessie's shadow in the foreground – a narrow shape topped by a hat – and when I scanned Glen's face again, I thought I detected a bit of impatience. Perhaps she had wanted to take the picture, something she could paint from later, and he was itching to explore.

I was surprised at my son's changeability from one photo to the next. I thought I knew his face better than I knew my own, but in the pictures he looked like two or three men. Sometimes hard. Sometimes as handsome as a Hollywood cowboy. And then in other shots merely a boy attempting a pose.

By the same lights, I couldn't help noticing that Bessie always looked the same – thoughtful, composed – just as she did in person. She often stared squarely at the camera, one hand tucked in a pocket. Then we came to one of the later photographs, and my impression changed. She was posed beside a rapid choked with boulders, a furious stretch of water, wearing her leather jacket and boots. The negative was grainy, but you couldn't miss the fear in her face. She seemed to be saying, 'For God's sake, will you look at this?'

There were only a few more negatives. One sheet at a time, Kolb exposed the paper and slipped it into the developing bath. Two more photographs of the scow. One of Bessie crouched against a sheer wall with a bunch of driftwood in the foreground. Something about that pose made me swallow hard. She looked so tiny against the cliff, so forlorn. There was hardly enough light to take the picture. Kolb said that from the look of the rocks it was probably taken in the Inner Gorge. Hard to tell exactly where. Then he slipped in the last negative and I stood over the basin watching my son's face sharpen up – half dizzy from the wet metallic smell. The safe light rippled in one corner of the pan like a red sun. Glen looked up at me through the slosh of the liquid, his face ready, full of purpose. He didn't look broken or tired. His face was a bit thin, his jaw set, but he looked like himself.

I reached down without thinking, but Kolb caught my wrist. 'Watch the chemicals,' he said, and pulled the picture out with a pair of tongs.

Glen and Bessie Hyde

In the morning, the river had dropped, and Glen was able to break free of the eddy without trouble. They ferried to the beach on the other side, made a quick breakfast, and started downriver. But their luck didn't change. Only a mile downstream, they smashed a sweep in a rough rapid, and they had to lay over for a day to mend it. They set out the next morning, November 24, and quickly came to a drop that looked unrunnable – the current split in two. Both sides of the rapid were full of rocks and bad waves. They spent most of the afternoon lining along the bank, nearly losing hold of the scow at one point. Thinking swiftly, Glen lassoed the rope around a rock, dragging the boat to a halt. When they got to the bottom of the rapid, they were too exhausted to go on. Two days' work, three miles.

The next two days were long hauls. They tore through fourteen miles each day, one rapid after another, working in wet clothes, in too much hurry to stop and dry them. The temperature was hovering near freezing – there were fringes of ice in the bucket when they woke for breakfast – and the water level was dropping steadily as they moved downriver. Each morning they found the scow beached higher than it had been the night before. Sometimes it was hard work to pry it off the sand. Low water made some rapids easier and others – the ones thick with rocks – into minefields. By late afternoon on the 27th of November, they had run six big rapids and covered nineteen miles. Then they came to Lava Falls. For nearly a week Glen had been thinking about it – the name loomed ahead of him, a nagging unpleasantness, like the foreknowledge of punishment. Emery Kolb had talked to him for an hour about the rapids from Phantom Ranch to the Grand Wash Cliffs. He spent a quarter of that time giving pointers on Lava Falls. By Kolb's account, no one had ever run it. 'And on low water, I wouldn't try to be the first,' he said. One look and Glen understood why – it was a thundering cauldron of water, full of jagged volcanic rocks and huge holes lined up like slalom gates in the channel. Hardly any way to skirt them. His stomach felt sour just looking at it.

He walked briskly along the bank, trying to see if there was a route he was missing. But no matter which way he studied the water, he couldn't see a way through. It seemed certain they would smash into something, and the volcanic rock would rip the boat like wet cardboard. He decided they had to line, although that didn't prove much easier. After four hours of arduous work, inching the boat around fangs of rock, skirting perilously close to the current, they pulled into an eddy below the rapid and spotted the warm springs, just as Kolb had promised.

Cold and tired as she was, Bessie pulled out their dirty shirts and underwear and a bar of soap and carried them to the spring. A slow trickle of water spilled from the lava, catching in a shallow pool. It was drizzling softly. When she looked up, the cliffs downstream rose up like the walls of a stage, a gray curtain of rain between them. How fitting, since the drama behind it had yet to be revealed. She dunked the fabric in the steaming pool. Sleeves billowed out in the water. She didn't mind the chore. It was a mercy to have warm hands. In Chinatown she used to take her clothes to the laundry on Jackson Street – it was surprisingly cheap. She remembered one customer – a man – who carried his fresh laundry away in a cardboard suitcase, as if each week he considered taking the pressed shirts and leaving town. It was an impulse she suddenly understood.

They made ten miles the next day, facing into a headwind, and on November 29, Thanksgiving Day, they made twenty-two – their longest run yet – and camped on the right just as darkness fell. Glen pulled the mattress onto the sand while Bessie made a fire.

'Hard to believe it's Thanksgiving,' she said. Down in the bottom of the canyon, there was nothing to mark the date. It had been three years since she had passed the holidays in her childhood home, and suddenly she missed it. Pushing cloves into oranges for the centerpiece, her brother kicking her under the table while Mr. Gorman, a dull bachelor her mother had adopted, said his interminable grace. Thinking of these details, she was overtaken by a quick pang. But in the end, she decided it was a comfort – to know, even from this great remove, exactly what they were doing.

In honor of the holiday, she decided to heat up the last of Mr. Sutro's smoked ham. She rummaged through the food stores for something to go with it. 'I don't think I could stomach another lima bean,' she said, tossing a can onto the sand. She found the last Prince Albert peaches in the bottom of the crate and held them up. 'How about these?'

Glen was strict about rations, always worried about getting caught short, but now he shrugged. 'Might as well,' he said. 'We're almost out of here.'

Such elation at the thought of this bit of fruit – it made her laugh. 'Look at what we've come to,' she said. 'Drooling over canned peaches. We're about as far gone as that half-naked Pate.'

Glen smiled and set the can on a boulder, where it looked oddly like an advertisement. 'Prince Albert peaches,' he said, pointing like a pitchman, 'they make a hermit feel like a king.'

They ate until they could hardly move – so hungry from cold and exertion they couldn't help themselves. Ham seared over the fire, biscuits made with eggs and Swift's lard, fresh coffee instead of the thrice-boiled dregs.

'Twenty-two miles today,' Glen said. 'That's worth giving thanks for.'

There were only two bad rapids ahead – Separation and Lava Cliff. Only sixty-six more miles to the Grand Wash Cliffs. At the rate they had been traveling, they could make it in three days. They had nearly pulled it off – the thing everyone had said was impossible.

'Hard to believe that only a year ago I was eating turkey in Elko, Nevada,' Bessie said, pouring the last of the coffee into their cups. She palmed the warm tin, looked up at the cliffs, cold and jagged in the moonlight, as if they were glazed with ice. That was the power, she supposed, of traveling to such a strange place, beyond comfort and the lull of the known: it seemed to break you free of your own past, so that you could hardly remember what your old life had been like.

In November 1927, Bessie moved to Elko and took a room in the house of Mrs. Delpha Jewell. The following February, as soon as her three-month residency was established, she would walk five blocks to the courthouse and file for divorce. Elko was set on a salt pan a mile above sea level, and beyond the small knot of wind-whipped buildings that made up the center of town the high desert stretched away on all sides. Bessie's room was on the second story, a beige box with creaking floors and a woodstove. The windows faced south and took in the cold winter sun.

Twin Falls was 180 miles north – a grueling day's drive over dirt roads – but after he dropped her off, Glen wasn't allowed to visit. The lawyer they retained had made it clear: small-town judges accepted gossip as evidence. Any whiff of adultery would damage her case. Mr. Griswold was a rotund man, with a net of broken capillaries across his nose. 'As long as your husband doesn't show up to contest, it'll be pro forma,' he told Bessie. 'We'll present you as a lonely young girl, abandoned without support.'

At times, in the coming months, Bessie was inclined to think this was the truth. She had no companions. Glen wrote once a week, his letters hasty and badly spelled. They were filled with descriptions of the state of the orchards, preparations for their river trip. She read them over carefully, looking for signs that he missed her. He only veered toward feeling at the end. 'I've put in some cash for the week. Wish it could be more. Love, Yr humbel boatman.'

She smoothed out the bills and tried to decide: drawing paper or food? She had taken the room without board, thinking she could be more resourceful on her own, but there was a steeper price to her feelings when Mrs. Jewell, seeing how her tenant fell short at the end of the week, invited her down for a bit of leftover roast. Hunger sapped her several ways; it kept her awake at night, made her faint when climbing the stairs. But working paid her back in others. When a sketch came together in an unexpected way, she felt a surge of gladness that burned cleaner than food.

But by the time the third letter came, she had no choice. She went straight to the dry goods and bought tinned beef, butter, cans of condensed milk. She had been forced to take in her skirt with a safety pin – the rich foods might put a little of it back. In her letters to Glen, she never mentioned her struggles. She felt sure he would drive down with a load of supplies, and a strange car, coming out of the desert at night, would get as much attention as a traveling circus. If they ruined their chances here, she'd have to start all over in another town, and she could hardly stand the thought. On the feed calendar in her room, there were already three weeks crossed out.

Down to her last sheets of vellum, she kept her mind clear with a series of pencil drawings, twelve to a page – each the size of a soda cracker, floating in white. At first she reveled in this compression, the way it cropped the forms of everyday things: a teacup, a skeleton key, three speckled eggs. But one night, in a dream, she covered her bedroom wall with casein and began a mural: steamships plowing through curling waves, yellow-lit dance halls that fell away to scaffolding like film sets. She paced the wall, laying down swaths of color, happy to be using her arm instead of her wrist – then woke and took a quick breath of relief to see the walls were still drab. Mrs. Jewell had been so kind.

She threw back the covers and went to the rickety table:

Dec. 15 – It's early – the light only minutes old – and I already feel the need to write something here. The thought of two more months like this fills me with dread. Don't think I can do it. But even as I write these words, I know it's not true. I'm always astonished at what one can bear.

She dressed and made coffee in the chilled kitchen, then went for a walk along the Humboldt River. It was a fast-rushing muddy stream, gouging a rut in the hardpan without offering much to the surrounding scrub. Still, it restored her, to watch the current rushing past, to soak up the thin sun. Happiness wasn't everything. One by one, she was slipping all the knots – the baby, the foolish marriage. It took work to make a good life.

Back at the house, she wrote two letters – one to her mother and father, one to Glen. It was a comfort to think that someone knew the details of her day. It made her feel tethered, out there in the desert wastes. The corner post of her afternoon was a trip to the post office to drop off her mail. She walked the three blocks down the crushed shale streets and loitered in the drafty room – nothing but a barred window, a bench, and pillars of chilled sun. The clerk might have been someone to chat with, except he wasn't inclined to chat. He took her envelopes without looking at them, nodded, and went back to his ledgers.

That night, after supper, Mrs. Jewell invited her to sit in the parlor and listen to the radio. They were playing a hole through 'Ain't She Sweet,' and she kept time on the arm of her wing chair. When the news came on, she turned down the volume and went to the kitchen for two slices of pie. During the silver boom, she told Bessie, passing a plate, Elko had been a bustling town. 'We had two banks, forty saloons, and ten whore-houses,' she said, gripping her fork as if a wave of the old iniquity might wash her away. That seemed unlikely, Bessie mused. Mrs. Jewell was as solid as the gullied hills above the river, a soft mountain of flesh.

'You got accustomed to gunfire,' she said. 'You'd be eating, hear a shot, stop a second, then go on chewing. I'm not sorry the mines went bust. This town's dried up. But at least they aren't killing each other like dogs in the street.'

Mrs. Jewell had other reasons to hate the mines – they had made her a penniless widow. Her husband, prone to drinking away his paycheck while alive, had left her a large debt at the company store when he died. There were plenty of people in town who didn't approve of the state's divorce laws – 'We're attracting the wrong types,' they said. But Delpha Jewell found herself rooting for the women who passed through her rooms. Let them cut loose if they could.

'Why didn't you remarry?' Bessie asked gently. 'There seem to be plenty of bachelors in town.'

The old woman tipped her head to one side. 'Well, my dear, the odds are good, but the goods are odd.' Then she took the pie plates to the sink.

Lying in bed that night, Bessie tried to remind herself what Glen was like. They had spent so little time together, and it had been almost a month since she'd seen his face. It was probably good to have some distance, so she could consider him more clearly. But she didn't have clear judgment. She had a jumble of remembered scraps. What was it he'd said when she'd told him she went to see the first talkie? 'Will Rogers calls them *noisies*.' She had laughed, not because she agreed, but because it was almost too quaint: an Idaho rancher who quoted Will Rogers. But then he surprised her in other ways. Much as he hated to write, he loved to read. He kept a stack of books on the mantelpiece at the ranch, books on shipbuilding and geology, and accounts of previous expeditions through the Grand Canyon – Major Powell's *Canyons of the Colorado*, Robert Brewster Stanton's articles in back issues of *Scribner's*, *Through the Grand Canyon from Wyoming to Mexico* by Ellsworth Kolb. Every night after dinner he would settle there for a few hours, tipping the pages toward the fire. He had an easy way of occupying a chair, canted back, one hand on his chest, legs crossed at the ankles. Having summoned this picture, she felt a twinge of longing. She guessed he was about six feet, but he was lean and looked taller. What else? His eyes narrowed slightly when he listened – in fact, he cocked his head and offered his complete attention, and this courtesy wasn't reserved for her. He was widely curious. On the train to Parkersburg, he had talked for several hours to a man who organized dance marathons, asking him all manner of questions; what was a good turnout, and what did they do with the ones who collapsed?

Still, she sometimes heard a scrap of news on the radio and realized that if Glen were there, she couldn't imagine what he would say. Did he think Sacco and Vanzetti were innocent? And Harding's adultery, what did he make of that? Not that these opinions added up to the man. But she had married once in a rush, and she didn't want to make the same mistake twice. She tried again to consider him, but it was all too fresh – the way he'd collided with her life, all the decisions she had made since then, under a kind of physical sway. When she tried to think of his drawbacks, she ended up thinking of his long fingers, the way he smoothed the cover of a novel she bought him or the sweating neck of a bottle. Or how at night, when he was sleeping, he made a soft swallowing sound to soothe his throat. The only sensible thing she came up with, in favor of his suitability, was that she liked what she made of herself in his company. He encouraged her to be bold.

And so the days went by:

Feb. 20 – Filed the papers today. I would have done it on the 18th, the first day I could, but the court was closed over the weekend. Walked home in a howling wind – sand scouring my face – and felt wonderful. Then Mrs. Jewell remembered I had had a letter and brought it up to my room. It was my note to Greta, posted over two months ago. I wept when I saw the postmaster's black pen: Moved – No Forwarding Address. How could I have waited so long to write. At first it was preoccupation – the trip back to Parkersburg, the plans to get settled here – and then pettiness. The things she said about Glen before we parted, my deserving better and all that, kept ringing in my head. Now it seems that I've lost her, my dear friend, who helped me when I was sick and alone and no one else would. For a moment I thought of boarding a train to Los Angeles. But I don't have the money for the fare, and I wouldn't know where to begin to look for her.

Feb. 24 – Horrible day. I've just learned that my court date is set for April 11. Mr. Griswold says this is a normal interval (he might have mentioned it earlier). I don't know where I got the idea it would be quicker. But apparently they must send Earl a summons. I've counted the days left, and cursed the fact it's a leap year, since it adds one to the number.

Apr. 11 – It's done. I took the stand this morning in my good suit (the same one I'll wear tomorrow) and answered their questions. The judge hardly deliberated. Mr. Griswold said that's the way it always goes, unless the husband shows up to contest. When they called Earl's name I thought my heart would burst, but the judge just looked up from his papers and, seeing he hadn't shown, struck the gavel – bang. One life changed (or two, or three, depending on how you look at it). Now I'm waiting for Glen to pick me up – we'll drive straight to Twin Falls. Odd to think that for the next twenty-four hours, I'll be a single woman.

At noon that day, she came home from a walk and saw a mud-spattered Model T in front of the boardinghouse. The apple crates in the back gave it away. She took the steps two at a time, rushed through the door, and found Glen sitting with Mrs. Jewell, a cup of tea in his hand. The sight of him made her chest contract. He stood quickly, and Mrs. Jewell made a flustered excuse to clear the china. After the kitchen door had swung closed behind her, they stayed a few feet apart, grinning foolishly. Bessie had been so used to imagining him and now here he was, wearing a denim shirt, his brown face and white teeth thrown into relief. It must have been a dry winter in Hansen. He must have been out working in the sun. She took all that in. Then he came forward and kissed her, put his hands in her hair. A pulse of pleasure went down her spine.

'How did you get here so early?' she asked.

'I drove halfway yesterday and spent the night in the back of the truck.' He drew back at arm's length. 'Has Mrs. Jewell been feeding you?'

She flushed and looked away.

'Hey,' he said, cupping her cheek. 'You look beautiful.' He looked at her steadily. 'It's just that I've been worried.'

She saw the feeling in his face, and suddenly the complaint she had been gathering toward him over the past months came apart. As long as he noticed. Knew it hadn't been easy.

'Come out to the truck for a second,' he said, tipping his head. They went outside into the icy sun. He threw back the oilskin over one of the crates. Inside were sandwiches wrapped in wax paper, jars of jam, a pie, and a silver thermos. Tucked beside all this was a patchwork quilt. 'All your letters had the word *cold* in them,' he said. 'We'll bundle you up for the ride.'

Bessie went in to thank Mrs. Jewell and gave her a few jars of the Hydes' apple butter. Then it was time to her gather her things. 'Bessie will be missed,' Mrs. Jewell told Glen, as she followed them up the stairs. 'Of course, she's probably pleased to go. It's a modest place.'

They all stood awkwardly in the doorway, pretending to admire the spartan quarters. Bessie buckled a belt around her sketch pads, and Glen fiddled with the flue. Suddenly the stove stopped leaking smoke. 'The handle was loose,' he said apologetically.

Mrs. Jewell waved her hand at the thick air. 'Bessie, you should have mentioned the flue was leaking. I can't have my boarders cured like ham.'

'Oh, it wasn't so bad,' she said, smiling at Glen. All of a sudden it seemed to be true.

It took them eight hours to make the drive back to the ranch, jolting over the poor roads. When they arrived, Reith was already in bed. They washed up in the big kitchen sink and made sandwiches, and then, discovering that neither one was tired, went out to sit on the porch.

'Your father made this?' Bessie asked, running her hands along the bent-willow armrests.

'No, I did. That's why it's about to fall over. The rest are his.'

'In Parkersburg everyone has wicker,' she said.

'Wicker's nice.'

'It creaks, though.'

'Well, it would do more than creak after a few winters here.' He gave her an appraising look. 'I wonder how you'll feel about this place in the winter.'

She smiled at him. 'West Virginia isn't the tropics.'

'It seems colder out here than it does in a town.' He looked off at the stars, scattered like sugar. 'My mother had trouble with the winters.'

'What kind of trouble?' Bessie asked.

'I think she got lonely.' They were quiet for a while.

'Are you nervous about tomorrow?' Bessie asked.

Glen leaned forward in his chair and took her hand. 'No,' he said. 'I was nervous you'd get sick of waiting and give up on me.'

Later, the months after their wedding would stand out in Bessie's mind – the dry heat, her passion for Glen, the sense of having arrived somewhere after a long journey. The ranch was its own universe – set up in the high desert, with orchards watered by the river and miles of sagebrush all around. She and Glen had coffee together each morning – Reith would be up and out already – and she spent her days writing and drawing. In the evening, when it was cool, they went for long walks. Glen's sisters, Edna and Jeanne, lived with their husbands a few miles away, and came over for supper once a week. Edna was meek and jittery – something a little strange about her – but Jeanne was like a tank. It was clear she didn't like having a new woman in the family home. She showed up for their first supper with an entire meal, cooked ahead of time and kept warm in towels, as if Bessie was incapable of lighting a stove. But slowly they got used to each other. And when Jeanne saw that Bessie didn't mind work, she began to teach her a few things. When to weed the kitchen garden. How to make bread.

Bessie went up to the spare bedroom, warm from the afternoon sun, and punched the dough down in its earthenware bowl. Then she draped the cloth over the top and stared down at the vegetable patches, the orchards marching outward in soldierly rows. A week after she arrived, her father-in-law had invited her up to this same room, his face set as he mounted the stairs. She dragged her feet, wondering what she'd done wrong. Then he reached the sill and turned to her. 'I thought you might like to draw in here,' he said. 'We don't have any use for it, now that the girls are gone.'

So she made herself a studio, pushing the bed against one wall, pulling a table under the western window. There she arranged her pads of vellum, her jars of brushes and pens, and began to sketch scenes of the desert.

When she first moved to the ranch, she was afraid she would be restless. So far from the city, from the changing sea of faces, the bustle of shops. But she was surprised to find herself happy. Something about the quiet, the stillness of the landscape, made her turn inward. She was working on line drawings, and had started a series of oils. But there was another piece to her happiness: the evenings spent with Glen. They talked about everything, but always circled back to their trip. If they made it through all of the canyon, it would be a way to lift themselves into a wider world, giving lectures, writing books, perhaps showing her pictures at a gallery. It was an entrancing dream: that mix of private and public life. And it was Glen's dream as much as hers. If he had been content to spend his days confined to the ranch, she could never have married him. But he was a strange hybrid, at home in the country as well as the city. He wore plain, sensible clothes, but when she went with him to the dry goods in Twin Falls and observed the other men from surrounding farms, she saw the subtle style in the way he carried himself. He favored shawl-collared sweaters, as his father did, and wore his hair parted and slicked. The other men dressed in denims from head to heel, and wore their hair short, cowlicks popping up at the crown. They looked like big, awkward boys. It added shading to her portrait of him, to see how he stood out among other men.

She checked on the dough – it had risen again – and turned for the stairs. Looking out once more at the orchards, thick with fruit, she flashed for a moment on the day of their wedding. They had been married in a meadow by the river, a justice of the peace presiding, the family assembled in the shade of a wind-leaning apple tree. It was in flower, the blossoms scattered among the branches like paper stars, no leaves to hamper their starkness. She had felt so calm – calm and elated at once – as if everything around her had acquired an extra sharpness. She looked into Glen's face, the curve of his mouth, his warm eyes. And then up at the blossoms, the way they made room for each other, as if they knew what the structure of the branches had given them – a kind of backdrop or frame, so the flowers appeared like a finely spaced cloud of seed pearls. It gave her a vision of what two people could be. It was about holding each other steady, about being bolstered by one another's moments of bravery and grace. The judge was reciting the litany – 'Do you take this man . . .' – but she met Glen's gaze and heard another question: 'Do you promise to offer the best of yourself?' She took a deep breath and answered, 'I do.'

They pushed the scow back from the bank on the morning of November 30 in a fine rain, but the winds were light, and they managed to run fifteen miles by midday. When they came around a slight bend and saw a huge side canyon opening on the left, they decided to stop for lunch. Bessie consulted the map. 'I think this is Diamond Creek,' she said.

'Makes sense,' Glen said. 'Kolb mentioned it. You can hike to the rim from here.'

They tied off at the sandbar and walked up the canyon a short distance. Suddenly the clouds tore and light poured over the edge of the drainage, making the opposite wall flare up in oranges and reds. On their right, the cliffs were still in shadow, and in that dusky light the foliage came alive: bushes the eerie green of tarnished copper, bare trees that made a whisk of purple against the cliffs. They walked in silence. Bessie picked a stalk of dead weed and chewed it.

The creek braided through a rocky bed. They crossed it, stepping on boulders and crunching through the wet gravel on the other side, and then caught sight of a few shacks, set against the edge of the canyon. Floodlit by the sun, they looked strangely theatrical – the weathered wood and slanted roofs straight out of a Hollywood western.

'This must be the old drill camp,' Glen said. He went to the door and stepped into the gloom. Emery Kolb had told them about it: a camp set up to test the local rock. They were thinking of damming the river nearby.

There was a splintered shelf along one wall, a set of rusted bedsprings, a pile of empty cans in a corner. A column of dusty light came down where the chimney once went through.

Suddenly Bessie heard a strange chattering and clutched at Glen's arm. 'What's that?'

He laughed. 'I think it's rain.'

Of course. She hadn't heard rain on a roof in months. Only the sound of rain on water, rain on rock, rain on her hat brim. Now dashes and drops fell through the chimney hole.

'We could have lunch in here,' Glen said. 'Get dry.'

By the time they had carried the stove up from the boat, it had started to pour. Bessie set the box just outside, under the narrow eave, and started lunch. To the left, the creek curved up through a wide valley. It was hard not to find it tempting: the last sure route to the rim before they ran the final stretch of the canyon.

'In five days I'll be twenty-three,' she said.

Glen smiled. 'We should be out of the canyon by then. Two things to celebrate.'

She set a pan of biscuits on the stove, then sat on the rusted bed, trying to wipe the flour from her hands.

'Let me see those,' Glen said, coming to sit beside her. Her knuckles were scraped, and the sides of her fingers, split by the cold and the silty water, had started to bleed. 'I've got just the thing.' He went out into the rain.

'What's that?' Bessie asked when he came back. He was prying open a small tin with his pocket knife.

'Sheep balm,' he said. 'Reith swears by it.' He dipped a finger in the salve and smeared it on her palm, then worked her hand open with his thumbs, as if fanning a deck of cards.

She tipped her head back and sighed. 'We're almost through, aren't we?'

He nodded, dipped into the tin, and picked up her other hand.

'Would you call this the end of the canyon?'

He looked at her carefully. 'Not exactly. There are a few more rapids left.'

'Bad ones?'

'A couple,' he said, keeping his eyes down. No point worrying her.

When he was finished daubing her hands, Bessie pulled the biscuits from the stove. They were out of jam, almost out of lard. Still, even dry, the warm bread gave her strength. She brushed the crumbs from her coat, then pulled her diary from an inside pocket and made notes on the day's run. For the last week, they had been running so hard she had barely had the energy to write, so she had devised a system of code. Dashes for flat water, zeros for riffles, and upright slashes for rapids. Often she pulled it out in the calm stretches and marked a slash for the rough water just run, a way of putting it behind her. Now, having reconstructed the day's progress as best she could, she lay down on the bedsprings, one arm curled under her head. The bed was pushed under a shelf, and Glen lay down beside her, ducking his head.

'Can I borrow your pencil?' he asked.

It was a small stub by now, whittled by the knife. He reached up and dug their names into the underside of the plank: Glen and Bessie Hyde, November 31, 1928.

She noticed the mistake – only thirty days in November – but she didn't point it out. Her mind was on something else. 'Glen,' she asked. 'If we hiked out here, do you think anyone would quibble about the last few miles?'

He sat up and stared out the doorway. 'Of course they would. What are we going to say – we almost made it? I don't know where you got the idea that hiking out is easy,' he said, getting up to pace the room. 'Rain down here means snow on the rim. If we lose the trail we could freeze to death.' He couldn't help thinking of the Powell expedition, which had come to a hopeless division just a few miles downstream. Separation Rapid. The ones who had stuck to the river had made it through; the three who had hiked out had been killed by Indians. He'd read all the books. This canyon was full of junctions where old showdowns had taken place. It always boiled down to the same thing: Give up or keep going?

Glen crouched down and worried the floor with a stick. He could just picture what it would be like to drag himself back to Twin Falls, frostbitten and broke, having nearly killed his wife, only to point out on the map where he'd turned yellow and quit. They were 250 grueling miles from Lee's Ferry, about fifty from the Grand Wash Cliffs, most of them easy. He knew they could make it.

He tossed the stick into a corner and took a deep breath. 'You heard what Kolb said. They're gonna dam this place,' he said. 'They've already surveyed for it. The whole canyon downstream will be underwater, and they'll be farming the desert. People will come visit us when we're sitting in our rocking chairs, asking us to tell them what it was like.'

Bessie had been listening with her head turned aside, but now she faced him squarely. 'I don't have any faith I'll live that long.'

He lit the box stove again and set water for coffee. 'You're not going to drown down here, Bess. I won't let you.'

He didn't sound boastful, merely resolute. It struck her as a fatherly phrase: *I've got you. I won't let you fall.* Two weeks ago – weeks that felt as stretched and full as years – she might have believed him. It was such an easy tumble into helplessness, into faith. But that was before she saw how close he had come to missing that rope in Sockdolager – it was sheer luck – and how close to drowned he had looked when she dragged him out. After that, she had vowed to stay alert.

They were quiet while the coffee boiled. Glen poured two steaming cups and brought her one, holding it by the rim.

'Look, this is the roughest water I've ever seen,' he said. He meant it as a compliment, but it came out like a warning. He tried again. 'Jeanne has never run anything like this – no woman has. Why not just ride it out?'

She looked up at him, barefaced. 'Because I'm chicken.'

He smiled slowly and glanced out the door. 'Toughest chicken I've ever seen,' he said. It was still drizzling – a slow downward graininess to the light. He put his cup on the shelf and crouched in front of her. 'When we get out, we'll kick our feet up and be lazy. Winters are slow on the ranch. You can write your book.' He slid his hands under her coat flaps, and the shearling lifted around her neck. 'Look, it was one thing to quit at Phantom Ranch – we were hardly a third of the way through. But now, with so little left? Why don't we just finish what we started?'

He didn't know it, but he'd snagged something there, the

hulk of an old argument she'd had with herself. She was afraid she'd never see anything through. Her marriage to Earl, the baby, her studies in art – they had all been left unfinished. On good days, she told herself that she'd followed her instincts, but then sometimes it came over her in a cold wash: she was a quitter.

'All right,' she said. 'But when we get to Needles, you're going to owe me a thing or two.'

He looked relieved. 'You name it.'

Of course he would agree to anything, so she made a litany of the things she'd been missing. 'Silk stockings and a new dress.' She lifted a forefinger. In her mind, she pictured a beaded sheath, like the one she'd been wearing the night they met.

'Done,' he said. 'What else?'

'Steak. Medium rare, with a heap of mushrooms.'

'Oh God, don't talk about steak.'

'You said anything.'

'All right.'

She lifted another finger. 'I want to go to the movies,' she said. 'No westerns, though. I never want to see another western as long as I live.'

He smiled. 'Go on.'

She looked out into the middle distance, her face shifting with memory. 'I want to find Greta.'

'We will,' Glen said softly. 'Or she'll find you. They don't put your picture in the papers without saying where you're from.'

'Do you think so?'

'I'm sure.'

Bessie took a deep breath and went on, naming other pleasures she had given up for lost: a rainy afternoon in a bookshop, a bed without sand, pouring glass after glass of clear water from the tap. Just imagining these things made her mood rise, and then she realized what they equaled – a life. Ordinary days that would go on once this was over. For weeks now she had given up imagining a single moment beyond the river – she had only thought of the present and the past. Now naming these desires was like building a delicate bridge, a way out of this place.

She had all her fingers in the air – one for each request – and she reached out and touched Glen's cheeks. He was suddenly so dear to her, so familiar. These last weeks she'd barely had the peace of mind to notice, but now it stunned her. His dark eyes, his big ears and widow's peak – this lovely, bony face, come to her by chance.

'A baby,' she said. The wish rose in her like a bubble in a frozen pond.

'What?' he asked softly. His mind had wandered off.

She cupped his face. 'When we get out of here, I want to have a baby.'

Reith Hyde

Francy and Harbin were due at Diamond Creek in two days, and I was waiting on pins and needles, as they were Glen and Bessie's last hope for rescue by boat. Kolb needed to attend to his business, so he introduced me to John Nelson, a local rancher with knowledge of the canyons, and on the 30th of December, he and I went down to Diamond Creek and started hiking upstream. We figured we would intercept Francy and Harbin on their way down. Nelson was quite a good tracker. When we came to small side canyons he would hike up a ways to look for prints or broken brush. I waited along the river, so as not to miss the boat when it came through. The canyon was steep and dark in this section, never getting any sun at the bottom. I'd walk briskly up and down the beach to keep my blood moving. Every time I pivoted and turned upriver, I expected to see a boat rounding the bend. It occurred to me that I would have my answer in that first instant – one glance, and I'd see four heads or two. I wouldn't even have to wait for them to land.

By dusk on the 30th, we had reached a small beach a few miles upstream of Diamond. There was still no sign of the boat. We camped and made a big fire. When Nelson saw I was still watching the river, he said there was no way they'd do any running after dark, but I remembered Glen telling me that once, on the Salmon River, he and Jeanne had come to a stretch without any place to land and they had ended up having to drift by torchlight until they found a beach. If the rescue boat was in such a bind, I suppose they would have stopped at this spot just the same, but a good blaze would guide them to our side of the river. I stayed up late and then stoked the fire before laying out my bedroll. The light leapt up against the cliffs, making strange figures appear in the rock. I lay there for what seemed like hours watching them. At some point I must have dropped off, because when I opened my eyes the sky was pale gray and the fire had sunk down to coals.

We boiled coffee and made biscuits and then packed up and started walking again. The sun still hadn't hit the rim. We were scrambling along a narrow shelf, the rocks slippery with dew, when we looked down and saw the boat. I counted – one, two men – and felt an anvil drop on my chest.

Nelson yelled hello, and the two of them looked up and waved their hats. I made myself lift a hand. By the time we backtracked down to the small beach below, Francy and Harbin were already tying off the boat.

I said, 'You didn't find them.'

Francy said no, but they'd seen signs all along: traces of fire, big square scuffmarks where the scow had been pulled up on the sand. 'We saw his prints at most of the big rapids,' he said, 'going down the beach and then back to the scow – he must have been scouting.'

I told them I was grateful that they'd been so thorough.

Harbin spit in the sand. 'Well, knowing Patraw, the Park Service will take all the credit,' he said. 'We'll just have to settle for the cash.'

I wasn't sure what he meant by that, but I didn't ask. We got into the boat and floated down with them the last few miles to Diamond Creek, where we spent New Year's Eve. I had brought along the whiskey Harbin asked for, and though I didn't partake and Nelson only sipped, the two boatmen managed to polish off the bottle. That's when things took a bad turn.

Harbin was grumbling about how they'd risked their necks

for nothing. Then he said, 'Maybe gramps here knows where they are. Maybe he knows something he's not telling.'

Francy tried to get him to shush. Nelson just shook his head, said he was going to bed.

I stared at Harbin across the fire. 'What are you saying?'

He stared back. 'I'm saying I think your son hiked out and went home.'

I jumped up. 'You son of a bitch.' It was all I could do not to leap across the fire and strangle him.

'Hey now –' Francy staggered to his feet, holding his palms up. 'That's the whiskey talking,' he said. 'It's been a long two weeks. Maybe Nelson's right, we should all get some sleep.'

I never spoke another word to Harbin or his companion. In the morning, we hiked out to Peach Springs. I went straight to the telegraph window and sent a wire to the bank, stopping payment on the reward checks I'd placed in their names. They hadn't found anything of use, and I was damned if I was going to let them spit in my face and then take the profit.

That was when I decided to go over to the North Rim and search the canyons on that side of the river. I figured there was a fifty-fifty chance that Glen and Bessie had been on the right bank when they lost hold of the boat. With no way to get across, they'd have to hike out to the north. There were hardly any settlements on that side of the canyon. John Nelson said they'd have to go a long way before they found anyone. He agreed to drive me down to Pearce Ferry in his Ford and then across to St. George on the north side of the river. From there we could hire a few men and outfit them for a search.

Jeanne had been sending telegrams, urging me to come home, but the fact was, I felt miserable all the time except when I was down in the canyon, putting myself to use. Searching for them was a kind of relief. All my thoughts were on the task at hand: climbing up and down those narrow gullies, sidling along ledges, thinking about where to get a handhold, where to gather firewood, where to make camp. I was like a blood-hound, my whole mind narrowed down to the trail. All that mattered was to be thorough. To figure out where they might be and go after them. When I slept at El Tovar or at Nelson's house in Peach Springs, I had troublesome dreams, but when I was in the canyon, I never suffered them. I hiked hard from sunrise until dark, trying to cover as much ground as I could, then slept the sleep of the dead.

We got to St. George on New Year's Day, 1929. It wasn't any trouble to find a few cowboys willing to work for quick cash. We outfitted three parties, and gave each one an area to search. I rode with Nelson – some people called him Hualapai Johnny, because he'd practically been raised by Indians. He certainly knew his way around those canyons. I'd think I saw a clear route along a bench, but he'd point his mule down a bit of scree and hit a lower shelf, and sure enough I'd look up a few minutes later and see the ledge we'd been on had dropped off into thin air.

After a day of hard riding, he and I got down to the river and went upstream as far as we could go, but we didn't see any sign of them. We spent the night there on a small rocky sandbar, and in the morning headed back downriver. Through some tough work with the mules – coaxing them along ledges as wide as a shoe box – we came to another beach. There we found the remains of a campsite. I tied off my mule and walked every inch of the tiny beach, the hairs standing up on my arms. They had been here – my son, my daughter-in-law – they had walked this very sand, not more than a month before. It broke my heart to come so close. You could see their footprints, sharp as cobbler's molds in the wet sand. There was a fire ring filled with ash and four broken eggshells, each half nested carefully in the other. Next to the cold fire was an empty lard can and a full can of lima beans perched on a rock. I recognized the brand from the pantry back home. The strange thing was, it wasn't opened. I turned it over in my hands. It was just an ordinary can of beans, but I read it like a telegram. It told me they hadn't been stranded at this campsite – they had to have been with the boat, or they would never have shucked off supplies. Nelson and I had come down to the river at every major side canyon downstream and there weren't any more camps along the beaches. So this had to have been their last overnight. They must have hit trouble on the river the next day.

I sat down on a wet driftwood log and put my head in my hands. I don't think I'd wept like that since my wife died. 'I'm sorry, Reith,' Nelson said. Then he had the decency to walk up the canyon a ways and leave me to myself.

Glen and Bessie Hyde

They left the shack when the rain let up and pushed the scow into the river. Just below Diamond Creek was a long, easy rapid. They ran it without shipping a drop. Around the bend, they passed through a series of riffles – quick bumpy rides that didn't require scouting, just enough to keep them sailing along. The air was moist and cold and strangely still, and the cliffs, which had flared open around Diamond Creek, were closing in again. The narrow canyon amplified sound. Soon they heard the unmistakable rumble, the low bass tones, of serious water. Glen pulled over to scout.

It looked bad, all right. A short, steep drop, the current running along the right and then driving around a big boulder near the end. If they stayed clear of that, they ought to make it. But just to be safe, Glen walked all the way to the eddy at the bottom, crouched down, and waited. Sometimes the waves would fall out of phase, and in the sudden lull, a hazard would surface. He counted slowly to ten and was about to stand up when the water dropped and he saw the trap. Not twenty feet from him, just when you would think you were in the clear, a ridge of jagged rocks cut crosswise to the current. They were as sharp as cat's teeth. Sure to rip a hole in the scow and send them flying.

When he got back to the boat, Bessie was bent over the map. The rapid didn't have a name – just one of the anonymous hazards that marked the route. 'What do you think?' she asked.

'We'd better line it,' he said, looking around at the cliffs. It wouldn't be easy. The shore eroded in the middle of the rapid, leaving them nowhere to stand. They would have to inch along a ledge above the water, and hope the rope was long enough to reach.

'Let's get it over with then,' Bessie said. Fifteen minutes later, they were side by side on the narrow bench, easing the boat down along the rocks. They held it well over the first drop, but the rapid was steep and fast and kept tugging at the scow, trying to draw it toward the tongue. She was on the bow rope and he took the stern – the back end was most likely to swing wide.

'Keep your knees bent,' Glen said. 'Don't give the rope any play.' And no sooner had he said this than the boat caught the current and the stern rope went taut.

'Jesus!' he shouted, and then teetered, his hips thrown back for balance. If they lost the boat they were trapped. The scow stalled for a moment and then a wave slapped the stern and yanked him out over the water. Whole seconds passed as he fell. He let go of the rope and wheeled his arms, trying to land feet first, but there wasn't enough time to correct – the rope had pulled him out flat – and that was the way he landed, hitting a rock with a sickening thwack. Bessie dropped her rope, pressed her hands against the cliff. A stupid phrase bloomed in her head: That can't be fixed. Below her, Glen stayed limp in the water, nudging the rock. Then slowly he spun and started to drift downstream.

A pain pierced her chest. She should have jumped without thinking – Glen would have – but that awful sound kept echoing in her head. The boat was halfway through the rapid, it was all over so quickly, and still she froze there on the ledge.

Then she saw him coming back to her, carried on an eddy, facedown, his shirt puffed with air. The river boiled and turned him to the side. She caught a glimpse of his face, his ear, shining with water. Then he lifted an arm – a limp, helpless gesture – and looked straight at her.

She called his name, picked a clear space between the rocks, and leapt.

The air whistled past her ears, then the water closed over her – dark, agitating cold. She was tumbled and folded and then driven deep, thrashing her arms, fighting the impulse to gasp. The water was calmer down there. She started to kick toward the surface – that turbulent zone. Again the current grabbed her, swept her downstream, then tossed her to the surface. She took a great gulp of air, panicked for a moment – where was Glen? One, two strokes toward the bank and then she was yanked down, as if pulled by her feet. A force pressed from above, only this time it wasn't a jumbled ride, she was driven straight down, deeper than she'd gone before, and even when she felt something hard beneath her the water went on pressing. *What do you want?* It seemed to be animate, something with a will. She paddled frantically. Then suddenly the pressure shifted – she felt it move to the side like a passing storm cell. She pushed off the bottom, lifted a little, and then stopped. Something was stuck. Pure darkness. Aching lungs. She tried to pull free, struggling like an animal caught in a trap, then folded herself down and felt with her hands. Her foot – pinned fast. No pain really. Too cold. She let go of her shin, floated to the end of her tether. For a long moment she held there, then exhaled.

It was a relief at first, that eruption of bubbles. A pleasant emptiness in her chest. Then the pain came back, only fiercer this time. So that when she gave up and took that first breath of water, she felt no fear. Only an odd thought: So this is how it ends. Her arms swung up. One leg pointed to the bottom, the other stretched behind. Her body turned from side to side – a jewelry-box ballerina, stirred by the wash.

At the surface, Glen was being pulled farther downstream. He struggled to keep his head above water, but his right arm was useless. His clothes were filling with silt. The cold made his mind slow, but when he got a breath of air, he held it and tried to go limp. Floating that way, he felt himself strike a boulder. His left hand shot out and grabbed hold. He lifted his head. It was a big rock, slick and hulked out of the river. He was pressed against the upstream side. Scissoring his feet, he tried to pull himself up. The rock face was steep. His hand slid down the stone. One by one, the waves slapped at him, twisting his legs back into the current. As the river pulled him past, he grazed the side of the rock, his fingers trailing, looking for purchase. Then nothing but water again. His mind going dark. When he gave up trying, he was swamped by a sorrow stronger than the river, sorrow at the last sight of his wife, stepping off the ledge to save him, her grave face turned toward the water. He had tried to raise his hand, tried to tell her to stop –

But a body has no regrets. Glen's moved downriver, bouncing quickly through rapids, then drifting through the calm stretches, snagging for a while in some rocks near the shore, then slowly working free and moving on again. He bobbed through the last riffle with his back humped above the froth, and slid out between the Grand Wash Cliffs. Here the sheer walls dropped away, and the river relaxed and spread wide. It was sunrise, the water like a glittering skin. Swallows cut the air. The current pulled him over its braided bed, past the sandbars and the empty salt flats where, in a matter of days, his father would walk the bank, searching for him.

This winter, holed up at the ranch, I haven't been myself. I often dream that I am hunting for Glen – in the hayloft, through the waist-high weeds by the river – only he's still a boy, and it's all like a game to him. I'll hear his whistle, a two-note call we used to find each other in the orchards. The mist will be up and I'll wander through it, hearing his voice as clear as when he used to wake from nightmares. Pa! The word like a hook in my flesh. Then I wake, jerking upright in bed, and there is a brief moment before it all comes rushing back at me. But instead of lying there, I take a lantern to the barn and sharpen the lopper blades. Or sit at the kitchen table and go over the orchard books. Sometimes I find I'm off by as much as fifty cents.

I left the canyon on the 5th of January, 1929, nearly three months ago. It took everything I had not to go back to the South Rim one more time. But I was ashamed to admit that I was holding out hope, when everyone else – Jeanne, John Nelson, the Kolbs – had given them up for dead. For so long the only thing that kept me sound was trying to find them. I had gone on in a kind of dry hope. Who could I write to? Who might be persuaded to aid in the search? I saved copies of the telegrams and the answers that came back, and in a notebook I kept track of the steps taken: which portions of the canyon had been searched, what tracks or clues had turned up.

Even after I came home, and there was nothing left to do, I kept pulling out each possible scenario and comparing it to the facts. There were awful rumors floating around – that Bessie's jealous first husband had caused foul play; that Glen had forced her to continue on when she wanted to quit, and she shot him and went into hiding. Hard for me to imagine her capable of such a thing. But I didn't know her well, and hardship does strange things to people.

Still, even if she had been desperate enough to commit murder, there was the rifle to account for. It was found in the boat and it was loaded. My daughter-in-law had never fired a gun – she told me they frightened her – and whatever she might have done in a fit of passion, I couldn't imagine her so cold-blooded as to stop and reload to cover the evidence.

Mr. Haley wrote me a few letters. He's convinced they became separated from the boat, hiked out, and got lost on the mesa. I tried to tell him: I walked or rode a mule along every major route out of the canyon above and below Diamond Creek, and I never saw a single clue. You'd think they would have left a bootprint or evidence of a fire. Even the Indians from Havasupai swore they'd never seen sign of them, and I'd offered a reward, even for bad news.

Eventually I came to believe the river did them in. The Kolbs found the boat with the painter down in the water. My son would never run a rapid with a rope overboard. He was too careful for that. Most likely it was thrown for rescue. Glen was an excellent swimmer – a champion in the distance races – but Bessie might have had a hard time in that current. No doubt she fell in, and when the rope didn't reach, he jumped in to save her.

Much as I've stewed over all this, in the months since I've been home, I haven't so much as looked at their things. But yesterday was my son's birthday – he would have been thirty years old – and in the evening I was passing by the room they shared, a cup of coffee in my hand, when it came over me. This was all I had left. I pushed open the door, listening to the hinges squeak, and stood there on the sill. Her drawings were still tacked to the walls, the corners curled by sun. Her brushes and pens sat in a jar on the table. It was so strange to look at those pens, to think that she had touched them, and wouldn't touch them again. There was a black sketchbook, lying closed on the desktop, and even from across the room, I could see her fingerprints smudged on the cover. This was why I hadn't come in here. I couldn't bear to look at it all, lying haphazard, as if they had just stepped out and were expected back. And I couldn't box it away either. It seemed too cruel. As if you could just tidy up after a life.

But now I made myself stay. I went over to the window and looked at the orchards, the grid of trees leafing out toward the south. It was near sundown, the light coming at a golden slant. Glen used to lie on the bed while she was sketching, and when he looked up from his book, this is what he would have seen. Once in a while, before they left for the canyon, I would pass by the closed door and hear them talking, his voice low and easy, her laugh bubbling up. My son and I were close, but we didn't talk a lot. So it surprised me – and, I'll admit, pained me a little – to hear his voice behind that door. I couldn't help wondering: all those years, had he been dying to talk?

At last I was in the room where those conversations took place. After a while, I could almost breathe right. I pulled a chair in front of the trunk at the foot of the bed and remembered how I had come down that April morning one year ago – she and Glen had driven up from Elko the night before – and seen it sitting by the door. I remember thinking, I hope he's made the right choice. Then she came in, with her hair combed neat, and her jaunty clothes, and that frank, lovely face, and it all made sense.

I set my cup down and opened the trunk. I suppose it wasn't right of me. I would have hated to see someone rifling through my effects, but the thing is, I don't believe the dead are watching us. Glen and Bessie were gone, and if this gave me some solace, I didn't see how it mattered either way.

On top was a volume of poems, written by someone named e. e. cummings. No one I'd ever heard of, and he didn't see fit to capitalize his name, but it looked like it had seen good wear. Underneath that was a sheet of newspaper. I don't think it was packing – it was folded too neatly. The *San Francisco Daily News,* nearly three years old. I read all four sides and the only reason I could see for her having saved it was the mention of that gal who swam the English Channel. Trudy Ederle. Stout little thing. They had a picture of her on the beach, smeared with white grease, grinning. Nineteen years old and she beat the fastest man by two hours.

Then I saw a sheaf of onionskin, with the title typed neatly on the first page: 'Wandering Leaves.' I guessed they were her poems. Glen had great faith in Bessie's talents. She certainly had a vivid way of talking. But her diary of their river voyage was nearly written in Braille. I wasn't sure what she would have put in that book they planned, even had she been granted the time and quiet to work it out. So I picked up the manuscript with great curiosity and started to read.

I'm no judge of poetry, but it didn't do much for me. A lot of stuff about foghorns and moonlight and ships setting out for sea. Each poem was numbered – there were exactly fifty – and they had titles like 'Incense' and 'Broken Dreams.' She was twenty-three, for Christ's sake. I don't know what I was hoping for. But once I got over my disappointment, I read the manuscript again, and found clues to the things that had occupied her. She went to jazz parties and wished she was walking under the pines instead. She craved adventure. That must have been where Glen came in.

I was almost to the bottom of the trunk when I saw the letters. I'd know my son's hand anywhere – that slanting scrawl. There was a whole packet of them, addressed to Bessie

Haley in Elko, Nevada. Must have been written during those months while she was waiting for the divorce. She had tied them with a piece of green ribbon. I sat there for a good while, sipping my cold coffee and trying to talk myself out of snooping. Then I picked open the knot.

They were short letters. I grazed over them, as if reading quickly would soften the intrusion. I don't know what I was looking for. Glen talked mostly about the plans for their trip, but here and there were other things – things I hesitate to recall – the private talk of marriages. I could see how he'd won her over, writing letters like that. Then I came to one that was thicker than the rest.

'I'm sarry for my boring letters,' he started. 'I'm pretty tired at night.' I almost folded the pages and put them away. But when I came to this passage, my gut pulled up:

Reith probly thinks I'm planning this trip to get back at him for the whole deferment business. And the truth is, I stewed about it for years. Every time I walked through town and saw the boys coming back from the front I was ashamed. Casper Nygord, my best friend, was killed in France and I always meant to go visit his mother to give my condolances, but I just couldn't do it. Then one day I ran into her at the store. I tried to say something about how it had been busy on the ranch, but it sounded bad, so I just stared at the floor. People were milling around us, but she didn't pay them any mind. She said, You thot it would pain me to see you well and whole, but it doesn't. Make the most of your life, she said. That's what you can do for me and Cas. And I promised her I would.

Of course Reith didn't force me to take that deferment. He just let it be known that my help would be missed around the ranch. But I could see that he was just plain scared. He probly thot he couldn't live if I didn't. And I suppose I figured he had already lost enough. So I convinced myself I was doing my part, staying home. Food will win the war and all that. But after I saw Mrs. Nygord something changed. Reith always says, Better safe than sarry. But I don't agree. The only thing I've ever felt sarry about was playing it safe.

I got up and walked around the room a few times, my throat in a knot. When that deferment option came up, I tried to make the case lightly, but I suppose my fear bled through. He was eighteen years old. Not a line on his face. I felt responsible. Still, I always worried that it was a mistake. Worried that he thought I was trying to run his life. That was why I kept mum about his plan to run the river. I didn't want to be the one always barring his way. But now I knew: he didn't sit out the war because he felt tamped down. He did it because he saw my dread, and pitied me. Grateful as I am for that, I'm glad he broke free of it.

My son was a grown man when he left for the Grand Canyon, but often I would stare at him and remember the child. He was a towheaded baby, his hair sticking straight up, like a dandelion gone to seed. He had his own will, right from the start. How could I have stopped him from doing what he loved? He knew the risks better than I did, and took the chance, and if this was how it came out, well, it was his life to gamble and not mine.

I sat back down, my legs watery, and stared at the scattered effects. Hard to get myself moving. Finally I folded up the letter, tucked it back with the rest, and knotted the ribbon. Then I saw a last piece of mail, loose in the bottom of the trunk. This one was in Bessie's hand – posted from Elko to someone named Greta Grandstedt, in Los Angeles. For a moment I couldn't place the name. Then I remembered: Glen had mentioned her. The actress Bessie was traveling with when they met on the ship. Across the envelope, someone had written: Moved – No Forwarding Address.

I was going to put it back, but then I realized: she doesn't know Bessie's dead. I thought maybe the letter would give some clue to her whereabouts. I could find a way to let her know. Or so I told myself. Maybe that was an excuse.

My dear Greta,

Your note arrived today – Glen forwarded it from the ranch. When I saw the familiar writing on the envelope, my heart leapt and I ran upstairs to devour it in private. I am well and safe, and I'm terribly sorry to have made you worry. I have no excuse for taking so long to write. Or only a thin one. I suppose things felt a bit strained between us, after I left Los Angeles. I had the feeling you disapproved – of Glen, and of my darting from one plan to the next like a drunken bee. Perhaps I wanted your blessing then because I had my own qualms. But of all the things I have to thank you for, topmost is your having taught me the value of first instincts. You won't believe where mine have landed me at the moment. After a trip home to confront Earl (a disaster, apart from showing me what a steadfast friend I have in Glen), I'm living in the world's dullest town, in northern Nevada, waiting to file for divorce. My only companion is the boardinghouse proprietress, who chews Sen-Sen to make up for years of bad dental care, and dispenses wisdom on everything from marriage (avoid if possible) to slaughtering chickens (don't bother with a hatchet, just break their necks). Perhaps someday she'll make it into a story. Meanwhile, I'm counting the days until Glen appears on the doorstep and I can see his face again.

Greta, I know he didn't make a good impression – quiet people rarely do – but he really is a gem. Brave and patient and kind. I've met so many men that only want to gab about themselves, but Glen has the most unusual composure. I think it's what I love most about him. All my life I've felt this inner agitation – I worry about the most senseless things – but he's as steady as a level, not least in his devotion to me. In the few months we've been together, I've never felt less alone. He's managed to give me a sense of family. He and his father – who we plan to live with until we can afford a ranch of our own – share a loyalty that I find a constant surprise. After growing up in the Haley household, I'm always looking for hidden fissures, but here there seem to be none. I know it sounds like I'm describing some impossible ideal. But I'm sure when you spend more time with Glen you'll see his merits on your own. We're still planning to make this trip through the Grand Canyon in the fall – our honeymoon – and while I don't know a thing about boats, I'm keen for the adventure, and for the chance to draw and paint in a fresh landscape. Of course, I had my jitters at first – I haven't changed *that* much – but I've decided it's time to soak up a bit more of this country than I've seen in my twenty-two years.

Please write and tell me of your life, which at the moment sounds glamorous and very far away. I keep expecting that one day I will walk by a motion picture marquee and see your name.

With much love,
Bessie

I dropped the pages into my lap and looked up. The sun had gone down. The windows were full of orange light, and the crickets had started up. My knee was aching. I sat there, not moving, until the sky turned black, and I could no longer make out the room or anything in it.

I ended up sending Bessie's stuff to the Haleys in West Virginia – the letters and drawings, all the things they found in the scow. I packaged it up and spent more time than usual phrasing a note. Nothing sounded right. We had this terrible thing between us, her mother and father and I, but it was finished, and it made us into strangers. Finally I settled on the wording.

Dear Mr. and Mrs. Haley,

    Painful as it might be to look on these things, I thought it right that they be returned to you.

In deepest sympathy,

R. C. Hyde

Later I heard that Mr. Haley destroyed her diary. Someone was looking for it, someone interested in their story – they would have been glad to hear that – but it seems that he burned it.

Glen and Bessie Hyde, Grand Canyon, 1928

Author's Note and Acknowledgments

This is a work of fiction, based on actual events. While all of the principal characters are historical figures, and the narrative follows the few known facts of Glen and Bessie Hyde's 1928 trip through the Grand Canyon, the portraits of the characters are wholly invented. The skeleton of the story was pieced together from archival material collected by Otis Marston, whose papers are held in the Huntington Library in San Marino. Bill Frank, curator of the Marston Collection, was of particular help with this project. I am also indebted to Richard Quartaroli, at the Northern Arizona University Special Collections Library, who was unstintingly generous with his time. The following books were also of special assistance: *River*, by Colin Fletcher; *Through the Grand Canyon from Wyoming to Mexico*, by Ellsworth L. Kolb; *River Runners of the Grand Canyon*, by David Lavender; *The Doing of the Thing*, by Vince Welch, Cort Conley, and Brad Dimock; and *Cadillac Desert*, by Marc Reisner.

I am grateful to the reference librarians at the Seattle Public Library's quick information line, who provided instant answers to many strange questions. To Ted Melis, Grand Canyon hydrologist and history buff, thanks for taking me down the Colorado River and for offering an expert's eye on the manuscript. Lizette Melis made me welcome on several visits to Flagstaff. Bernard Cooper, Bill Hayes, Tony Horwitz, Ann Lewis, and Wendy Lesser gave me invaluable editorial input. The folks at the Wylie Agency, Sarah Chalfant and especially Jin Auh, lent their constant support and expertise. Jill Bialosky is an editor in the old-fashioned sense of the word; her sympathetic reading made for a better book. And to Mauricio, with whom I made several trips in Grand Canyon, always in unseasonably cold or wet weather, thanks for encouraging me to push my limits.

LISA MICHAELS

Lisa Michaels is an award-winning poet and contributing editor at *The Threepenny Review*. Her critically acclaimed memoir *Split: A Counterculture Childhood* was a *New York Times* Notable Book of the Year. She lives in northern California. *Grand Ambition* is her first novel.

Fred and Edie
JILL DAWSON

Shortlisted for the Whitbread Novel of the Year Award

Set in the early nineteen twenties, this mesmerising tale is based
on the true story of Edith Thompson, an attractive, ambitious
woman who was charged with conspiring to murder her
husband. Drawing on newspaper reports of the time as well as
letters by Edie to her young lover Fred, the novel creates an
intimate, tantalising voice for Edie as the story unfolds of how
she came to be on trial for her life at the Old Bailey. Was Edie
simply ahead of her time or did she collude in her own fate?
Teasing out answers to a compelling mystery, this is a novel
of entrancing imagination, sensitivity and grace.

'A captivating account of a strangely impassioned, and
compelling, love affair' Caryl Phillips

'It will captivate readers . . . Edie is so wonderful, so bitterly
honest about herself, especially her understanding of her own
sensual nature. And the sex is beautifully written about. Jill
Dawson magnificently gets into a woman's skin and makes
the whole act sublime' Margaret Forster

'Jill Dawson's novel about the famous Thompson and
Bywaters murder trial makes compelling reading . . . Edie, as
envisaged here, is a latter-day Emma Bovary, whose
passionate wish to live life to full leads in the end to her
destruction. Dawson has given her a hauntingly authentic
voice, and imparted an edgy, contemporary resonance to
her story' Christina Koning, *The Times*

∫

SCEPTRE